P9-DMR-868

Kiss and Tell

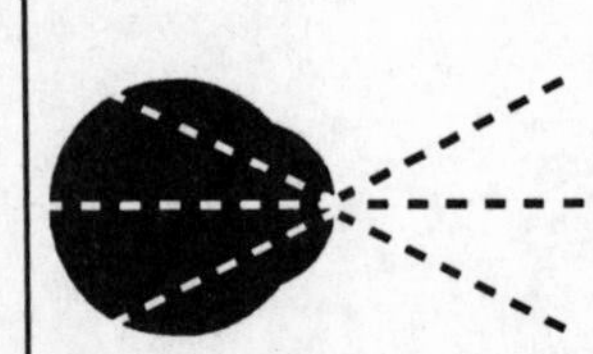

This Large Print Book carries the Seal of Approval of N.A.V.H.

Kiss and Tell

Fern Michaels

WHEELER PUBLISHING
A part of Gale, Cengage Learning

Farmington Hills, Mich • San Francisco • New York • Waterville, Maine
Meriden, Conn • Mason, Ohio • Chicago

Wheeler Publishing, a part of Gale, Cengage Learning.

Wheeler Publishing Large Print Hardcover.
The text of this Large Print edition is unabridged.
Other aspects of the book may vary from the original edition.
Set in 16 pt. Plantin.

LIBRARY OF CONGRESS CATALOGING-IN-PUBLICATION DATA

Michaels, Fern.
Kiss and tell / Fern Michaels. — Large print edition.
pages cm - (Wheeler publishing large print hardcover)
ISBN 978-1-4104-6673-0 (hardcover) — ISBN 1-4104-6673-6 (hardcover)
1. Female friendship—Fiction. 2. Vigilantes—Fiction. 3. Swindlers and swindling—Fiction. 4. Large type books. I. Title.
PS3563.I27K57 2014
813'.54—dc23 2014016150

Published in 2014 by arrangement with Zebra Books, an imprint of Kensington Publishing Corp.

Printed in the United States of America
1 2 3 4 5 6 7 18 17 16 15 14

Kiss and Tell

Prologue

It was a beautiful day. The sky was blue, the clouds like marshmallows. Not that he'd ever had a marshmallow or seen one in real life, but Billy Bailey knew what they looked like because he'd seen pictures of them. But then again, most days in August looked like today. It wasn't too hot, just perfect, he thought when he sat down on the bench under the monster apple tree that was as old as the orphanage where he'd spent the first seventeen years of his life.

Billy looked up the hill at the huge building made from gray stone. The windows glistened in the summer sunshine. He could hear all the children screaming and laughing, and knew that one of the teachers was spraying the little ones with water. He was too big now to participate in that. As he sat there, he kept his eyes on the vast expanse of lawn, waiting for his two best friends, Marie and Sally, to come running down the hill. He'd already found the perfect red apple for Marie and shined it till he could almost see his reflection in the glorious red skin. The one he had for Sally was red, too, but not as perfect. His heart kicked up a bit when he saw the two girls appear at the top of the hill, then, holding hands, skipping their way down to the old slatted bench where he was waiting for them, apples in hand.

The secret he was holding close was almost more than he could bear. He knew today was the day he had to tell Marie and Sally what it was. He knew they would cry, and he'd come prepared with a length of toilet paper in his pocket. He might even cry himself, he wasn't sure. Big boys of seventeen didn't cry. At least that's what the nuns had told him. Girls, it seemed, were allowed to cry any old time and over nothing. If they saw a mouse, they could cry, or if a bug crawled up the wall, they could both cry and scream. Then it would be up to him or one of the older boys to catch the mouse and eliminate the bug.

Just six more days, and he wouldn't be catching any more mice or squashing bugs. In six days, he would turn eighteen. Time to leave the only home he'd ever known. He was beyond excited, almost giddy with the thought of being on his own for the first time in his life. But he was sad, too, that he would have to leave Marie and Sally behind. Marie was only fifteen and Sally was thirteen. Something clutched at his heart at the thought. He wasn't sure what love was — the nuns didn't talk much about that — but he had feelings for the tiny girl with the golden curls. He liked Sally a lot, but the feeling was different. Way different.

And then they were both standing right in front of him. Marie smiled that beautiful, winsome smile of hers and held her hand out for the apple in his. Sally stood to the side, somehow knowing this was some kind of special ritual between Billy and Marie. She knew she'd get an apple, she always did, but hers wouldn't be as red or as shiny or as perfect as Marie's, but that was okay. It tasted just as good. Marie was special to Billy.

Billy was pacing now and he looked, Sally thought, worried. She asked him what was wrong.

Marie stopped eating the shiny red apple and looked up at Billy. Her voice was soft and gentle when she said, "You look like you have a secret, Billy. Remember, we promised each other we'd always share whatever was on our minds. Do you want to talk about it?"

Billy nodded. "I'm leaving next week. I'm not going to wait around for them" — he jerked his head in the direction of the big gray building — "to decide what to do with me. When things have settled down and we have enough to live on, I'm going to the big city." The girls knew that the big city Billy was referring to was New York City. Everyone they knew in Syracuse, in or out of the orphanage, meant New York when they referred to the city. Not Rochester, not Buffalo. The Big Apple.

"Manhattan? Not one of the other boroughs?" Marie asked in a shaky voice. They had learned all about the geography of New York City in their social studies classes.

Billy nodded. "Do you want to come with me? I'll take care of you." In his heart, he knew that was the part that had been bothering him, asking Marie to go with him. He hadn't planned on asking her, but the words just popped out of his mouth.

Marie thought about what he had said. She looked down at the half-eaten apple in her hand, then she looked at Sally, who had also stopped eating her apple. "Do you mean like run away from here? I'm not allowed to leave until I'm eighteen. And I can't leave Sally behind. Can she come, too?"

Billy thought about it. At first he said that taking a thirteen-year-old would be a problem, but after a while, when Marie did not give in, he agreed.

"What will we do, where will we live? I think I'd be scared." Tears pooled in Marie's eyes. She wasn't sure she wanted to stay here if Billy left. Billy had been her and Sally's protector for as long as she could remember. Life wouldn't be the same without him.

"I'll take care of you and Sally. I'll be eighteen. That means I'll be considered a man. I have a plan."

"Tell me what the plan is, Billy," Marie said in her soft, gentle voice, which, to Sally's ears, sounded excited.

"Someday, I am going to be so rich, everyone in the whole world will want to be my friend. I'll build you the finest house, and you'll have servants to do everything for you. You can sit in a chair that has gold arms and do needlepoint like Sister Alice does on Saturday afternoon. I'll buy you fancy dresses and diamonds. We'll have a big car and someone to drive us around. Sally, too," he added as an afterthought. "Sally will always be our little sister."

Marie looked down at her scuffed shoes. "We would have to get married first."

Billy's face turned beet red.

"You know what happens to people who live in sin. You go straight to hell, and I don't want to go to hell. Neither does Sally."

"I know all that, but you are too young to get married. We would have to wait till you turn eighteen. That will give me three years to make money and turn that money into a fortune. I can do that, Marie. I know I can. That's why I want to go to the city. Because," he said, his eyes wide, "*that's where Wall Street is.* I'm going to make money first. Then I'm going to invest that money and make us all rich. Not just rich, filthy rich. I'll find someone to teach us how to act when we get rich, so people won't laugh at us orphans. What do you think, Marie?" His voice was so intense, so anxious, Marie wanted to reach out to grab his hand, but she didn't. She wasn't sure what she should say, so she nodded, her blond curls bouncing all over her head. Sally nodded, too, and took a big bite out of her apple.

Finally, Marie spoke. "Sometimes you think too much about money, Billy. What if it doesn't work out? Then what will we do?"

"Life is all about money, Marie. Think about it. The three of us do not have any money. In fact, the three of us have never held any money in our hands. I want to know what that feels like. I want to have so much money that I can burn it if I want to. I want to be someone. I don't want to be an orphan. I want people to want to know me, to want to shake my hand, to look at me with respect. I know I can do it."

"Sister Julie said you have to earn respect," Sally said.

"Yes, she does say that, and I will earn that respect by making lots and lots of money. I'll buy you hair ribbons every color of the rainbow. Will you respect me if I do that, Sally?"

"Sure."

Marie laughed. "Will we be able to get holes in our ears so we can put diamonds in them?"

"And rubies and sapphires, too." Billy laughed out loud. "So, do we have a deal, girls?"

Both girls nodded in agreement.

"This will be the biggest adventure of our lives," Billy said, smacking his hands together.

"Tell us what we have to do, Billy?" Marie said.

"Nothing, actually, except to get your things together. Each of you take one sack, and that's it. We'll have to travel light. Don't talk about this, we need to keep it a secret. I'll take care of everything. We're leaving the day before my birthday. That's six days away. I know it's going to be hard to keep a secret that long, but you have to do it, okay?"

Both girls nodded again. They knew how to keep a secret.

Ever practical at the age of thirteen, Sally asked if they were going to need money.

"Of course we're going to need money. I'm going to steal it from the office. Oh, don't look so shocked. We will pay it back and add a little extra to show our good intentions. I've been watching for months now, and I know how to get the money. Every Thursday, Sister Helen goes to the bank and brings money back and puts it in her desk drawer so that on Friday she can pay the workers, the milkman, the bread man, and the man who mows the grass and does all that outside stuff. The envelope is always filled to the brim with money. I'm going to take the whole envelope the night before we leave, after everyone is in bed. Sister Helen never pays anyone till four o'clock, so if we get up, eat breakfast, then leave, we will have almost a seven-hour head start."

"Will you make a confession about stealing the money?" Sally asked.

"First chance I get," Billy said airily. *Like that is really going to happen,* he said to himself. He smiled at the girls. "Who wants another apple? I see two really red ones up high. See them?" he said, pointing to a branch in the middle of the tree.

Billy climbed the tree, agile as a monkey. He tossed down two apples. The girls caught them, shined them on their cotton dresses, made from flour sacks, and bit into them.

Billy eyed the girls from his perch high in the tree. The first thing he was going to buy for Marie was a pretty dress with colored flowers on it and a hair ribbon to match. He'd buy one for Sally, too, maybe with some ribbons or lace on it.

There was no doubt in Billy Bailey's mind that he was going to be one of the richest men in the world. Sooner rather than later.

All he had to do now was wait six days before he embarked on the biggest adventure of his life.

Chapter One

Annie de Silva blinked, then blinked again at the e-mail she was seeing on her computer screen. Her hand snaked out to the phone to the right of her computer, only to withdraw it a moment later. Another one of those weird e-mails she and Myra had been getting lately. She read it again. Only three lines, it was the most ominous-sounding of all the e-mails to date:

> If you don't act quickly, it will be too late, and it will be on your conscience. Open your eyes wide TODAY and SEE what is in front of you.

Annie didn't realize that she had been holding her breath until it exploded from her mouth like a gunshot. She clicked the keys to bring up her saved mail, then scrolled down and read through her past e-mails, not that she really needed to read them. Over the past months, she'd memorized them and talked them to death with Myra and Charles as they collectively tried to figure out what the cryptic messages could possibly mean. All to no avail.

The first e-mail, sent three months ago, had only one line:

Nothing is as it seems.

Sent by someone named kat@gmail.com. Well, Annie thought to herself, that was true of most things in life. But why did the man or woman who went by the name of Kat send it to her and to Myra? She and Myra had both tried to respond to the e-mail to ask questions, but their replies bounced back.

The second e-mail, like the first, had only one line. But this time there were two sentences, both questions:

Why haven't you acted on my e-mail? Do you need a road map?

They had tried to reply again but had the same result — neither reply went anywhere. Well, yes, they did need a road map. Even as brilliant as Charles was, he couldn't figure it out. Nor was he able to trace the IP address.

The third e-mail consisted of three insulting sentences, expressing their correspondent's fury. An insult Myra, Charles, and she took personally:

> I thought you were the Vigilantes. You people are a joke. I spent a lot of money and time trying to trace you to get your help.

Again, as with the first two e-mails, their replies did not reach their intended destination.

The fourth e-mail was short and to the point. Again, it had three sentences, breaking the pattern of adding a sentence to each e-mail:

> Go to the source. Wake up, ladies. You are such a disappointment to me.

The source of *WHAT*? They tried to respond once again, to no avail, at which point they were almost pulling their hair out in sheer frustration. What good, they asked themselves, was calling for help, then not allowing the people from whom you seek the help to find out what the problem was?

Annie rubbed at her temples. She felt a headache coming on. Each time she brought up one of the e-mails, she got a headache.

Myra said the same thing. Charles, however, more practical, shrugged it off. She should call Myra. It was early, so maybe her friend hadn't checked her e-mail yet today.

There were six more e-mails, but Annie decided she'd seen enough. She turned off the computer and looked at her watch. It was early, not yet seven. She decided to take a shower, have coffee, then drive over to Myra's.

As the steaming water pelted her body, Annie let her mind race. What was *today*? Nothing special as far as she knew, unless Myra had something planned that she hadn't shared. What was she supposed to *see*? She wasn't blind, and she sure as hell wasn't stupid. So why wasn't she seeing what Kat at Gmail wanted her to? And, perhaps even more to the point, where was she supposed to be looking for whatever it was?

Annie toweled dry, fluffed at her wet hair, then looked out the bathroom window to see what kind of day it was outside. Her jaw dropped when she saw snow flurries slapping at the window. Whoa! Well, it was the week before Thanksgiving, but the weatherman hadn't said a word about snow, flurries or otherwise. So much for meteorological science. About as reliable as bets on the roulette wheel in her casino.

Within minutes, Annie was dressed in fleece-lined sweats, heavy wool socks, and ankle boots. Minutes after that, she had a pot of coffee going. While she waited, she sat on a stool at the counter, drumming her fingers on the granite surface. Why couldn't she figure this out? *This,* of course, meaning the anonymous e-mails. Anonymous because she knew in her gut that there was no way Kat at Gmail was the real name of the person sending them. So who was Kat? What kind of stake did Kat have in whatever game he or she knew was going on? Annie threw her hands high in the air and let loose with a few choice expletives that only succeeded in turning her ears pink.

Annie doused her coffee with cold milk and gulped at it. She was so anxious to be on her way to Myra's that she barely tasted it. After setting the cup in the sink, she looked around to see if she was leaving a mess for her day lady, who came to work at nine. Then she was out the door and buttoning her jacket as she ran through the snow flurries to her car.

Ten minutes later, Annie ran through the open door to Myra's kitchen. "Did you get the e-mail, too?" Myra asked by way of greeting.

"That's why I'm here. What's going on *today*? What are we supposed to *see*? Do you have something planned you didn't tell me about? I don't have a clue what this person is talking about. Do you, Myra?" Annie asked as she poured herself a cup of coffee.

"Of course I don't. How could I? Kat refuses to give us anything concrete to go on, and do not say we are stupid, Annie, because we are not stupid. This whole thing could be something as simple as that person jerking our chain. Why, I have no idea. Then the Vigilante part of me kicks in and tells me Kat is afraid and is trying to tell us something without giving himself or herself away. There is also the mention, if you recall, of its being expensive and time-consuming to find us. Assuming that, at least, is true, it pretty much means that Kat is not jerking our chain."

"I agree," Annie said, snatching a piece of cold toast off Myra's plate. "By the way, it's snowing out. Flurrying, but the weatherman didn't mention snow at all."

"And this bothers you . . . why?" Myra asked.

Annie grimaced. "Which just goes to prove what Kat said, to wit, *nothing is as it seems.* Get it?"

"I get it, Annie." Myra sniffed.

"So today seems important to Kat. Today is the day we're supposed to *see* something. But the only thing going on that I know of is our twice-monthly therapy-dog visit out at King's Ridge. Unless you have other plans. Do you, Myra?"

"No. I gave Lady a bath last night and brushed her out. She smells great, and she just loves going out there. All that ear scratching and those delicious belly rubs. What's not to like? I like it myself to see how happy those oldsters are when Lady prances in and does her routine. That dog is a real ham. She loves applause."

Suddenly, Annie pounded both hands on the old oak table so hard that the coffee cups danced with the force of the blow. "Maybe that's it! Quick, Myra, get out a calendar. Let's see if those other e-mails came in around the dates we took Lady out to King's Ridge."

Excited to finally have a possible clue, Myra raced into the laundry room, where a colorful calendar featuring magnificent golden retrievers marked the months. She ran back to the kitchen and shoved it under Annie's nose.

"Do you remember the dates those e-mails came in, Myra?"

"No, but it won't take more than a minute or so to find out." Myra whirled around and hit a key on her computer. Within a minute her saved-mail folder popped up. Looking at the e-mails from Kat, she rattled off the dates, which Annie scratched on a pad on the counter by the phone.

"Aha! I think we're onto something, Myra! Look at this!"

Myra leaned over Annie's shoulder. "Aha is right! They were all sent either the morning of our therapy visit or the night before. Oh Annie, how could we not have seen this? Maybe we *are* stupid. But what were we supposed to see?"

Annie shrugged and rolled her eyes.

"I can't think of a thing, but obviously there is something out there that Kat thinks we should see. Having said that, perhaps Kat lives out there in one of the facilities and what she thinks is obvious to her should be obvious to us. I don't remember seeing anything out of the ordinary, but by the same token, I wasn't looking for anything. My attention was on Lady and the other animals with their owners. Does anything ring a bell, Annie? Anything at all?"

"One visit we stayed for lunch. It was quite good as I recall. I liked the part where we didn't have to clean up. The lunch was a thank-you for all the volunteers. Nothing unusual happened. If something did happen, then I missed it."

"I'm with you. It was just a nice luncheon, and they even had plates for all the animals. I thought that was nice. There was that time when Ellen and Abe Speer sought us out to talk about . . . nothing, as I recall. Do you remember what we talked about, Annie?"

"I don't. I vaguely remember them, nice couple. Didn't they say they moved out of Olympic Ridge to King's Ridge, the assisted-living section? Am I wrong, or did they make a big point of telling us that?"

Myra frowned. "I can't say that I remember that specifically, but I do remember thinking either then or later on that they were new to King's Ridge. I guess that means subconsciously it did register on me. The only way to move to King's Ridge is if you have a disability of some sort and need the help of the trained staff. Didn't Charles tell us you have to live in Olympic Ridge in order to move into King's Ridge? Then, if you become more disabled or sick, they move you to Queen's Ridge, which is the nursing home. From there it's Angel Ridge, the hospice. Which, by the way, kind of creeps me out."

"It creeps me out, too. Once you move

into that complex, you know where you're going every step of the way. That would not be for me, that's for sure. You said you checked out King's Ridge before you signed up Lady to be a therapy dog. You never told me what you found out. Is there anything you can remember that might shed some light on what we're facing now?"

Myra shook her head. "Charles checked it out. Olympic Ridge is a 150-home community. You have to be a client of Emanuel Macklin, that financial wizard who has more money than Fort Knox, to buy in there. The houses start in the seven-figure range and go up and up and up. One-of-a-kind custom-built homes. Each applicant is vetted thoroughly. And you can't sell to just anyone if you want to move. You need to go through a whole, long, drawn-out process to sell. You need to be at least sixty years old to move into Olympic Ridge. You can, however, move to the second tier, King's Ridge, the assisted-living facility, and so on until you end up in Angel Ridge, the hospice."

"Sounds like the guy has a lock on everyone who lives out there. Think about it, Myra. He's got you once you move into the high-end house, then to assisted living, on to a nursing home, and, finally, at the end, into a hospice. And he owns all of them and pretty much controls to whom you can sell what you bought. Like I said, it gives me the creeps."

"That's exactly how Charles feels," Myra said fretfully.

"Maybe we need Charles to do a background check on Mr. Emanuel Macklin. I think it was the fourth e-mail — check it out, Myra — that said we should look to the source. That has to be a reference to Emanuel Macklin."

Myra clicked the keys. "Yes, Annie, it was the fourth e-mail, the one Kat sent after she said she was disgusted with us. It has to be Macklin. What other source could it be?"

"Maybe I should call Abner Tookus to do a financial hack job on the man. The papers are always saying Macklin has more money than the government and should bail out said government. But don't be upset, Myra, since I do not think he has as much money as I do, not by a long shot. But even so, I'd kind of like to know where he got it all. Wouldn't you?"

"I absolutely would love to know that. The money people call him a one-of-a-kind financial wizard. I remember someone saying, or else I read it somewhere, that he owns one of the homes in Olympic Ridge.

He also has an apartment in the Trump Tower in New York. And a big spread in Carmel, California, where he is supposedly a neighbor of Clint Eastwood, the guy who has conversations with empty chairs. Don't look at me like that, Annie. It's just lazy-Sunday-morning reading in the Life section of the *Post.* In case you have forgotten, you are the owner and publisher of that paper. Don't you ever read it?"

"Not really. Why should I? I've got good people, including Maggie and Ted, running it. Speaking of whom, let's kick this up a notch and call in the kids to see what they can come up with. Out of our archives. There's always stuff that never gets printed for one reason or another. This is made to order for Maggie and Ted. Should I call them, Myra?"

"Before or after you call Abner? Of course you should call them. Make arrangements for them to come out here ASAP. Later, we can all go out to lunch after our therapy session. I'm thinking this is right up their alley, something for them all to sink their teeth into."

Annie made the calls while Myra brewed a fresh pot of coffee. They then looked at each other across the table. "Are you going to say it, or am I going to have to say it first?" Annie asked.

Myra sighed. "I have to say, Annie, that I am very distraught that there are only two of us now. If we count Charles, three. Marti is off with Peter Ciprani, and it looks like wedding bells. She doesn't have time for us these days. Pearl is knee deep in her underground railroad, helping women and children. That's her first love, and we can't fault her for that. As for Nellie, she's taking Elias's advancing Alzheimer's seriously and won't leave his side. Even though he has round-the-clock care. She *wants* to be there, and we can't fault her for that either. It's the way it should be. It's just a shame that all those special gold shields are going to waste."

Annie sniffed. "If that's your way of saying we're chopped liver, I'm not buying it. So our numbers are down by three. We're still three, counting Charles, and don't forget the kids. They really came through for us in Baywater. And we still have Abner. I'd say that makes it all okay unless you, Myra, are getting cold feet?"

"I am not getting cold feet. I'm just reminding you that there are only three of us, counting Charles, and I'm not sure how good Charles would be out in the field."

"For God's sake, Myra, Charles used to

be a spy. He worked in clandestine operations. What makes you think he couldn't cut the mustard these days?"

"He's out of practice," Myra said lamely.

"Then maybe we should put him through his paces."

"It's just that he's so good at what he does behind the scenes. And he worries about us. He would see danger where you and I won't. He'd try to stop us if he thought we were doing something wrong even though you and I would know it would come out okay. He'd be more of a hindrance, and I say that with all due respect for my husband."

"You have a point, Myra. Okay, then it's just you and me and the kids."

"That works for me," Myra said smartly as she offered up a sloppy salute. Annie laughed.

"So, when are you going to call Charles to do that background check?"

"Will right now work for you, Annie?" Myra said as she headed for the intercom that would reach Charles in the underground catacombs. Annie shrugged.

Ten minutes later, Charles appeared in the kitchen, a look of concern on his face. "Is something wrong?" he asked, looking at the two women, "or did you call me up here to make breakfast? Good morning, Annie. Nice to see you so bright and early. My word, it's snowing out!"

"We're not hungry, dear. We have some orders for you. We'd like you to get right on it. We got another e-mail this morning that we'd like you to see. And to remind you that today is therapy day out at King's Ridge."

Charles leaned over Myra's laptop to read the latest e-mail from Kat at Gmail. "Hm-mnn. I'll get right on it. Anything in particular?"

"Macklin," Myra and Annie said at the same moment.

"My thoughts exactly. I'll call you when I have something. By the way, are you two going to wing it on your own or call in the second string?"

"We don't have a second string, Charles," Myra snapped.

"I know that, dear," Charles said as he prepared to beat a hasty retreat. Myra threw a wadded-up dish towel at him.

"No one likes a smartass, Charles," Annie said as the swinging door to the kitchen closed behind him. Myra rolled her eyes.

"Let's confirm right now, Myra, that it is just the two of us handling this mission."

"It's just the two of us," Myra said solemnly.

"We can kick ass and take names later. Knowing how squeamish you are, I'll do the ass kicking and you can take names," Annie said airily.

Myra fingered the pearls at her neck until she saw Annie glare at her. "I like the way you think," she said in a strangled voice.

"I knew you'd see it my way," Annie said sweetly.

Maggie Spitzer parked her car in the underground lot of the *Post* building. She walked over to the concrete railing and stared out at the world, not that she could see much with the swirling snowflakes. She felt antsy, the fine hairs on the back of her neck warning her that something was up. She could feel it in every bone of her body. Somewhere, something was happening or about to happen that would involve her. A confetti of memories assailed her as she recalled other instances when she had felt the same way. She went still and waited, knowing somehow that her cell phone was going to ring any minute. Every fiber in her body told her it would happen. Her fist shot in the air when her cell phone buzzed to life. Reporter gut instincts, something to never trifle with. She identified herself and listened to Annie's excited voice. She continued to listen as she walked over to the door that would take her to the elevator and on to the newsroom. Finally, it was her turn to speak. "I'll get the guys, sign out the van, and we can be out at the farm in an hour, give or take, depending on traffic and the weather. See ya!"

Maggie was walking on air as she breezed into the newsroom, to see Ted, Espinosa, and Dennis West already at their desks. "Get your gear, guys, we're going out to the farm. Annie and Myra are on to something!"

"Wow! You sounded just like Gibbs on *NCIS.* He always says that to his team when they find a dead body," Dennis said, whirling around in his red leather chair, the chair he had to use because he was a newbie and he had to wait until the others told him he could move on. It was a rule he accepted without any fuss even though he already had a Pulitzer to his name.

Jackets were slipped into, backpacks slung on backs, and the four-man team headed for the elevator, everyone talking at once. "You can ask me all the questions you want till the cows come home, and I can't tell you anything other than it involves that ritzy commune, or whatever you want to call it, that Manny Macklin owns. That plus ten or eleven e-mails Myra and Annie have been getting over the past few months. That is the sum total of what I know, so just shut up and let your minds try to figure out why those two sharp-eyed women with gut instincts that are better than all of ours put together are asking questions."

"This sounds like it's right up there with the time they took on the guy who ran the World Bank. Ooh. I gotta say, that took guts," Ted said dramatically.

" 'They' as in the whole crew," Espinosa said, a frown building on his face. "There are only two of them left, three if you count Charles. That's not a comforting number from where I'm standing."

"Well, gee whiz, Espinosa, there are four of us to take up the slack. That has to count for something. Plus Ted said we're fearless, but I'm not sure that's true. What I mean is, I'm not —"

"Shut up, Dennis," Ted said as he signed out the van.

Dennis shut up. Ted was his idol, and when his idol spoke, he, Dennis, hopped to it.

Behind the wheel, Ted checked the gas, saw that he was good to go, and barreled out of the underground garage.

Maggie, riding shotgun, spoke. "Ted, how many stories has the *Post* done on Macklin over the last ten years?"

"A boatload. Crazy-ass kind of guy. As far as I know, he's only ever given two face-to-face interviews, one I did and one Jed Lyons at the *Times* did. He's on his third trophy wife. Macklin, that is, not Lyons," Ted clarified.

"Where's the original?" Dennis asked. "By that, I mean the first wife, not any of the trophy wives."

"I don't know, kid. You said you're a reporter, so why don't you find that out for us, along with the other three. Remember what I told you: information translates to power. The more you can garner, the quicker you get to the goal line," Ted snapped as he maneuvered the van around a slow-moving Toyota.

"Got it," Dennis said as he worked his phone.

The rest of the trip out to Pinewood was made with Maggie discussing the weather and how the weatherman never got it right. "I just hate when he's so far off the mark. It's not even Thanksgiving yet, and here it is snowing."

"It's just flurrying. It's not even sticking," Espinosa said. "Here's a bit of trivia for you. There's a guy in Florida whose name is Al Sunshine."

"And his weather reporting is so accurate he's won prizes. I researched him, and he said he goes by the *Farmers' Almanac,*" Dennis said.

"Should we care about this, Dennis?" Espinosa grinned.

"It's up to you," Dennis said, busy clicking away on his new phone, compliments of the *Post.* "I sure as hell don't care. And you know why I don't care? I'll tell you why. Because there is nothing we can do about it. The weather is the weather. Period."

"Put a cork in it, Dennis," Ted said as he steered the van off the highway to a secondary road that would take him to the main entrance of Pinewood.

"I wonder if Charles is cooking breakfast," Maggie said, more to have something to say than anything else. "I didn't even have time for coffee this morning. When I saw the snow, I beat feet."

"Cross your fingers that Myra isn't the cook this morning. Worse yet: Annie," Ted said.

"I can cook breakfast. My mother made me learn how to cook. I make a wicked omelet. The trick is to make them fluffy. I can do fluffy to perfection, but I don't do cleanup. If I cook, you clean up," Dennis babbled as he kept clicking the keys on his phone.

"That's going to work for me. Ted and Espinosa love to clean up," Maggie said as Ted sailed through the open gates at Pinewood.

The greetings were perfunctory as Maggie presented Myra and Annie with Dennis's offer to make breakfast. Myra showed him where everything was and they all sat down at the table as Dennis went to work. Within minutes, Maggie and Ted had the story and were bouncing ideas off each other. "This reminds me of the time we took on the World Bank and that skunk we took care of."

Annie was busy setting the table. Myra moved over to her small desk in the kitchen alcove and showed Ted and Espinosa the e-mails that had come in from Kat at Gmail.

"We're taking Lady out to King's Ridge today. It's therapy day for the seniors in the assisted-living section. Why don't you all come with us and perhaps write up a human-interest story for the paper tomorrow. Maybe if we do that, we can flush out some information. I say that because Annie and I have always gone alone. The e-mail this morning indicates something's happening today, so between all of us, we should be able to come up with something. Unless you all have a different spin on it."

"Old people like me," Dennis chirped from his position at the stove. "For some reason, they think of me as a grandson because I look so young and have a chubby face. At least that's what my mother said, and everyone knows that mothers are never wrong. I know when to listen, and I know *how* to listen."

"The kid's right. We couldn't have gotten half the information we got on the Ciprani twin judges without Dennis. He does have a way with people, not just older folks," Ted said magnanimously. Maggie seconded Ted's endorsement of the young reporter. Dennis flushed a bright pink as he expertly slid an omelet onto a plate and handed it to Espinosa.

Five minutes later, they were all seated at the table wolfing down Dennis's five-star omelets. Dennis beamed his pleasure at the profuse compliments.

Annie poured refills of the coffee as Ted and Espinosa dutifully loaded the dishwasher. When the last of the coffee was gone, they all put their coats on to head to King's Ridge. Lady waited patiently at the door, wearing her colorful neckerchief decorated with pumpkins and little ghosts.

She barked once to show she was ready.

Myra looked back at the four pups, Lady's offspring, sitting in the doorway to the dining room. "I know you guys want to go, but you're too rambunctious. Maybe next year." She handed out chews and led Lady out the door to Annie's racy car.

Before the others climbed into the van, Maggie turned to the others. "Okay, our cover is that we're doing a story on therapy animals, right?"

"Right," Annie and Myra said in unison. Lady let out a soft *woof* to show she was in on the cover story.

Settled in Annie's car, Myra grabbed at her pearls. "There is no need to drive like a bat out of hell, Annie. We have Lady in the car with us."

Annie ignored her and laid her foot on the gas pedal. Lady howled in the backseat. "I'm so excited, Myra. My skin is tingling. We're on to a big one. Do you feel it?"

"What I feel, Countess de Silva, is a migraine coming on. Slow down."

"Myra, I'm only going sixty, and the speed limit is sixty-five."

"I don't care. Slow down to fifty."

"Then I'll be a hazard on the road and people will start blowing their horns and Lady will get upset and you will get upset with Lady and me. Play with your damn pearls and let me do the driving, okay?"

Permission from Annie to play with her pearls. That was a new one, Myra thought as she clasped the lustrous necklace in a death grip.

"Look! I got us here all safe and sound," Annie said ten minutes later. Myra rubbed at her temples as Lady nudged the back of her neck.

Ted parked the *Post* van next to Annie's car. Everyone piled out and waited for Myra to attach the leash to Lady's collar. They walked in single file to the entrance of the community building available to all the Ridge inhabitants.

"Showtime, people! Look and stay alert," Annie said.

Chapter Two

The clubhouse used for all Ridge inhabitants was a luxurious-looking building on the outside. Inside, it was just as luxurious, a community center unlike any Myra's group had ever seen. Priceless art hung on the wheat-painted walls. Carpeting, ankle deep, matched the walls. Drapes embellished with lightning bolts of color adorned the wraparound windows overlooking lush gardens that were bare now but were a veritable rainbow of color in spring and summer.

Inside a medium-sized foyer, a pleasant-looking woman was sitting behind a massive, hand-carved desk that appeared to be some kind of antique. It took up most of the foyer, which was probably the intention of the builder. There was no place to sit. Visitors or guests signed in and were immediately ushered to wherever they wanted to go.

Soft music could be heard from somewhere in the back of the building. "How big is this place?" Maggie whispered to Annie.

"Thirty thousand square feet," Annie whispered back. "I only know this because the first time we were here, I heard someone ask the receptionist. There is a ballroom for festivities, a full kitchen, a dining room for banquets that seats two hundred, five different full bathrooms, a fully equipped gym with all the latest exercise equipment, and the community room, which is where we're going. Wait till you see it. One whole wall is a fish tank, with the most beautiful exotic fish in the world. They say watching fish is very restful. And all the plants you can see are also tropical, and someone comes in twice a week to care for them. Another wall has a hundred-inch plasma television. Watching it is like being in a movie theater. There is also a computer room with wi-fi and five computers. They have fax machines, copy machines, and five separate telephone lines. One time I was here, Lady wandered off, and I saw the room when I went to look for her. There's a sign on the door that says the room is soundproof. I do not quite understand why they need a soundproof computer room."

"A lot of money went into this operation,"

Myra said. "Top of the line in everything. The furniture is custom made, and whomever the decorator was, he or she did a great job. This place, big as it is, is still comfortable and welcoming. Everyone who lives at Olympic, King's, or Queen's Ridge has the run of this building. They even have concerts here from time to time. Famous people give them, and it's always free to the residents."

The pleasant-looking receptionist, whose name tag said her name was PAULINE, motioned for Myra and her team to follow her. "I'm afraid with the weather, you might not have a full house today. There are coffee and donuts on the credenza. And a bowl of dog treats. I'm sure Lady could use one."

Annie stepped forward. "It's hard to believe Thanksgiving is next week. Do you plan anything out here for the residents? Like this week, today in particular: is anything planned, aside from therapy day?"

"Well, having the reporters you brought with you is certainly out of the ordinary, not that we mind. Our residents dearly love therapy day. Personally, I wish the residents were allowed pets, but no one cares what I think even though I live in Olympic Ridge. I just volunteer here at the center to keep busy since my husband passed away in January."

"I'm so sorry," Myra said, patting the woman's arm as she made eye contact with Annie.

"My grandmother turned to the Internet when my grandpa died last year. She made a lot of friends on there. She loves e-mailing. Do you do that?" Dennis West said as he moved to stand next to Pauline.

"I do, but I'm not very good at it. I don't blog or tweet or anything like that. I just e-mail my children and grandchildren and a few friends. Well, I'll leave you now. I hear the bell, so someone is out front. We still have twenty minutes before the residents get here. I'll check and see how many calls went out to the shuttle and let you know if we're going to be running late.

"Oh, I'm sorry, you asked me about next week. This isn't new since we do it every year, but Santa comes on Thanksgiving day in a horse-drawn carriage. Mr. Macklin himself plays Santa as he's done every year since this community was built. He looks so much like Santa, he doesn't have to wear a beard or put on a white wig. You should see his suit and boots. It's the real thing. And he gives gifts to everyone. Not junk either."

When the bell rang again, Pauline literally

ran out of the room.

Dennis whipped out his phone, clicked twice, then waved it under everyone's nose. Smiling into the camera was Emanuel Macklin, and even Santa would have had to admit he was a dead ringer for Father Christmas.

"Do you think that counts as something we need to see and pay attention to?" Annie whispered.

Myra responded with a shrug. "Could be. I don't see anything else jumping out at us. Maybe the weather will prevent us from seeing or hearing whatever we were supposed to. Maggie, why don't you go up front and see if you can find out if Pauline knows anyone known as Kat at Gmail. You know how to interview people. She seems a chatty sort."

"I think Dennis should do it. Not that I don't want to do it, but he's young enough to be her grandson. I just think he'll have better luck."

Dennis was half out the door before Maggie had finished speaking.

Owners with their therapy animals started to trickle into the community room. Lady moved off to greet them as they were old friends. Maggie and Ted separated to start interviewing the owners, while Espinosa had his camera at the ready.

Myra and Annie made their way over to the credenza, where an elaborate silver service was set out. The donuts were fresh and the coffee a special blend that was delicious. Annie poured real cream into her coffee as she looked around. "I'm not seeing a damn thing, Myra. What about you?"

Myra brought her coffee cup to her lips. "Ellen and Abe Speer just got here. I told you about them and how they sought me out. They look . . . just the way they always look. They aren't even looking at us. I think this is going to be a washout."

Fifteen more minutes went by before the community director blew her whistle, which was the signal that the animals were to line up to get their assignments. A chocolate Lab barked as if to say, it's about time. A fluffy white cat hissed his disapproval, broke ranks, sauntered over to Lady, and started to purr. To the amusement of everyone, Lady nudged him back to his place in line.

The therapy hour flew by quickly, with the animals doing what they did best: offering comfort and love to anyone who needed to stroke them or murmur sweet words in their ears. The hour ended as it always did, with a parrot named Dominic who did a flyover not once but twice as he squawked,

"Good-bye, good-bye!" to everyone in the room. The audience clapped loudly in appreciation. The animals preened and looked to their owners for their treats. Therapy hour was over until next time. Now the owners and their therapy animals went to their next assignments. Lady's assignment was to visit Queen's Ridge nursing home to visit with Sara Overton, a recovering stroke victim.

Guests and residents of the Ridge milled around for the social hour that followed the therapy for those without special assignments. Maggie and Ted worked the crowd as Espinosa continued clicking away with his camera. There was no sign of Dennis West.

Myra reached for her jacket. "I'm not getting it, Annie. No one has come up to us, no one has said a word, and the director hasn't made any announcements other than to hand out our special assignments. I wonder if perhaps Sara Overton is someone who can give us a clue. The only thing we learned is that Emanuel Macklin, who looks like Santa Claus, is playing Saint Nick on Thanksgiving Day, when he will arrive in a carriage. And he gives everyone a gift that is not junk."

"That's not giving me the shivers, Myra.

So the guy is living up to his looks. He's probably bored making money and needs a diversion. My vote is, it means nothing to us at this moment. If it means anything, my money is on young Dennis. He does have a way of ferreting out information."

Dressed again for the outdoors, Myra called to Lady, who came on the run. Annie held out the leash, Myra hooked it onto Lady's collar, and the three of them walked ever so slowly out of the community room, hoping that someone would approach. No one did. Myra sighed. "This was a dead end."

"You can say that again," Ted said. "I didn't get a single thing. These people are not into computers and e-mail and handles. That's not to say they don't use computers; they do, but it's just to stay in touch with friends and family."

"Ditto for me," Maggie said, a look of disgust on her face. "I hope Dennis made out better than we did. Where *is* he?"

"Are you looking for me?" Dennis bellowed, as he loped down the hallway of the west wing.

"We are. We're leaving now to go to Queen's Ridge. We have to drive. Lady is going to visit a Ms. Sara Overton, who is a recovering stroke victim. After that, we go home. How did you do?"

Dennis reached for his jacket on the coatrack by the front door.

"Good-bye, Dennis. Now don't forget to come by on Monday for that pot roast dinner I promised you. Bring your friends if you like. The more the merrier."

"I won't forget, Pauline. It was so nice talking to you." Dennis turned to the others and said, "I told her she reminds me of my mom. Don't you all agree?"

"Absolutely." Maggie smiled.

"She even looks like your mother." Ted beamed.

"Let me take a picture of you and Dennis so he can show his mother," Espinosa said, as he shoved Dennis behind Pauline's chair. Dennis grinned like a Cheshire cat, and Pauline showed a lot of teeth, her hand reaching up to pat Dennis's hand, which was resting on her shoulder. "Say cheese!"

Picture taking done, everyone waved good-bye as they scooted for the door.

It was still snowing. Lady loved it, and she tried to catch the flakes on her tongue.

"What'd you get, hot shot?" Ted demanded.

"What you sent me to get. What do you think? Don't I always come through for you? Well? Huh? I felt terrible picking that nice lady's brain, and she's lonely. She's cooking a pot roast for me on Monday. I love pot roast. She liked me. She kept patting my hand."

"Kat at Gmail. You know who that is? Spit it out, kid."

"Well, not exactly. Sort of. Kind of. It's gonna take some legwork. Pauline does not like to gossip. Stop poking me, Ted. I'm freezing out here. Let's get in the van, and I'll tell you what I learned."

"This better be good, Dennis," Ted said, slamming the sliding door of the van so that Dennis and the others could get in. Somehow, Myra and Annie managed to squeeze in, too. Lady bounded into the front seat and tried to sit on Maggie's lap.

Ted turned over the engine. "Talk!" he bellowed.

"Okay, okay! Gee whiz, Ted. Look, in the computer room is a list of all the people who use the computers. Just their e-mail names. There are several variations of Kat. One is k.a.t. at yahoo and there is another one that is Tak at hotmail. That's kat spelled backward. Then there is the one you got e-mail from, the Kat at Gmail. Those are all free e-mail accounts. I don't know who the names belong to. There are over a hundred posted on the list. Pauline said she got an e-mail once a while back from the k.a.t at yahoo about something or other, but she can't remember what it was. She's going to search her account when she goes home and call me. That's it. And before you say it, I can see by the looks on all of your faces that I got more than you all got. Am I right? I am, I can see it! And the cub reporter strikes again!" Dennis said jubilantly.

"That's good work, Dennis," Maggie said. "I wonder if I can get Abner to hack into that computer to find out who the real Kat at Gmail is. He's good with that IP stuff, but then we already know what computer was used. Hey, he might be able to come up with something. By any chance, Dennis, did you get the times of day that Kat at Gmail logs on and off?"

"Late in the evening and early in the morning, that's all I could get. If there is no function going on here in that building we were just in, Pauline said it closes at six. So then how did Kat at Gmail get in? You said your e-mail came through early this morning. The center doesn't open till eight o'clock. Pauline opens and closes," Dennis said. "I asked her who else has keys to the center, and she said only the maintenance staff and Mr. Macklin. Oh, she also mentioned that someone named Luther Kelly had had a key, but he died last year. She doesn't know what happened to his key. Luther was a kind of security guard. No one replaced him that she knows of, and she pretty much had the skinny on this whole operation. I'm sure I'll get more during our pot roast dinner on Monday."

"Send Abner a text, Maggie," Myra said. "We have just arrived at Queen's Ridge, and Ms. Overton awaits us."

The Overton house was a pretty little building that resembled a Swiss chalet, and with the snow coming down, it was easy to imagine that they were in Switzerland. Myra rang the doorbell, which was a brass stag rearing up on its hind legs. The sound within was like a bongo drum. She stepped back, as did the others.

"Maybe she's hard of hearing," Maggie whispered.

The door was opened by a woman in an immaculate gray uniform with a white apron that was so pristine, it matched the falling snowflakes. She stood aside for the little group to enter. Lady held back and growled deep in her throat. Myra and Annie stopped in their tracks as the others tried to urge the golden dog farther into the foyer. Lady moved, but only unwillingly.

Myra turned her head so that no one

could see her speaking to Annie. "She's never done this before," Myra whispered in Annie's ear.

"I know," Annie hissed back.

And then they were in a pleasant, brick-walled room with comfortable furniture and a blazing fire in a fieldstone fireplace.

A tiny woman bounced off an oyster-colored sofa and bellowed, "What took you so long?"

"Ah . . . the weather . . . some of the therapy people were late. I'm sorry," Myra sputtered at the aggressive little woman with big hair. "Are you Ms. Overton? We were . . . expecting . . . Pauline at the clubhouse said Ms. Overton was a stroke victim. You . . . ah . . . are we at the wrong house?" Her grip on Lady's leash was so tight, the golden dog tried her best to back up. Ted and Espinosa closed ranks so there was nowhere for Lady to go.

The little woman boomed again. "Oh, don't pay any attention to that. I didn't have a stroke, I just wanted to move over here to Queen's Ridge, so I had Tressie lie. This is Tressie," Ms. Overton said, pointing to the woman who had opened the door.

"I don't understand," Myra said.

"I think I understand, Myra," Annie said as she took a step forward. "You're Kat from

Gmail, aren't you?"

"Took you long enough to figure it out, now, didn't it? Who are you? I was expecting the Vigilantes, not the geriatric patrol. I know what they look like, I've seen pictures, and the Vigilantes are *young.* You're *OLD.* I need young along with piss and vinegar, not warm milk and Bengay."

Lady reared back and howled.

"Oh shit!" Ted swore under his breath. "Those are fighting words."

"No shit," Espinosa growled.

Evidently, Lady thought they were fighting words, too. She balked, jerked free of Myra's hold on her, and raced to the door and lay down. She took turns growling and whimpering.

Annie, her eyes narrowed, opened her purse, and faster than lightning, was next to the little woman and had a gun pointed at her head. "Just goes to show, *nothing is as it seems.* Right, Ms. Overton?"

"Oh my God, that's a gun! She has a gun! A real gun! Do something," Dennis squealed.

"Shut the hell up, Dennis," Ted said, his eyes glued to Annie and the gun in her hand.

Before the others knew what was happening Myra had her arm around the maid's neck in a hammerlock and her knee in her back.

"Espinosa!" Maggie shrilled.

"I'm getting it! I got it! This will look great on the community bulletin board."

"Is she going to shoot? Is it loaded? Oh my God, what if it goes off?" Dennis sagged against the sofa, his face as white as the falling snow outside. "Gee whiz, I never saw a real gun up close before. Holy cow!"

"Talk!" Annie bellowed. "Otherwise, I am going to shoot up this place, five rounds, then I'm going to blow out your brains and hang your body from the flagpole in the common ground."

"Oh shit!" Ted said again.

"All right! All right!" Sara Overton said. "You made your point."

"Apologize. Right now!" Myra ordered.

"For what?" the little lady queried.

Annie cocked the hammer.

"Oh, you mean about the *OLD* comment I mentioned?"

"And . . ."

"The warm milk and Bengay? Okay, okay, I'm sorry. Now put that silly gun away. We all know you aren't going to shoot up my house or me. That's just . . . ridiculous."

"Oh shit," Ted said for the third time, as Annie shoved Ms. Overton onto the couch and fired off three rounds, shredding two club chairs, the coffee table, and a hutch filled with what looked like fine crystal. "I hope you're insured," Annie drawled.

"I am, and you'll do," the old lady said, cackling. "It's not the first time I've been wrong. I like your style. In my day, we called it moxie."

Annie blew on the end of the smoking gun and grinned. "I don't think we're interested, right, Myra?"

Myra, her ears ringing, nodded.

"Oh my God, what if someone comes and sees all this?" Dennis wailed as he flapped his arms like a bird in preparation for flight.

"Then Ms. Overton will have some explaining to do." Maggie grinned.

"Do you have a license to carry that gun?" Dennis bleated. Annie eyed him with such disdain that Dennis buried his face in a pillow, his whole body shaking.

Lady pranced into the room, looked around, and sniffed before she sat down next to Myra. Obviously she wouldn't be doing any more therapy and was smart enough to know it. Myra scratched her behind the ears to show things were right-side up. Messy but right-side up.

Annie shoved the gun back into her purse. She dusted her hands dramatically. "I think we've wasted enough of our valuable time here. We'll bill you, Ms. Overton."

"What? You're just going to walk out of here after you . . . you destroyed my living room. *I'm* the one who should be billing *you.* You're way too old to be PMSing, so let's all just sit down over a nice cup of coffee and discuss this like intelligent people."

"There's nothing intelligent about people wanting help who deal in riddles and don't have the guts to sign their name to their e-mails," Dennis West said, getting up on wobbly legs.

"And who might you be, you little whippersnapper? And the rest of you, who are you?"

Dennis rushed forward. He leaned over so that he was eyeball to eyeball with the little woman, who was wearing too much cheek blush. "I'm a Pulitzer Prize winner, that's who I am. I work for the *Washington Post,* these are my colleagues, we are going to do a number on you, and I will earn another Pulitzer, that's who I am."

"Ballsy, that's for sure. I like that. You'll do, whatever your name is. And I can personally guarantee you a second Pulitzer after you hear what I have to say."

"Maggie Spitzer," Maggie said.

"Ted Robinson."

"Joseph Espinosa."

"I recognize all your names except for the whippersnapper. I read the *Post* religiously. Now, this is what I suggest. We start over and pretend nothing happened. We adjourn to the dining room and have some coffee. I love coffee, and Tressie makes unbelievable coffee. Tressie, by the way, is my only friend in the whole world, my housekeeper, my pretend nurse, and my *confidante.* She doesn't talk much, but that's okay. She's also my eyes and ears as to what goes on outside my front door. In case you're wondering why that is, it is because I like to keep a low profile. I just want us to be clear on that. Are we?"

Everyone in the room nodded as they followed the little woman, who was skipping ahead, to the dining room.

Tressie poured coffee into fine bone china cups and handed them around the table. Silver cream and sugar pitchers were then passed around. The silver spoons were to be envied. Obviously, Sara Overton liked and owned fine things. Tressie returned to the kitchen and came back with a colorful Christmas plate piled high with fat sugar cookies that she passed around. Within minutes, they were all gone.

"Can we get on with it? It's past noon,

and the weather doesn't look like it's going to get any better," Annie grumbled.

"Fine, fine! I was just trying to be hospitable. Where to start?"

"Try the beginning," Annie snapped. "Don't make me pull out my gun again. I only have two rounds left."

"Yes, well, you might have young reflexes, but, like most *old* people, you have no patience," Sara Overton snapped in return. "I do understand, but first I have a question. Why did you bring these reporters here?"

"So we can nail your skinny ass to the wall if you brought us here under false pretenses. You are taking up our time, lady. Our time is valuable. Other people need our services, so let's just say they are our insurance. Now get to the point!" Annie literally bellowed.

Lady, liking the sound of Annie's agitation, barked loud and long before she started to howl.

"I'm going to tell you a story. You need to hear the story; otherwise, none of what I'm going to tell you will make sense. What I mean by that is, why I need you now. Not just me but hundreds, maybe thousands of people are going to need you. If you want to get all antsy and superior, go right ahead."

Myra reached for her pearls. "We're listening, Ms. Overton."

"For starters, that's not really my name, but that's immaterial at this point."

"You use an alias?" Dennis West squawked. "What, are you some kind of criminal?"

"Yes and yes, Son: I use an alias, and yes, I am a criminal. *Was* a criminal. But I gave up my wicked ways a long time ago. I even made restitution, so rest easy on all of that."

"Your story, Ms. whatever your name is," Myra said gently.

"A long time ago . . . forty or so years ago . . ."

Chapter Three

Sara Overton had everyone's attention, and she played to it. She looked like a precocious squirrel making faces as she let her memory go back to what she considered *her story* and the reason she was now playing to the audience she had requested.

"Actually, it's more like fifty years if you're counting, and I stopped doing that a long time ago. I was an orphan, as was Tressie, who is a little younger than I am. We had a third friend at the orphanage, a boy named Billy Bailey. My name was Marie Palmer and Tressie was Sally Dumont. None of us knew if those were really our names or just the names someone had assigned to us. We were taken care of — we had plenty of food, clean clothes, and beds to sleep in. And, believe it or not, we got a bath every single day. There were no tuck-ins at night, no hugs, no kisses. None of the things all kids secretly wish for. We had rules, we had school, and we had playtimes. And books, of course. The three of us were readers, and to this day, Tressie and I read constantly. Mostly trash, I'm sorry to say. Billy liked to read about the world, about government, how to build things, educational things. He was obsessed even back then with money and what a person could do if they were wealthy. He promised Tressie and me that someday we'd live in mansions with swimming pools and have so much money that we wouldn't know what to do with it all. Of course, we didn't really believe him, but it was fun to pretend, and Billy could weave the most exciting stories about what our lives would be like in the future. We wanted to believe, and maybe we did for a while.

"Somehow or other the three of us banded together. We were so tuned in to one another we knew what the other was thinking before they could give voice to the thought.

"Billy was two years older than I and four years older than Tressie, so that made him our leader if you will. He looked out for us and made sure none of the other kids bullied us or anything like that. Not that they did, but he still took care of us; he was our protector in every sense of the word. We felt safe with him, we really did. We seemed to know instinctively that as long as we were with him, nothing bad was going to happen to us.

"Just before Billy's eighteenth birthday, he said he was going to leave and strike out on his own. He asked me to go with him. He had no intention of taking Tressie. I suppose that was because she was just thirteen and . . . she wasn't . . . *quick,* if you know what I mean. I wanted to go with him, but not without Tressie, and he agreed to take the two of us. We left after breakfast on the day before he turned eighteen. We didn't have much to take with us, just a few clothes, our rosaries, and our catechism books. Billy left his behind, but Tressie and I took ours. Billy stole the money Sister Helen had gotten from the bank to pay the workmen, and that's all we had. It was the first time that any of us had ever held any money in our hands.

"We lived wherever we could, washed up in gas-station rest-rooms. It wasn't much of a life, and Tressie and I wanted to go back, but then Billy got the idea to try panhandling. We were quite successful; he was the older brother taking care of his two little sisters. People gave generously. We moved around a lot so no one would turn us in to the authorities. We lived in a number of different cities as we slowly worked our way south and east toward New York City.

"Eventually, we found a ratty apartment in Scranton that had a real bathtub. We thought we had died and gone to heaven. By day we panhandled and by night we were burglars. We broke into businesses, homes, stole whatever we could carry. Then we'd fence it. Billy kept our money, gave us an allowance, and bought us decent clothes. We eventually got a better apartment and learned to cook to save on money. This went on for three years.

"I was eighteen when Billy said he wanted to move to New York since the pickings were better there than in Scranton. When we got there, however, we only stayed in Manhattan long enough to get bus money to take us on to Washington, D.C. Billy said that staying in New York could get us caught and that Tressie would be sent back to the orphanage. Actually, we moved to Virginia and worked, if you want to call it that, in the District. Billy bought us scooters — secondhand, of course — tinkered with them, and that's how we traveled back and forth.

"Then, a year and a half later, Billy said he'd go ahead of us to New York, get the lay of the land, and make arrangements for Tressie and me to follow. Tressie was of age by then, and he said no one would be looking for us. He left money for us and told us to lie low till he got back. There was a pay phone out on the street, and he called every night at eight o'clock and reported in.

"That worked fine until the tenth day, when the building we were living in caught on fire. The fire trucks knocked out the phone booth on the street, and our building was nothing but ashes the next day. Tressie and I escaped with just the clothes on our backs, our purses, and the money Billy left for us, most of which had been spent. We panicked. The only thing we knew how to do was rob and steal and panhandle. Tressie said we should go to the Salvation Army and ask for help. So we did, and they did help us. They got both of us jobs in a nursing home of sorts. They even found us a rooming house. For the first time in our lives, Tressie and I knew what it was like to be what we thought of as normal. We went to work, cashed our paychecks, paid our room rent, paid for our food, and saved the rest of our money. We even made a few friends. And we never saw Billy again.

"The patients at the nursing home adored Tressie. There was this one elderly lady, a grandmother type, who was bedridden. Tressie was assigned to her. I always helped, but because of my diminutive stature, I couldn't move the patients. Tressie did all that. I had to stand on a stool. I would comb and brush Mrs. Meredith's hair, put a little rouge on her cheeks. She really liked that. She said she wanted to look her best in case someone came to visit her. No one ever did. I guess you could say Tressie and I were her family. On her birthday, we even bought a bottle of perfume for her at the drugstore. She was so moved, she cried.

"Mrs. Meredith died in her sleep a year and a half after we started to work at the nursing home. No one was more surprised than Tressie and me when this lawyer showed up at the nursing home and asked to see us. We almost ran away, thinking that somehow the police had found out what we used to do. But by the time we got to the door, our floor person caught us and took us to the conference room. Long story short, Mrs. Meredith had left Tressie and me her house, her brokerage account, her car, and all the furniture in her house. The house and car were paid for. Neither one of us knew how to drive, but we learned. The brokerage account had fifty thousand dollars in it. Back then, that was a fortune. Tressie and I talked and decided to take half of the money and donate it to different charities as a way to make up for what we had stolen when we were with Billy. And we started to feel good about ourselves.

"We continued working at the nursing home, and the same thing happened twice more. Patients left us what they had in their wills. Nothing on the scale of what Mrs. Meredith had left us, just a simple kindness. We weren't set for life, but we were quite comfortable.

"Flash forward. We stayed at the nursing home for ten years until it was sold, and new management took over. Tressie and I didn't like how they were all about the money and not patient care. We tried anonymously to blow the whistle on them, but no one paid any attention. We quit and decided to go into business for ourselves. We even changed our names. That was Tress's idea, and I went along with it. I suppose that she realized how it was important that Billy not be able to identify us should we become successful and well-known.

"We cleaned out Mrs. Meredith's garage to provide workspace and, using most of our funds, started making medical welcome packets for people going into nursing homes, hospitals, and therapy facilities. The Salvation Army people helped us and even got us customers. Before we knew it, we were making so much money that we couldn't count it all. Perhaps you've heard of our company. It's called WELMED."

"WELMED is *YOU*!" Annie exclaimed. "I own stock in your company."

"That's nice to know. And no doubt you like that handsome dividend we pay you every quarter."

"I do! I do!" Annie said, excitement ringing in her voice.

"This is when the people at the Salvation Army who were helping us explained that we needed financial help — lawyers, accountants, financial planners. We did all that.

"Tressie said, and I agreed, that we wanted to remain private, so we never gave interviews, never allowed our pictures to be taken because always in the back of our minds was the fear that someone, somewhere, would remember us, and we'd go to jail. And we didn't want anything to happen to the company we'd worked so hard to build. When the lawyers took our company public, Tressie and I went to Europe. To this day, as hard as it may be for you to believe, no one knows who we were or are. Our lawyers at the Quinn Law Firm talk for us."

"So you're rich!" Dennis said. "There are

a lot of people out there who are rich but who don't send anonymous e-mails threatening doom and gloom. What is it you want?"

"Just you hold your horses, sonny. I'm getting to it." Sara looked at Dennis with a critical eye, then smiled. "You know, Son, I'm thinking if I'd ever had a grandson, he'd probably be your age and maybe even look like you. If I have any regrets, that's it, not having children and grandchildren."

Dennis, softhearted mush that he was, backed up, and before he knew what he was saying, said, "I'm available. I mean, I don't have grandparents anymore. If you need a stand-in, I'm yours." Damn, did he just say that? Obviously, he had, from the way everyone was looking at him.

"Well, now, that's the nicest thing anyone has ever said to me, young man. How would you feel about having Tressie as an aunt? Aunt Tressie."

Dennis decided since he'd put his big toe in his mouth, he might as well shove his whole foot in. "I'd be honored . . . Granny."

The little old lady cackled happily. "Then, grandson, it's official. You're all witnesses. You are now my grandson and Tress's nephew. At some point when all this is settled and put to bed we can celebrate. Is that okay with you?"

"Well, sure. Whatever you want. My other granny never let me argue with her. She said she was always right. Are you always right?"

"Most of the time. Tressie and I have made our share of mistakes. We don't talk about them, though, because we like to think we're perfect."

"I guess that works for me. So, Granny, can we speed this up? I'm really getting hungry," Dennis grumbled. "And look outside. We have to drive home in this weather."

"Oh, to be that young again and to have to live with no patience. All right, grandson, spoil my day for me. Now be quiet and listen to your granny and aunt."

Dennis shut up after receiving a glare from his idol, Ted.

"Our financial people invested a ton of our money with this financial wizard who enabled Tressie and me to move out here to this complex. We were getting a 20-percent annual return on our money. My financial people were over the moon, as were we. Since we did not really need it, we donated that 20 percent to every worthy charity we could think of and even started up a few of our own. And to this day, we donate handsomely to the Salvation Army and their people who made all of this possible."

"I'm not following you," Annie said. "Why do you need us?"

"Because the person our people invested with turned out to be Billy Bailey, known to the entire world as Emanuel Macklin. And his entire operation is all one big Ponzi scheme. I want you to stop him. In his tracks. We've seen the signs, the cracks; we've heard the disgruntled investors. At first, Tressie and I weren't sure, but then we did our own checking, and, sure enough, it's Billy. We immediately pulled all our money, which was well over 100 million dollars, out of his hands. That started a bit of a panic. We're safe now, but there are thousands who aren't."

The room was quiet, jaws dropped, and eyes gaped in stunned surprise.

Annie had her cell phone in hand and was hitting her speed dial. She got up and walked into the kitchen so the others couldn't hear what she was saying. "Just say yes or no, Connor. Did you invest any of my money with Emanuel Macklin? How much? When?" Annie swayed as she fought to ward off a wave of dizziness. "Okay. I'm glad to hear that it is a very recent investment and we're no more than even. At least we haven't lost any money. Anyway, I'm giving you five minutes to clean it out. FIVE damn minutes. Otherwise, you are going to be mowing your own lawn, and your seventh wife will be doing her own nails, compliments of Walgreens' nail-polish department. Oh, and you'll be on the unemployment line. The minute you finish that, check with Bert and see where they have Babylon's profits going. If it's Macklin, pull it all out. Five minutes, Connor."

Annie's second call was to Charles, where she repeated everything she'd just said to her financial guru and gave instructions that he was to give to Myra's financial people.

Somehow, Annie managed to stumble back to her chair. She looked at Myra, and said, "I called Charles. I just got out, and so will you. I hope that you have not been invested with this guy for very long." She looked over at the little lady with the big see-through hair, and smiled sickly.

"Good for you, ladies. I'm glad I could help."

"Hold on here a minute," Maggie said, wagging her hand in the air. "Are you saying all these years that you never saw any pictures of Manny Macklin? You never put two and two together? I'm finding that hard to believe."

"Why, dear? Tressie and I had people taking care of things for us, people we trusted. I rarely if ever read the financial section of the newspapers. Manny Macklin, if I did see the name, didn't ring any bells with either Tressie or me. Now, if it had been Billy Bailey, then yes, we would have known. Tressie and I are readers, not television watchers. The name Emanuel Macklin or Manny Macklin meant nothing to us. We knew someone named Billy Bailey, someone who had taken care of us for more than a decade, both inside and outside an orphanage. The other thing is, Billy does not now look anything like he did back then. Today he is chubby and has a full head of white hair and a full white beard. The media say he is a double for Santa Claus himself. If I had passed him on the street, I would not have recognized him. Time and age. . . ." Ms. Overton said, letting what she didn't say hang in the air.

"I guess it makes sense," Myra said, just as Annie's cell phone chirped. She watched as Annie scampered off toward the kitchen. The others could hear Annie's sigh of relief all the way in the living room. She gave a thumbs-up to Myra, who simply nodded.

"It would seem, Ms. Overton, that Myra and I owe you a debt of gratitude. Thanks seems hardly enough."

"*Countess,* I'm not looking for thanks. I want you to *do* something. At our first inkling that something wasn't kosher, Tressie and I set out to find out everything we could about Emanuel Macklin. What bothers me the most is the people here in King's Ridge and Queen's Ridge who are going to see their money disappear overnight. I know most of them in one way or another. I do not even want to think about all those poor souls who are living out their final days in the hospice at Angel Ridge. When those poor souls die, all their assets go back to Macklin. That's part of the deal you sign up for when you move here. Once you're here, you're hooked. Now that we've engaged your interest, Tressie and I will be moving on. We'll just walk out, get in our car, and go abroad. We know how to get lost. Our money and the company are safe, at least for now. As I understand it, these last seven years or so, Billy, or Manny, has been signing up middle-income and low-income investors, people who can't afford to lose what little they have. He uses their money to fund the returns to his wealthy clients and pay off any withdrawals, in order to keep them happy and, most of all, quiet. It's the little person who is starting to ask questions. Think Bernie Madoff but twenty times worse and much bigger."

Dennis West felt his eyes roll back in his head. He could *smell* a second Pulitzer.

So could Maggie and Ted. Annie's eyes sparked, and Myra gripped her pearls in a death grip.

"Well! Aren't you all going to say something?" the little woman said tartly.

"You're absolutely sure about all of this?" Maggie said.

"Honey, do dogs get fleas? I just love that saying. We are sure. Manny Macklin is definitely Billy Bailey. The orphanage is still in Syracuse, but of course new people are running it these days. Tressie and I went there once and donated a hefty amount of money for them to buy books, computers, printers, and the like. Ask to see the orphanage records. There might be something in them that can help you identify Billy. Somewhere, there have to be the yearly pictures from the time we were there. They were taken during the summer months. All the old records used to be kept in the subbasement. I'm sure they're moldy and might even have some dry rot on them, but you all need to satisfy yourselves."

"We could come out here on Thanksgiving on some pretext or other and take pictures of Macklin playing Santa and handing out his tony gifts. You know, his arrival in the carriage. Human-interest stuff," Ted said.

Annie started to gather up her belongings. Lady got to her feet and whimpered. "How do we get in touch with you, Ms. Overton?"

"How about if we just leave it that Kat at Gmail will get in touch with you."

"Now, you see, that is *not* going to work for any of us. None of us work that way. The client — you, in this case — must always be available to us. That's our rule, so take it or leave it. Right, people?" Maggie said forcefully.

Everyone agreed.

"All right." Ms. Overton rattled off two cellphone numbers. Maggie inputted them into her phone, then sent them to Myra's, Annie's, Ted's, and Dennis's phones. Espinosa said he didn't need it since he was just a photographer and not a reporter.

"When do you plan on leaving here?" Myra asked as she slipped into her jacket.

"Right after you. We have a few things to take care of first. I'll be in touch. Tressie and I want to thank you for tracking us down."

"It would have been a lot easier and quicker if you had given us a way to get in touch with you," Annie grumbled.

"You got here, and that's all that matters,"

the little woman said tartly.

Tressie spoke for the first time. She had a gentle, musical-sounding voice that surprised everyone. "Security at the gate keeps a record of everyone who drives through the gates. It might not seem like it to an outsider, but everyone who lives here is watched."

"That's why I wanted you to come on therapy day," Ms. Overton said. "You've been coming here for months and months, so no one will think twice about your visit or if you come back on Thanksgiving. Your people from the *Post* are legitimate, so be sure you really do print something in the paper to back up this visit as soon as you can to give legitimacy to the visit. I don't mean to sound like an alarmist, but one can't be too careful. Manny Macklin has billions of dollars' worth of incentives to make sure that nothing gets in the way of his scheme. He knows what happened to Bernie Madoff when his shenanigans were exposed, and I am sure that Emanuel Macklin — Billy Bailey — would stop at nothing to prevent the same thing from happening to him. So be careful."

The good-byes were brief and quick, with Lady running ahead out into the snow and heading directly for the van. She danced around, barking and pawing the ground. She wanted to go home, it was that simple. Everyone smiled when Granny Sara embraced her new grandson. Dennis beamed happily.

"Looks like an inch or so of snow on the ground," Maggie said as she slid the door open for Lady. "I didn't think it was going to stick, and that weatherman needs to be fired."

"One can never predict what Mother Nature will do, not even the meteorologists, who make their living being half-right and half-wrong," Dennis said philosophically. Ted gave him a shove as he flew into the rear seat of the van.

"Lord, Ted, turn on the heat," Annie said, hugging her arms across her chest.

Ted laughed. "By the time the heat comes on I'll have you in the parking lot of the clubhouse, and you'll be getting into your own cold car. Not to mention you'll have to clear the windshield. Dennis will be happy to do that for you, won't you, Dennis?"

"Absolutely. I will be thrilled and delighted to clear the snow off your windshield with my bare frozen hands. Yes siree, I can't wait. That lady was something, wasn't she? I believe her, though."

Ten minutes later, Myra, Annie, and Lady

were sitting in their own car, waiting for it to warm up. Sweet, snarling Dennis had indeed cleaned off the front and back windshields. No one seemed to care that his hands were red and looked chapped, not even Dennis, as he raced to get back into the van.

Lady made her presence known as she tugged at the seat belt Myra had patiently taught her to use. The minute she was secure, she barked again, meaning, "I'm buckled up, so let's hit the road."

"In a minute, Lady. We have to get warm first. Settle down, we're going home. What did I tell you about patience?" Myra fixed a steely gaze on the retriever, who had the good grace to look ashamed. But like most females, she needed the last word so she let loose with a ferocious howl, then settled down. Both Annie and Myra tried not to laugh.

"Whatcha think, Myra? Did any of that sound strange to you?"

Myra knew Annie wasn't talking about Lady and her seat belt. "The part about them not knowing all these years that Manny is Billy, yes, it doesn't ring true, but in some ways it does. My personal opinion is they are still emotionally tied to Billy Bailey. They want him stopped, but by us, not the authorities. Are you reading it any differently, Annie?"

Annie shrugged. "They could have gone to the SEC anonymously. Ask yourself why they didn't do that? The Securities and Exchange Commission has to pay attention to any and all complaints, so why didn't they do that? This is just a wild thought on my part, but I think Ms. Overton still has feelings for Billy Bailey. Buried deep, of course, but young love sometimes lasts forever."

"I don't know, Annie. It's a stretch but entirely possible. Did either one of them say how long they've been living out there? For some reason, I'm thinking they only moved there recently. To have lived there longer they would have seen Manny Macklin at the clubhouse; someone said he goes there once a month or so and actually had a house of his own at Olympic Ridge. That's bothering me. Then again, they didn't sound like the type of women who mingled with the other residents. They admitted they were loners."

"I think a lot of things are going to start bothering us once we delve into all of this. The kids are excited. Could you tell?" Annie said.

Myra laughed. "This is right up their alley

or down their alley or whatever that expression is. This is definitely something for the four of them to sink their teeth into. I don't think it's a good idea for you and I to go out there on Thanksgiving, however. I say we send the kids and let them run with it. Mr. Manny Macklin might be getting a little testy about now with two, or is it three, redemptions. Did Bert invest Babylon's profits with Macklin?"

"He did, and Connor redeemed it along with mine, and Charles did yours. That's not just a boatful of money, Myra, it's a *yacht*ful. He's going to be squirming. But we're out, that's the important thing."

The rest of the ride back to Pinewood was made in silence as Annie paid attention to the road, ever mindful that she had precious cargo in the backseat, namely, a golden retriever named Lady, whom Myra loved and adored, possibly more than she loved and adored Charles, her husband.

Chapter Four

Sara Overton stood at the bay window and stared out at the snow. For some reason, she was feeling jittery, and it wasn't the falling snow working on her nerves. She hated second-guessing herself, she really did. She liked the people she'd just said good-bye to. But was it a mistake calling them in to handle what she saw as a problem belonging to her and Tressie? Wasn't it their own responsibility to do what needed to be done? They were copping out, and she knew it. So did Tressie.

Time will tell, she told herself. Then she smiled at the thought that she now had a grandson, and Tressie had a nephew. How sweet was that? Just like that, out of the blue, she had a grandson!

She sensed Tress's presence before she felt her hand on her shoulder. "We didn't make a mistake, did we, Tressie?"

"I don't think so. There was no other way,

Sara. We talked about this so many times, and we both agreed that Billy has to be stopped. I think what you're feeling right now is the same thing I'm feeling, which is, we should have figured it out sooner. But we were both so wrapped up in our own cocoon that we didn't want to see it. It's called *guilt.* Sara, this might be a good time for you to finally say the words out loud. I've always respected your feelings and never said a word. But I know, Sara, I just *know* that you still have feelings for Billy locked away in your heart. That's the reason we enlisted the aid of the Vigilantes. We're cowards, pure and simple. It's all right to have the feelings you have for Billy. We can't unring that bell, dear. But look at it this way: we got a bonus today. I got a nephew, and you got a grandson. We need to do something about that before we start out. Okay, okay, I can see by your expression that we are not going to be discussing Billy now or anytime in the future. Am I reading this right?"

Sara nodded. "Are you saying what I think you're saying?"

"There's no one else, Sara. We made all our bequests. All we have to do is type up an addendum and fax it to Miss Quinn. I'll do it; you call the firm to tell them of the change. Imagine the look on that young man's face when they tell him he's our residual heir! We're going to do just what Mrs. Meredith did for us years and years ago. I think that young man will do something wonderful with the inheritance we leave him, just the way we did with Mrs. Meredith's. What goes around comes around. We've done a lot of good things in our lifetime, Sara. I think we more than made up for all the sinful things we did back when Billy was in our lives."

"Just like that, Tressie! We're leaving our fortune to a young man we just met a few minutes ago."

Tressie cupped Sara's face in her hands. "Isn't that what happened to us, Sara? That's how we got our start. Without Mrs. Meredith's leaving us her estate, we wouldn't even be standing here. If you don't agree, then we won't do it. If it counts, I liked that young man. Look, we aren't going to die tomorrow. By the time that young man inherits our estate, his children will be in college and he'll probably have bills, a mortgage, the whole ball of suburban wax. It's a good thing," Tressie said softly.

Sara smiled as she patted Tress's hand. "You're right, of course. Go ahead. Type it up, sign it, then bring it to me to sign. I'll call the firm and let them know that the fax will be coming through. Are we going to need a witness to us signing?"

"I'll film us signing and upload it to the firm."

Ten minutes later, it was a done deed. Tressie unplugged the computer and the fax machine. "That was such a nice thing we just did, Sara."

"Yes, it was. I think Mrs. Meredith would be proud of us, don't you, Tressie?"

"I do, Sara. Are we done here?"

"We are. We should have gone to the SEC. Why didn't we do that, Tressie?" Sara asked fretfully.

"Because we're both cowards. And down deep, we both feel like we still owe something to Billy. In your case, your personal feelings for him. What else could it be? Think about it, Sara; we wouldn't be where we are today if it wasn't for Billy's taking us with him when he made up his mind to leave the orphanage."

Sara's voice was still fretful when she said, "But we made it on our own. He didn't help us."

"We wouldn't have been able to do anything if it wasn't for Billy. We would have stayed in the orphanage until we were eighteen, then gotten jobs as salesclerks or waitresses or something like that. You know it, and I know it. By calling in the Vigilantes, we are asking them to do what we can't or won't do ourselves. No matter how you look at it, we're cowards."

Sara reached up and patted Tress's hand, which was resting on her shoulder. "Yes, we are. Are we ready to leave? Should we double-check?"

"Our bags are by the garage door. All appliances have been unplugged. The fridge is empty. No wet towels anywhere. The safe-deposit keys are in my purse, and you have a set in your purse. Trash can is full and ready to be picked up tomorrow. I stripped the beds, washed all the linens, and put them in the closet. We're leaving things nice and tidy. Did I forget anything?"

"I don't think so. I don't like leaving the BMW, but a sports coupe is no good in this kind of weather. We need to take the Rover. It's snowing harder, Tressie. Maybe we should wait to see if it lets up."

"Maybe we shouldn't. Our whole life has been about waiting for one thing or another. We've driven in snow before. Are you saying you don't trust me behind the wheel?"

"I'm not saying that at all, Tressie. I'm just unnerved. We talked about this day for years and years, and now that it's here, I'm relieved. And yet, I'm terribly sad. You know me, Tressie, I always want happily ever after."

"You're going to have to settle for being happy ever after at the Best Western. Tomorrow, weather permitting, we'll be on a plane to Costa Rica, where we will live out our lives. You said you were okay with that, Sara. Tell me now if you want to switch up. You did tell the law firm we were going to Europe, right?"

"No, I don't want to switch up. And yes, I told them we were going to Europe. I'm a little antsy about that. Someone should know where we are, you know, just in case. We could be in a plane crash, we could have an accident on the highway, a bomb could go off in the Best Western. But I understand our need for secrecy. At some point, I do think we will have to tell Miss Quinn where we are. Someone needs to know. A plan is a plan, and we're sticking to ours. I'm ready, Tressie."

Tressie patted Sara's shoulder. She reached up, turned off the kitchen light, then opened the door that led into the garage, where their two vehicles waited. Sara picked up her bag, as Tressie did hers, and they secured them in the cargo hold. Tressie pressed the remote on the visor of the

Rover, and the garage door slid upward. Both women settled themselves as Tressie turned on the engine and backed the big SUV out of the garage. She waited until the garage door slid down before she backed out of the driveway.

"The snowplows should have come through by now. With all his money, Billy should have the maintenance crew on call the minute the white stuff starts to fall. Penny pincher." Sara sniffed.

Twenty minutes later, going no more than ten miles an hour, Tressie turned onto the interstate. The plan was to go to the first exit, get off, and head to the Best Western, and that's what she did. She turned on her signal light, and just as she turned the wheel, a monster eighteen-wheeler sideswiped the Rover, spinning it around, where a Dodge Ram pickup truck hit it head on.

Both women in the Range Rover died on impact just as Annie drove through the gates of Pinewood.

Lady howled her pleasure at being home. Myra climbed out of the car on wobbly legs and opened the rear door for the dog to jump down. She turned to Annie and said, "You are not going home and out on that road again. You're staying here tonight. I don't want to hear a word out of you either. Are we clear on that, Annie? And reach in the back and get those two thick folders Ms. Overton insisted we take with us to read at our leisure. Tomorrow will be time enough to go through them, I'm thinking."

"Crystal. And I was going to beg you to let me stay. I don't think I've ever had such a harrowing drive in my life. The snow is coming sideways; how weird is that, Myra?" Annie said as she grappled with the two thick accordion folders and tried to stay on her feet at the same time. "Gotcha," she mumbled as she slammed the door with her hip and trudged toward Myra's kitchen door.

"Everything is weird to me today, Annie. Right now, the only thing I care about is getting inside and having something nice and hot to drink. Oh, I do so hope that Charles is making us a good dinner this evening."

It was pure pandemonium when Myra opened the kitchen door. The small television on the kitchen counter was turned on high, the four pups were barking their brains out now that their mother was home to see to them. Charles had a blender working at high speed while his free hand was pressing down on a chopping machine that added to the clamor.

"Home sweet home!" Annie laughed as she leaned over to turn off the TV. "Guess you'll have to wait till tomorrow to see what is happening on your favorite soap opera." She laughed as Charles wrinkled up his nose at her. He loved soap operas and wasn't afraid to admit it.

Myra opened the door, and the pups barreled through, followed by Lady. Both machines under Charles's care went quiet at the same time. The sudden silence was deafening.

Myra broke the moment by saying, "Hot chocolate with little marshmallows would taste so good right now, wouldn't it, Annie?"

"Absolutely, it would," was Annie's response.

Miffed that he was missing the last ten minutes of his soap, Charles banged a few pots and pans to make his point that he was unhappy, but he knew that neither woman cared, so he carefully measured out milk and chocolate and set the pot on the stove. Five minutes later, he sprinkled in little marshmallows to Annie's delight and plopped both huge cups in front of his two favorite women. "Talk to me!" he ordered.

"We will as soon as you tell us what's for

dinner," Myra said, the cup to her lips, her eyes sparkling.

Charles sighed. Someday he was going to win, but he was smart enough to know that this was not the day. "Leg of lamb, mint jelly, Irish potatoes, my special lettuce bacon hot salad, yeast rolls, and chocolate thunder four-layer cake."

"I think that will work, don't you, Annie?" Myra said over the rim of her cup.

"It's better than weenies, that's for sure," Annie replied, giggling.

Suddenly the dogs slammed up against the kitchen door. Myra got up and opened it as the dogs, covered in snow, raced into the kitchen. They shook themselves all at the same time. The three humans ran to the laundry room for towels and mops as the dogs slipped and slid over the tile floor, barking and, as Charles said, having a hell of a time.

"My house is so quiet compared to this place," Annie said as she tried her best to dry off one of the pups, who clearly did not want to be dried off. One sharp bark from Lady was all it took for the pup to back up and submit to Annie's vigorous towel rub.

"Scoot, now," Myra said to the rambunctious dogs. "Go by the fire and warm up."

Charles checked on the progress of dinner, then poured himself some hot chocolate and topped off Myra's and Annie's cups. "Now, talk to me."

The two best friends talked. Nonstop for a full thirty minutes until Charles held up his hands, and asked, "Why didn't they just go to the SEC and file a complaint?"

"We asked ourselves that, too, Charles. Unbreakable ties to an old childhood friend. Guilt, we think, was the primary reason. They want him caught, but they don't want to be physically a part of it. Contacting us was their way out. They were just children when they knew Billy. We are all — meaning Maggie and the boys — having trouble believing that all these years they didn't know that Billy Bailey was Manny Macklin. I'm not calling them liars, but I am having a hard time with that part of it."

"They explained it away, though," Annie said.

"It is entirely possible," Charles said, agreeing with Annie. Myra just frowned as she fussed with the pearls around her neck.

"What's the game plan?" Charles asked, when the women went silent.

"To get as much information as possible on Emanuel Macklin. Maggie called Abner, and he's already on the financial end of it. I'd like to get some information on his first wife and what happened to her, but Annie and I can do that. Can you do Billy or Manny whatever he's called these days, this afternoon, Charles?" Charles nodded as he got up from the table.

"Macklin is on his third trophy wife. That means he has tripped down the aisle four separate times. All we really know is that he has a son and a daughter — by the first wife, I think. No one told me that, I just remember reading it somewhere. Both work for their father," Annie said. "Myra and I can see what we can come up with in regard to the four wives. And the kids, while you do what you have to do. Is dinner good, or do we need to watch and stir or anything?"

Charles clapped at his forehead. "God forbid. Do *NOT* touch a thing while I'm down in the War Room. Is that understood? Dinner will take care of itself."

"In that case, Annie and I shall retire to the family room and work by ourselves as we watch over the dogs, which is more to our liking anyway. Sometimes, Charles, you are just too cruel," Myra said, winking at Annie, who grinned from ear to ear.

"And you both are so full of it, your eyes are turning brown. I will be back up here at five thirty, so do not get into any trouble. Unless, of course, you two want to go out and clear the driveway with the snow-blower."

"I-don't-think-so!" Annie said, marching into the family room. The dogs cracked open their eyes and went right back to sleep as Myra snapped open her laptop. Annie sat down and did the same thing. "Amazing what you can learn on the Internet, isn't it, Myra?"

"It certainly is. I'll take wife number one, and you do numbers two and three. And together, we'll do the current Mrs. Macklin. The two kids come last, but they aren't really kids anymore."

"That works for me!" Annie said, offering up a devilish grin.

Myra and Annie worked side by side, making comments from time to time as they worked on their Internet searches. The only sound in the great room was the soft tapping of the keys and the dogs' gentle snoring. An hour into their Internet searches, Annie suggested coffee and said she'd make it.

While she waited for the coffee to drip all the way down, Annie stared out the kitchen window at the falling snow. To her untrained eye, it looked like there were about five inches of accumulated snow. She shuddered when she thought about her own mile-long driveway. She hoped the man she had on retainer was hard at work clearing the white stuff away. She had no desire for a fall or a broken bone. She hated thinking about her bones and the drugs she had to take to keep them from deteriorating. The good news was that her doctor said she was slowly rebuilding bones. "Golden years, my ass," she mumbled to the empty kitchen.

"What did you say?" Myra asked, as she entered the kitchen.

"I was talking to myself, Myra. About my bones, and hoping that guy, Dwayne, whom I have on retainer, is clearing my driveway. I was also mumbling about the golden years."

Myra joined her friend at the window. "Remember how as children we loved snow. And how our girls took after us. They could stay outside for hours and hours and come in all rosy cheeked and wanting hot chocolate," Myra said with a catch in her voice. She looked up at Annie, who had tears in her eyes.

And then the unbelievable happened. Both women saw the vision at the same time. Two young girls in cherry red jackets lined in white fur, waving to them from a snowdrift.

"You see them, don't you, Annie? Please, God, tell me you see our daughters," Myra whispered.

Annie reached out for Myra's hands. "I do. I can see them. We bought those jackets at the same time," she whispered in return.

"Look, Annie, they're going to throw us a snowball. We taught them how to do that, remember?"

Both women reared back when two snowballs hit the kitchen window. "No one will believe us if we tell them about this," Myra said.

"I know. And I know if we go outside, they will disappear. I was just standing here feeling so very melancholy."

"I told you, Annie, they come when we need them most. We have to accept it because there are no other options."

"They're fading away," Annie said, waving frantically. Myra did the same thing.

"Do you feel any better, Annie?"

"Yes. No." She shrugged. "I wanted more. I will always want more. They really did throw the snowballs. If only we could preserve that."

"It doesn't work that way, you know that. This is for now until the next time. Be happy we got this. And we *saw* them. It wasn't just a presence or a feeling or whispered words. We *saw* them," Myra said.

Annie wrapped Myra in her arms and

together they had a good cry. For the would-haves, the could-haves, and the should-haves.

"Okay, enough of this drama; we have work to do," Annie said, wiping her eyes on her shirt sleeve the way she had when she was a child. Myra did the same thing.

Myra poured coffee. "Did you get anything interesting, Annie?"

"Well, wife number two is named Carol Jones, if you can believe that. Macklin married her two years after his divorce from his first wife, Mary. She was a bookkeeper at an accounting firm when he met her. She went on to get her degree in accounting and finally, after four tries, got her CPA license. They were married six years, and the reason for the divorce was irreconcilable differences. I take that to mean he paid her off big-time because she knew what he was doing. No clue where she is today. She dropped off the grid and didn't show up in court the day they were divorced. No children; friends said she simply disappeared. People do that when there is a handsome payday. As to what she got as a settlement, that's sealed, but speculation was, 15 million dollars. True or false, I don't know. What did you find out on the first Mrs. Macklin?"

"Her name is Mary. No clue where she resides these days. There is no obituary, so I'm pretty sure that she's alive somewhere or other. She might have remarried, so she could have a new name, but I couldn't find anything in the marriage records in Virginia, Maryland, or D.C. She divorced Macklin after twenty-two years of marriage. She was nineteen when he married her. They had a son and a daughter, and the son was in college when she filed for divorce. The daughter was a high school senior when Mary walked out on her husband and children. The children elected to stay with the father since he was the one with the money. At least at that time. Mary walked away with pretty much just the clothes on her back. It appears she didn't look back either. Twenty-two years is a long time to stay married, then throw in the towel. So whatever happened must have been serious. They were divorced quietly. No record of a settlement anywhere that I could find, sealed or otherwise. She didn't work during the marriage. So I assume she was a homemaker taking care of her husband and children during those years. Macklin met her at a bakery where she worked. That's the only kind of job she's ever held as far as I could determine. No housing records, no records of her paying taxes anywhere, property or otherwise. It's like she disappeared, too, or as Maggie would say, she went off the grid."

Annie curled her legs up under her and asked, "What do you make of it, Myra?"

"Mary stuck it out for twenty-two years. I assume that means she's from the old school. The second Mrs. Macklin got a big payday. If you're thinking he *offed* them, no, I don't think so. One just got fed up and walked away, apparently not wanting anything. To me, that cries out dirty money. She found out, and that's why she left. The second wife got her payday and split for calmer waters. That might have been part of their agreement. She leaves and never opens her mouth.

"Wife number three lasted all of ten months. She was a stripper. Nothing there. Looks like she got fifty grand, and that's it. I guess that stripping did not qualify her to figure out that Macklin was dirty."

"What about the two kids? We should see what we can find out about them. I'll take the daughter, and you take the son, okay?"

"Okay. Let's finish this coffee first. Wonder what Sara and Tressie are doing right now. I thought they were scared. Did you think that, Annie?"

"Not sure if 'scared' is the right word.

Certainly they were apprehensive. Who knows?"

"Who knows is right."

Chapter Five

Maggie Spitzer paced around her cozy kitchen as she waited for her dinner to warm in the oven. She wished now that she had invited the boys to stay for dinner. She could have scraped something together to make a decent dinner for three big-appetite guys even if it was just scrambled eggs or hot dogs. She peeked into the oven to see the Stouffer's frozen TV dinner bubbling away. Ten more minutes. She thought about how many times impatience had won and she'd taken out a frozen dinner before it was done, only to find that it was still frozen in the middle.

Maggie pressed the switch that would turn on the outside light over the small stoop leading down to her postage-stamp yard. Snow was still swirling in every direction. It was too early for snow here in Georgetown; it wasn't even Thanksgiving yet, for Pete's sake, she thought glumly. She liked snow, liked to be inside all cozy and warm with a fire blazing in the fireplace — on weekends, when she did not have to go to work. Tomorrow morning was going to be a zoo. She'd have to get up at four in order to get to the *Post* building by six. She'd have to shovel the front steps, the sidewalks, then dig out her car. Sometimes she wished for the not-so-good old days, before she had quit as editor in chief to marry Gus Sullivan, who had been killed ten months later, and had a driver pick her up for the ride in to work. Well, that was then, and this was now.

She took a moment to wonder where her shovel was. Most likely the basement. That's probably where the rock salt was, too, unless she was out of rock salt, which wouldn't surprise her. Shopping was something she did on the fly. She really needed to get more organized.

Maggie peeked once more through the glass in the oven door at her dinner. She turned off the oven, knowing her dinner would continue to bake the remaining time. She might as well use up the rest of the time she had to wait to find the shovel and the rock salt. Five minutes later, she leaned her snow shovel with the rickety handle and a bag of rock salt by the front door and looked outside. It looked like a Norman Rockwell painting outdoors. She could see a man bundled up walking a golden retriever. She did a double take when she saw the *Post* van pull to the curb and park. She opened the door, turned on the porch light, and yelled to the occupants. She felt so relieved she actually felt light-headed. Why was that, she wondered. She squealed her pleasure as the boys ran through the snow and up her front steps. It was Dennis who had bags of food. "Chinese and Italian, lots of it. And beer!" he bellowed happily.

"Oh, you dear sweet boys!" Maggie said happily. "I was just thinking earlier that I should have invited you and made eggs or something. I'm so glad you came. You all can help me shovel out in the morning. You are staying the night, right?"

"We are," Dennis chirped. "Oh wow! Look, guys, Maggie has a fire going! I love a fire. I like sitting on the floor to eat, with the evening news playing on the TV. That's how I knew I wanted to be a reporter, even when I was ten years old. This is just so great. Do you guys want to eat in the living room?"

"If you promise to shut up, then yeah, we can eat in the living room," Espinosa snapped.

"You guys go on in, and I'll get the dishes and snack tables," Maggie said as she headed for the kitchen. She turned and called over her shoulder. "What is the weatherman saying now? Is he predicting a heat wave for Thanksgiving? I haven't had the television on since I got home."

"No clue. We went straight to the office, cleared things away, went home to check on Mickey and Minnie, and here we are," Ted said, taking out plates from the kitchen cabinet. Espinosa was rummaging for silverware and napkins. Dennis just stood in the doorway, marveling how at home Ted and Espinosa were in Maggie's cheerful kitchen. And he was part of it all. He almost, almost, felt like he belonged. He knew he still had more grunt work to do, but he was confident that he'd make the cut. They liked him. He knew they did. He wished he could cross his fingers for luck, but his hands were filled with the two shopping bags full of food.

"Eight to ten inches by morning," Dennis chirped.

"Oh crap," Maggie mumbled.

"You should have bought a snowblower, Maggie," Ted said. "And you only have one shovel!"

"I'm sure you'll figure out something," Maggie said as she set up the snack-tray tables by the armchairs. "I'll put that on my to-do list of things to buy, right up there with food for my empty refrigerator."

"You know, Maggie, there are people out there who can do the shopping for you," Dennis said. "It's a regular business. They are trustworthy and bonded. I did a whole big article on it. A group of seniors started it up, and they are making so much money they can't count it. It's a *twofer* — gives them something to do in retirement and helps out people who are too busy to do it themselves. And they put it all away. Reasonable rates, too."

Maggie gaped at the young reporter. "Are you serious?"

"I am. Do you want the number of the organization? Tell them I sent you. They like me. A lot. They said they would shop for me for free because they had to turn business away after I did my story. The AP picked it up. I'm upset that you didn't see it."

It was Ted's turn to gape at the reporter. "You never cease to amaze me. Do they pick up dry cleaning?"

"They do. Guess you want the number, too."

"We all do, kid," Espinosa said as he dumped food out of a Chinese container into a big serving bowl.

China clinked and silverware tinkled, the sounds competing with the warning musical notes that always preceded the local six o'clock news as the TV came to life.

Dennis twisted the caps off the beer and passed the bottles around before he settled himself on the hearth, his plate on his knees.

All eyes were on the television and the weatherman's dire comments on the weather outside. "It sort of came out of nowhere, folks." The audience in Maggie's living room snorted as one.

Scene after scene filled the big screen, shots sent in by viewers for the next ten minutes, followed by six different commercials. The little group had made a serious dent in their filled plates by the time the anchor took over the screen. "We are just now getting pictures from the deadly accident earlier on the off-ramp leading from the interstate, where two women died on impact. The driver of the eighteen-wheeler, who the state police say is responsible for the accident, is still in critical condition at Our Lady of Mercy Hospital. Four other drivers and their passengers from the pileup have been treated and released. The off-ramp is still closed because of the weather. At this moment we are not releasing the names of the deceased pending notification to family."

The hair on the back of Maggie's neck moved. She stopped eating and looked around at the others. Ted had also stopped eating, his eyes glued to the screen in front of them. Espinosa, oblivious to his colleagues' reactions, kept right on eating.

Dennis's gaze went from Maggie and Ted to the wide screen. "What?"

Neither reporter responded. Both were busy with their cell phones.

"What happened?" Espinosa finally asked. Dennis pointed to the television, then at Maggie and Ted.

Dennis felt his jaw drop, his eyes growing round as saucers when he heard Ted say, "Describe them to me, John."

And then he heard Maggie say to the other person on the line with her, "Where are they taking the vehicle? Yes, yes, I got it. Okay, thanks, Milton."

Dennis was up and on his feet dancing around as he waited for Ted to end his call. Maggie's face had gone white and Ted looked like he was in shock. "It's those ladies out at Queen's Ridge, isn't it?"

"What?" Espinosa barked.

"The accident, the two people who died. I think it's those two ladies we saw earlier out at Queen's Ridge. For God's sake, my new granny and Aunt Tressie!"

"Naah," Espinosa said.

"Yeah, it is," Ted said. "My source at the morgue described them perfectly. Said the two women died on impact.

"My source told me they're taking the car to the police impound lot. It hasn't come in yet, but that's where it's going to end up. Who are they going to notify? The ladies said neither has any family. Did they say who their attorney is when we were out there? Crap, yeah, I remember now, it's Nikki Quinn's law firm. I bet everything is in their vehicle. We need to get our hands on the contents of their car. They said they were leaving. It fits in. We left first. Then they were going to leave. Where did they say they were going?"

"If they did say anything, I didn't hear it," Espinosa said thoughtfully, all interest in the food gone. "Maybe they told Myra or Annie."

"Oh Lord, we have to call them. Ohhh, this is not good," Maggie said as she started pacing the living room. "This is definitely not good. Should we go to the impound lot and see what we can do, if anything?"

"If you think the cops are going to let us snatch their belongings, get that thought right out of your head," Ted said.

"You're right, you're right. I know that. Still, there has to be a way. Maybe we could say we're next of kin or something."

"You're going to *LIE*!" Dennis said, outrage ringing in his voice.

"No, I'm not. *You* are. You are their next of kin. Ms. Overton said she was your new granny. And the other lady was your new aunt. We were all witnesses. Who's to say if you are or not? By the time things settle down, you can just return everything anonymously. As next of kin, you are entitled to the deceased's effects," Ted said.

"No one is going to question you, Dennis. When we go to the morgue, you'll have the name and can give a description of the two women. It hasn't been on the news, so they'll believe you. They were loners. They don't have friends. Think about it. Who is going to ask any questions? They'll probably thank you for making their job easier by identifying the ladies. You *will* do this, right, Dennis?" Maggie said

"Before you reply, Dennis, let me be the first to tell you we'll kick your ass all the way to the Canadian border if you say no. I'm sorry, but there is simply no other way," Ted said ominously.

"Well, when you put it like that, okay. I

guess I can pull it off. When are we going to do it?"

"Right now," Espinosa said.

A mad scramble ensued as the foursome beelined for their outerwear hanging in the foyer.

Ninety minutes later, Ted pulled the *Post* van to the curb in front of the county morgue. He jammed his pass under the windshield, got out, and led the way into the building, the others stepping into the ruts in the deep snow his passage had created.

"How come you know your way around here, Ted? This is the *morgue*!" Dennis squeaked. Ted shot him such a withering look that Dennis cringed inside his bulky down jacket. However, he reared up when they stepped out of the elevator in the basement. "This is really creeping me out."

"Well, you better get over it right now so you can put on a convincing performance," Maggie said as she shoved the young reporter down the hall. "Just breathe through your mouth."

"Why? Why'd you say that? Are we breathing in . . . oh God, what are we breathing in?"

The stainless-steel doors were suddenly in

front of them. Espinosa reached out and pressed the buzzer, his camera at the ready in case it was needed. The door slid open on well-oiled hinges. A blast of arctic air made the little group suck in their collective breath. They advanced into a room where two men were bent over stainless-steel tables. One man stopped, looked up, and raised his hand, indicating they should stop right where they were. The little group stopped, bumping into each other.

"Showtime, kid," Ted hissed in Dennis's ear. "You screw this up, you'll be frozen solid on your flyover of the Canadian border. You'll end up in a room just like this, only it will be in Canada."

Maggie nudged Dennis forward.

"Ah . . . sir . . . I saw . . . I heard on the news that two ladies were in an accident on the off-ramp of the interstate earlier this afternoon. I think it might be my . . . my granny and my . . . my aunt. Can you tell me their names?"

"No, Son, I can't. EMS just brought in the bodies. What makes you think these two bodies are your relatives?"

"They . . . they would have been driving that way. I don't know for sure but . . . they haven't been answering their cell phones. They *always* answer their cell phones."

"Are you here to identify the bodies?"

"No . . . yes . . . yes, I want to know," Dennis stammered, as Ted pinched his ass to shove him forward.

"Son, have you ever seen a dead body?" the coroner asked.

"God, no! I've never been to a funeral." Another hard pinch from Ted, and Dennis started to babble. "If it's my granny and my aunt I need to know. I need to . . . to make plans. You need to make plans when someone you love dies. My . . . my granny and my aunt would expect me to do this so . . . so I'm doing it," Dennis said as he stepped forward to avoid a third pinch from Ted's willing fingers. His heart thundered in his chest as his legs turned to Jell-O. He tried to take a deep breath but found that he couldn't do it. He felt tears burn his eyelids. He needed to be strong, be a man. He could feel eyes burning into his back. They were depending on him to come through. He did his best to square his shoulders. He struggled again to take a deep breath, and this time he succeeded. He was ready.

"You sure, Son, that there is no one else to make the identification? Viewing a dead body — and in this case, two dead bodies — can be traumatic."

Dennis's head bobbed up and down. "I'm

it, sir. Can we just do it?"

The coroner looked at the others, and said, "You wait here."

Dennis sucked in his breath as he looked down at the two bodies on the stainless-steel tables. He swayed dizzily and was grateful for the coroner's strong arms. Tears filled his eyes, overflowed, and rolled down his cheeks. He didn't trust himself to speak, so he nodded.

The assistant coroner appeared with a clipboard. "Can you give us their names?"

"Names? Granny. I always called her Granny. Names? Shit. I just called . . . her Auntie."

"They have names, don't they?"

"Oh yeah. Yes, they do. Gertrude. And Millie," Dennis said, picking names out of thin air.

"Gertrude what?"

"What what?" Dennis said, stalling for time.

"Last name, Son," the assistant coroner said gently.

"Oh yes, last name. Mercer. Gertrude Mercer."

"And your aunt?"

"Millie. Millicent, I guess. Her last name is . . . was . . . is . . . Turner."

"Do you want us to perform an autopsy?"

"Oh God, no! No, they . . . they wouldn't want to be carved up. *NO!* You need to put clothes on them. My granny and aunt were very modest ladies. Can you dress them up?"

"They'll do that at the funeral home once you tell me where to send the remains."

"Remains? What remains? What does that mean?"

"The bodies," the coroner said bluntly.

"Oh. Well, I don't know anything about funeral homes. Let me ask my friends what they recommend." Dennis raced to the front of the morgue, and demanded in a whisper, "Give me the name of a funeral home." He ran back to where the coroner waited. "The Dyal Funeral Home."

"Son, would you like a few last moments with the deceased?"

God, no, that was the last thing he wanted. "Of course." Dennis sucked in his breath and squeezed his eyes shut. Cop-out, his mind shrieked. He opened his eyes and stared down at the woman who had said she wished he was her grandson. His eyes filled again. "I'm sorry, Granny. And, Auntie, I'm sorry for you, too. I know this doesn't sound right, but I'm glad you . . . you went together. I could tell that you were best friends. Thank you for thinking I was worthy enough to be related to both of you."

"What the hell is he doing over there?" Ted hissed to Maggie.

"I think he's praying. Leave him alone. Have some respect," Espinosa said.

Ted looked ashamed. "You're right. Sorry."

Dennis turned, swiped at his eyes, shook hands with the coroner, and asked. "Is there anything else I need to do?"

"No, Son. Just give me a phone number where I can reach you. I'm sorry for your loss."

Dennis rattled off his cell-phone number and joined his colleagues. He swiped at his eyes again as they left the morgue. No one said a word until they were on the main floor.

"You did good, kid, you really did. That was quick thinking when the names came up. You handled that real good," Ted said.

"I wasn't sure if we wanted them to know their real names until the Vigilantes get a bead on which way they are going to handle this."

"You took the bull by the horns, so we can't second-guess now. It's done, and now we have time on our side. First thing in the morning, we'll go to the funeral home, but right now we're going to the impound lot to see if we can get their belongings. I'm not hopeful, but we can give it a shot," Maggie said.

"I cried. It was sad," Dennis said, his eyes filling up again.

"It's okay, Dennis. If you didn't cry, I'd wonder what was wrong with you," Ted said.

"I really don't have a grandmother. I liked having one even if it was for just a short time. And it was nice to have an aunt, too. I feel really bad. Like I should do something. Like maybe go to church or something."

"Tomorrow, Dennis. There are no churches open at this hour of the night," Maggie said kindly.

"Okay, but I'm going tomorrow, so don't try to change my mind."

"Don't worry, Dennis. We'll all go with you," Espinosa said softly.

Dennis leaned back in his seat and sighed, the sound full of sorrow.

Chapter Six

It was a bright, sunny, yellow kitchen, much like the person who was standing at the doorway watching the falling snow.

Mary Macklin Carmichael brushed her hair back behind her ears and sighed. She was wishing, and not for the first time, that she had a snowblower. It wasn't a problem, not really, since the neighbors always cleared her driveway with their blower because, as Pete Anders said, that's what one neighbor did for another neighbor. Still, she hated to impose on anyone. As a payback, all she had to do was bake Pete a strawberry rhubarb pie, and they were even. The pie was cooling on the counter as she stood by the door.

Mary turned around to look at the pie and smiled. It looked good, evenly browned, with just a touch of the filling leaking out of the slits in the crust. Her gaze swept around the kitchen. She loved her kitchen. It was sunshine yellow. When she'd come to this house all those years ago, it was a dark, gloomy room that her half brother walked through but never stayed in long enough even to boil water. A bachelor, Lowell Carmichael ate out three times a day. Tears puddled in Mary's eyes. Lowell had been so good to her; but then he'd always been good to her even though they had different fathers. They were blood, as he put it, and being older, it was his job to watch over his little sister. He'd given her free rein to transform his dark, gloomy house to her liking, knowing she was there to stay. He liked that she was a good cook, and the fifteen pounds he put on the first year was a testament to her cooking.

Mary poured coffee and sat down at the table with the pumpkin centerpiece. She smiled through her tears. Lowell was gone. She'd nursed him right up to the end of his life and cried for weeks after he was gone. She missed her older brother something fierce.

Then she'd cried for months when his lawyer told her that Lowell had left her his charming little house, his substantial 401K, his new Jeep Cherokee, and some way, somehow, his Social Security came to her, too, along with two very nice-sized insurance policies. When she'd timidly questioned the attorney, he'd smiled and said not to look a gift horse in the mouth. So she didn't. Lowell had seen to it that she was taken care of for the rest of her life, bless his heart.

She'd come here to this little house on a day much like this one many years ago, with just her purse and the clothes on her back. It had been snowing that day, too, and it was bitter cold, her tears freezing on her eyelashes when she rang the doorbell. Lowell hadn't asked any questions, just took her in his arms, made her a cup of hot tea, and promised her that he would always take care of her no matter what. So many years.

While she was alone, she wasn't lonely. Some people just couldn't understand how that could be. There were days when she missed her husband. How could she not miss someone she'd lived with for twenty-two years? She missed her son and daughter, too, but she'd learned how to live without them in her life. She had friends she played bridge with one night a week. She went on senior bus trips with the senior group at her local church. She was active in the church activities, and she worked one day a week at the local bakery and volunteered at the local hospital two evenings a week. All in all, she was content with her life and had no financial worries.

A savory stew simmered on the stove, and a pumpkin pie was baking in the oven. She always liked to make comfort food on a snowy day like today, when her memories often rose to the surface of her mind. Though she felt sad, she knew from past experience that the memories would soon fade, and she'd get back to normal before the day was over.

Suddenly, coming out of her reveries, Mary heard the snowblower in front of the house. That meant she had ten minutes to slip the cooling pie into an oversize Ziploc bag for Pete.

While she waited for the knock on the door, Mary stared at the colorful calendar on the side of the refrigerator, compliments of the bakery she worked at one day a week. A succulent, gorgeous dessert always graced the page for the month. November's page had a pumpkin pie with a mound of whipped cream, with slivers of pumpkin dotting the snow-white cream. It looked too good to eat. She'd baked the pie, the owner of the bakery had taken the picture, and its placement on the calendar was the result.

November was Thanksgiving. How quickly it had arrived this year. It seemed, Mary thought, that the older she got, the quicker the time went by. All old people thought that for some reason. But it was true: time just literally seemed to fly by these days.

There was a time, a long time ago, when she loved the start of the holiday season. It was a time when the children were younger, and she still had some say where they were concerned. Then her husband had struck the mother lode, and suddenly they were rich. The kids went from saving for things for months on end to being given everything under the sun by their father. At sixteen, Adam drove a flashy sports car and had money to burn in his pocket. Ava had designer clothes, designer everything. She got manicures and pedicures, got her hair styled and dyed, and had a chauffeur to take her anywhere she wanted to go until she was able to get her own sports car. When Mary had tried to rein them in, they had turned on her like two snakes in a barrel. They were mouthy, disrespectful, and downright ugly to her. They called her square, told her to get with it, said she was a dowdy frump and no help to their father, who needed a little class at his side. God, how that had hurt. Especially when Manny had agreed with the kids and said she should fix herself up a little. Try some fashionable clothes, get your hair styled, Manny had said. Then he asked if it would kill her to wear some makeup. After which he told her that she looked like a scrubwoman. The only thing he hadn't said was that she embarrassed him, but sometimes what wasn't said was what was the most important.

One day, after a particularly harrowing blowup with both her children and her husband, as a result of which all three stormed out of the house, she'd gone into Manny's office to try and figure out what was going on and where the unlimited money was pouring in from. She was no rocket scientist, but she knew how to read a P & L sheet and bank statements. What stunned her, though, was that there were two sets of books. It had taken her hours to compare them side by side. When she was finished, she walked out to the foyer, got her coat, a warm hat, and her galoshes. She put them on, looked around at the opulent surroundings, and walked out the door into the falling snow. In a daze, she'd taken two buses, then walked many miles, all the way to Lowell's house, and rang the bell.

Mary blinked away the tears. So many years ago. She'd never seen her husband again. Nor her children. She'd filed for a divorce. It was uncontested since she didn't ask for anything. She didn't even have to show up in court the day the divorce was granted. Manny hadn't shown up either.

Months after moving in with Lowell and after the divorce was final, she'd finally confided in Lowell, and it was his idea for her to take the name Carmichael instead of her maiden name of Richardson so that when the dark stuff hit the fan, she wouldn't get splattered. She had agreed and changed her name legally. It was doubtful if Manny or the kids even knew or cared where she was. Lowell had never been on their radar. There were never any calls, never any mail; she was never mentioned in any articles that were printed in the paper about the Macklins. As far as her ex-husband and children were concerned, she no longer existed. For all she knew, they might not even know whether she was alive or dead.

The front doorbell took that moment to ring. Mary picked up the pie in its Ziploc bag and went to the front door. "Lots of snow out here, Mary. You be careful if you go out, you hear?" Pete reached for the pie, gave her a sloppy salute, and turned to leave.

"Thanks, Pete. I'll call you when the stew is ready. Another few hours, okay?"

Pete nodded as he gave an airy wave and made his way next door to his own house and his invalid wife, who had good days and bad days. On her good days, she was able to sit in a wheelchair. Nan would be so happy with this pie. No one baked pies like Mary Carmichael. Pete knew that later, the succulent stew that was cooking on the stove and smelled so good would find its way to his house near dinnertime. He smiled at the thought. Mary was what he and Nan called good people, that was for sure.

Back in the kitchen, Mary gave the stew a quick stir, sniffing appreciatively at the delectable aroma. Later, a few hours from now, she'd slide a pan of homemade bread into the oven. Perfect crusty bread with warm, melted butter to go with the stew. What could be more perfect? Nothing, was her answer. Absolutely nothing.

A fat yellow cat appeared out of nowhere and brushed against Mary's leg. "Well, Miss Winnie, you finally woke up," Mary crooned to the animal as she picked her up and cradled her close. The tabby purred louder. Mary smiled. The cat loved her. She had been a present from Lowell years after she'd moved in with him. She had just been a scrawny skin-and-bones kitten at the time. Now, to her dismay, Winnie weighed fourteen pounds. She loved unconditionally, and she was loyal. Tears pricked at Mary's eyes when she remembered the long months when Winnie stayed on the bed with Lowell, refusing to move except to hop off to run to the litter box or to eat. She'd been more of a comfort to Lowell than she herself had.

Winnie purred louder, licked Mary's cheek, then jumped from Mary's lap and scooted to the litter box.

Time to get a move on. There was laundry to do; today was the day she changed the bed linens and tidied up the house with a light dusting. She was a creature of habit and comfort. It all worked for her. Now, if she could just get rid of the bad dreams she'd been having lately and the feeling that something was wrong, she'd be a happy camper. She'd always paid attention to her feelings, and they rarely led her astray. This time, though, for some reason, she hoped her feelings were just because of the inclement weather, which would probably keep her housebound for a day or so.

Mary shook her head to clear her thoughts. She knew in her heart that inclement weather had nothing to do with her thoughts. She knew as sure as she was standing in her kitchen here that her ex-husband's day of reckoning was about to come. And her children's, too, and there wasn't a thing she could do about it.

As Mary went about her household chores, her thoughts stayed with her ex-husband and the early years of their marriage. Although they had been sweet and pleasant there had always been something off about the whole thing. Not that Manny wasn't a good, kind husband; he was. He was a good provider, but he was obsessed with money even at the beginning of their marriage. Oftentimes, he would work around the clock, waving to her from time to time if he had some deal cooking. Once, over too much wine, he'd told her the story of his two friends from the orphanage and how his biggest disappointment in his life was that he wasn't able to locate them after a fire had destroyed the apartment building in which they lived and the phone booth at which he had called them every night. He'd been sketchy on those details, but she had figured out that there was more to that particular relationship than just friendship. She knew that somewhere deep in his heart was a love for a young girl whom he could never forget. She even remembered her name after all these years. Marie. The other young girl was Sally. How weird that she should not only remember that but be thinking about it today.

Maybe what she needed was some music

or some noise; the house was just way too quiet. Television or music? She opted for the television — not that she was going to watch it, but the background noise would be helpful. And hopefully she could get caught up in some program and forget her melancholic, dire thoughts.

Would it work? Probably not. Things would, as always, just have to run their course. Mary sighed heavily as she gathered a load of towels to put into the washing machine.

Time. Time was the answer to everything. She just had to accept that.

Mary burst into tears. I should have done something, gone to the authorities, the SEC, someone. But she hadn't. That was the big sin on her shoulders. She had disclosed that sin so many times in confession, done her penance, and still she didn't feel the slightest bit better. She was just as guilty as her husband for not telling someone in authority that he was bilking his clients. At the time, she didn't have a name to put to what he was doing, but in recent years she had learned what it was called. It was a Ponzi scheme, the same sort of criminal enterprise that Bernie Madoff had been found guilty of. And her children were part of the whole scheme, aiding and abetting their father. All for money, so they could sail in yachts and fly in private planes and live in palatial estates.

Money truly was the root of all evil.

Three hours later, the front doorbell rang. Mary turned down the volume on the TV and went to the door. "Pete! I was just going to call you. All I have to do is ladle out the stew and take the bread out of the oven. Oh dear, what's wrong? It isn't Nan, is it?" she said, alarm ringing in her voice."

"Can I come in, Mary? No, it's not Nan. Well, yes, in a way it is Nan. Today was a good day, so she was in her wheelchair in the kitchen. When the mail came, I took it into the kitchen and left it on the table and forgot about it. Nan opened it. This . . . this is what came in the mail today. God, Mary, I . . . We're wiped out. It's all gone. Unless I'm crazy, and I'm not reading this right. Will you look at it and tell me what you think?"

Mary stared at her neighbor's face, which was as white as the snow outside the door. "Of course, Pete. Come along into the kitchen. I just made some fresh coffee. Is Nan all right?"

"No, she isn't. I got her into bed, gave her an extra pill, and she was asleep when I left. I can't stay. I just . . . just needed to talk to someone. Here?" he said, shoving his brokerage statement into her hands.

Mary looked around for her reading glasses but couldn't find them. Pete reached up and removed them from her gray curls. Mary just shook her head at her own forgetfulness. She sat down and smoothed out the two-page statement. Her heart flip-flopped in her chest when she saw *Macklin Investments* in fine script at the side of the page. Dear God. She knew what she was going to see even before she let her gaze rake the page.

"That was everything we had in the world, Mary. It's gone. We can't make it on my small pension and Social Security. As it is, we were dipping into our account every month. Nan's medicines have gotten more expensive. The insurance rates have gone up. We were just getting by, barely. Nan saw that and started to cry, saying she was a burden to me. We both know her MS is getting worse. She asked me . . . she wants me to . . ."

Mary reared up, her face full of shock. "Do not go there, Pete Anders. Do not even think what you are thinking. Do you hear me? I can help. Father Steve, the parish, they'll help. This is no time to be proud. Are you listening to me, Pete?"

Pete's big hands started to shake. "Explain that to me, Mary. How could this happen? The account was doing great, then slowed down, went back up, then last month, it started downward again. In just twenty-seven days, I'm not worth even the price of that piece of paper. Is it possible there's a mistake?" There was such hope in his voice that Mary felt sick to her stomach.

"Anything is possible, Pete," she said, trying to make her voice cheerful. She didn't succeed. "Listen, I know how this all works. Lowell taught me when he got ill. I used to take care of all his affairs. Let me look into it in the morning." She looked at the clock on the range and said, "It's too late today to do anything, but I'll see what I can find out first thing in the morning. I can call my brother's people and see if we can get a handle on all of this. I want you to go home now and take care of Nan and try to convince her things will be all right. Let me take the bread out of the oven, and I'll get the stew ready. Make sure Nan eats. She can't afford to lose any more weight, you know that. And, Pete, take all her meds and keep them away from her. Promise me you'll do that."

"I will, Mary. You're such a good friend. Thank you seems hardly adequate, but that and blowing away your snow and mowing your lawn in the summer is all I can do for you."

"And that's way too much as it is. I thank God every day that you and the others are such good neighbors. Now, here, take this and be careful going home. It's starting to ice up out there. I'll call you in the morning the moment I know anything. Give Nan a hug for me."

Pete would have hugged her, but his hands were full. He nodded as Mary led him to the door. She turned on the outside light. She blinked, wondering when it had gotten dark. Time was moving too fast again, was her first thought. She stood in the doorway until she saw Pete enter his garage through the side door. Then she collapsed against her own front door and let her whole body turn to Jell-O. "You bastard," she whispered over and over. "Well, we'll just see about that!"

The next morning, Winnie in her arms, Mary walked into the kitchen and turned on the lights. It was still dark outside. The range clock said it was 5:10. She hadn't slept a wink. She'd tossed and turned all night long. She itched, she ached, she felt pain for her neighbor. She had to do something. She'd stared at the ceiling for hours, trying to decide what, if anything, she *could* do. She set the cat down and walked over to the stove. She did everything by rote, but the two-page brokerage statement seemed to bore holes in her back. She whirled around. She should burn the ugly thing. But it wasn't hers to burn. What she would do was make a copy of it. She'd left her brother's home office intact after he'd passed away. Everything still worked although she never used any of the fancy machines. All she did was dust and clean and air out the room from time to time. Yes, yes, she'd make a copy and give Pete back his original.

And just what was she going to do with a copy of Pete's statement? To be decided.

Mary fed the cat, toasted an English muffin she didn't want, then poured herself a cup of coffee. She knew what she had to do. What she did not know was whether she had the guts to do it. She heaved a mighty sigh. She realized she was Pete and Nan's only hope. That meant no matter how hard it was going to be, she had to do what only she could do.

Sitting at the small, round, oak table in her kitchen, Mary looked around. Until last night, this room had been a comfort room. There was nothing like a warm kitchen to make a person feel good. The heady scents, the aromas of cooking food and baking bread made her so happy. She loved the bright, cheerful curtains hanging in the window, loved the waxy green philodendron hanging from the old beams in the little house. A place of joy and comfort.

But when the digital clock clicked to 9:00, would she still feel that way? Would her life change? Of course it would because once you woke a sleeping tiger, you had to deal with that tiger's wrath. *Dear God, please let me be up to this. Please. Please.*

Mary spent the next three and a half hours watching the digital numbers on the range clock change. Night turned to day, and her kitchen was bathed in blinding whiteness. She barely noticed. She took turns shivering inside her chenille robe, the same one that she used to wear when she nursed her children in the middle of the night. It was so old, most of the nub was worn off it, but she wouldn't part with it for anything in the world. It was an old friend that gave her comfort.

The clock ticked forward: 8:57. Mary drew a deep breath. She clenched and unclenched her fists, which were balled up in the pockets of the old robe. She blinked when the numbers changed to 8:58. Two more minutes. Her heart thundered in her chest. She needed to calm down. She let her breath out in a loud *swoosh* when the numbers changed to 8:59. One more minute to go. The paper in hand, she got up off the chair she'd been glued to and walked over to the old-fashioned wall phone. She zeroed in on the range clock the moment the numbers indicated it was 9:00. One more deep breath before she punched in the numbers for Macklin Investments. She knew her son's extension and wondered how he would respond. She knew full well that she had never, not once, called him at the office. Indeed, she had had no contact with him whatsoever after she left her husband and the two children he had, effectively, stolen from her.

A nasal-sounding voice asked how she could direct the call. Mary said, "Extension 478, please."

Mary heard her son's voice and almost lost it right then and there. She wanted to hang up the phone to end the call so badly, her hands began to shake. She said, "Adam?"

The silence on the other end of the phone was short but noticeable. "Mom! Mom, is that you?"

How wonderful that acknowledging word

sounded. Mary licked at her lips, and said, "Yes, Adam, it's me. I need to talk to you. Do you have time?"

"My God, Mom! Of course I have time. Where are you? Why . . . what . . . how . . . Are you okay? You aren't sick, are you? Why are you calling? Damn, Mom, it's so good to hear your voice. Dad said . . . never mind what he said. Can we meet, Mom? I'd like that. I tried to find you. But Dad said if you wanted to be found, you'd get in touch. Why did you abandon us like that? Why, Mom?"

Mary was so light-headed, she had to grab hold of the kitchen counter to keep herself upright. "That's all for another time, Adam. I'm calling you for a reason."

"Well, whatever it is, I'm glad you called. Talk to me, Mom."

And she did. She laid it all out quickly and concisely. She hated hearing her son's indrawn breath, hated that she couldn't see him to gauge his reaction. She just simply hated this whole darn call. Period. "And one more thing, Adam. When you cut the check for Mr. Anders, add an additional two hundred thousand dollars. That's not a suggestion, it's an order. If you don't follow through, I will do exactly what I said I would do. Now, repeat the fax number I gave you and tell me exactly when you will be faxing me the revised monthly statement showing the additional two hundred thousand dollars. Then I want you to close out the account and fax the closing statement. Are we clear on all of this, Adam?"

Adam's voice was hard. "I understand perfectly. Who is Peter Anders? Your new husband? Is he the man you left us for?"

Mary wanted to cry. She *was* crying, wiping her eyes and nose on the sleeve of her old robe. "Pete Anders is an old, dear friend. His wife has multiple sclerosis and is practically bedridden. They depend on the money they invested with your father. They need the money for medicine, for food on the table, and to help pay their mortgage. That's who Pete Anders is. I want you to think about that, Adam, really think about Pete and all the other Petes you and your father have been swindling all these years. I will give you fifteen minutes, not one minute longer, to fax me what I asked for. Send the check by messenger. Pete's address is on his account. I don't care if you have to use a dogsled to deliver it; just do it. This morning will be soon enough. Before noon. Good-bye, Adam."

Mary had to jab at the old phone three times before she could get the receiver into the cradle because she was so blinded with her tears. She unwound a length of paper towels, swiped at her eyes, and blew her nose. She'd done it! She'd actually done it.

Mary sniffed as she made a second pot of coffee, her eyes once again on the digital clock on the range. She poured a cup and hurried up to the second floor to Lowell's old office. She felt like her skin was on fire, that's how nervous she was. Would Adam do what she'd told him to do, or would he call his father? When the fax line rang, she almost jumped out of her skin. Her hands were trembling so badly, she could barely hold the paper in her hand. She tried to read it but couldn't. She had to go back downstairs to get her reading glasses.

Tears puddled in Mary's eyes again as she read through the newly revised statement. And the short letter explaining that a check would be hand delivered by noon for the full value of the account, and apologizing for the erroneous statement showing major losses that should have actually been a gain in value of two hundred thousand dollars. Mary blessed herself. God did work in mysterious ways. Sometimes with a little help from a well-meaning friend.

Mary dialed Pete's number and told him to come over. He blew in the kitchen door with a wave of swirling snow that was blowing off the roof. She didn't even bother to ask about Nan. She just waved the papers under his nose and told him about the check that would be delivered by noon.

Pete knuckled his worn, callused hands over his eyes. He was trembling so bad, Mary had to help him to a chair. She poured him a cup of strong black coffee and ordered him to drink it.

"How . . . I don't understand, how did this happen?"

Mary smiled. "Can we just say, and leave it at, that sometimes it's not what you know but who you know. When the check comes, take it to the bank if the roads are clear. I'll call Lowell's people, and they'll talk to you about investing the money. Now, I want you to go home and show the papers to Nan and make her a nice big breakfast. There is one thing, though, Pete. If anyone asks if you know where I live, please don't tell them. Just say I'm a friend and leave it at that. Can you promise me that?"

"Of course. It goes without saying. Mary, I don't know how to thank you. You're just like Lowell, always helping someone. Nan had a bad night, but I think this just might turn out to be a good day for her. I'll build us a nice fire, then we'll watch some old movies and wait for the check to come."

Pete's hug was bone crushing before he walked out into the winter wonderland. Mary smiled. The smile left her face when she trudged up the stairs to her bedroom, feeling every day of her age.

Mary didn't even bother to remove her robe. She climbed into bed, whistled for Winnie, who came on the run and leaped onto the pillow. Mary fell asleep making a promise to herself that she was going to take matters into her own hands and do something about her ex-husband's activities. She didn't want any more Pete Anderses on her conscience.

Chapter Seven

The reporters all piled into the *Post*'s van. "God, Ted, turn on the heater," Maggie said, her teeth chattering as she reached for Dennis's hand. She turned to the young reporter and asked, "Are you okay, Dennis?"

"Yes. No. God, no, I'm not okay. I never saw a dead body, and I just saw two of them. I should have given the coroner their right names. I just froze. They're going to know I lied because I gave them my real name and phone number. How's that going to look? I bet I broke some kind of law. I never break the law. Never. I respect the law." He was shaking uncontrollably, and while he knew he was babbling, he couldn't seem to help himself.

Ted turned around in his seat to glare at Dennis. "Will you relax. All you have to say is you were in shock and you mixed up your paternal grandmother with your maternal grandmother. No one is going to fault you.

We'll make it right. We needed to know if it was . . . them. Okay?"

"No, Ted, it is not okay. Who is going to claim the bodies? Who is going to bury them? They said they had no one. That leaves me. I have to do it! I don't know the first thing to do. I don't have money to bury them. Do you think the *Post* will give me an advance on my pay?"

Maggie took pity on the young reporter and tried to make her voice as soothing as possible when she said, "Dennis, the burial is not your responsibility. I'm sure the ladies have a will. They said the Quinn Law Firm represents them. I'm sure they'll handle everything."

"That's . . . that's so impersonal. A law firm burying a client. No. I want to do it. I can pay back the advance over time. I know what you are all thinking — that I'm nuts — but I'm not. For a little while yesterday, I was Ms. Overton's grandson. And Tressie's nephew. It seemed real at the time, and I remember what Ms. Overton said. She said that if she ever had a grandson, she would want him to be someone like me. Yeah, maybe they were just words, but coming from that feisty old lady, I really took them to heart, okay? I'm going to do this no matter what you say. If you guys want to make fun of me, go ahead. And if you don't want to go to the funeral service, then stay the hell away. I don't have any more to say," Dennis said, clamping his lips tight. He continued to shake as he clenched and unclenched his hands.

Ted swallowed hard after Espinosa jabbed him in the ribs. Maggie wrapped her arms around Dennis and crooned to him.

"Dennis, it's a wonderful thing you want to do. We're the schmucks for not thinking of it ourselves. I'm ashamed of myself because you are right. You make me proud to know you, kid. We'll help in any way we can, right, guys?" Ted said, a desperate note creeping into his voice.

Maggie and Espinosa agreed, but Dennis remained tight lipped. Finally, he unlocked his lips, and said, "I know you know those two ladies were rich and probably could pay for their own funeral, but that doesn't make it right. Paying for your own funeral just doesn't . . . it's wrong. Somebody has to care enough to do the right thing. I'm going to do it. I'll make the arrangements for a service, and I'm going to get up there and say how nice it was for a few minutes to think I had a granny and an aunt. Everyone needs someone at some point in their lives. I'm just sorry they're gone and won't know we cared enough to do this."

"Dennis, trust me, they'll know," Maggie said, squeezing his hand. Dennis squeezed back.

"Why are we still sitting here, Ted? The car's hot already, so turn down the heat," Espinosa said.

Ted turned around, his fists clenched against the wheel. "Are we going home or to the impound lot? Somebody needs to make a decision here."

"The impound lot!" Dennis said briskly. "We need to get the ladies' gear. I know what to do, and this time I'll do it right."

"Right on! Buckle up, guys, the roads are hazardous. This might take us a while, so be patient."

And patience *was* the name of the game. It took them a full ninety minutes to cross town to the impound lot and another twenty minutes to find a spot to park the van when they reached the lot.

The reporters hopped out of the van and raced against the wind and falling snow toward the office. Everywhere they looked, there were tow trucks, disabled vehicles, and shouting men and women looking for a place to stash a vehicle. Guard dogs barked and howled at all the unusual activity. Tow drivers cursed as angry car owners bellowed their outrage.

"See if you can identify a Range Rover, that's what the ladies were driving," Maggie said. "I saw it in the garage parked next to a little Beemer. They would never have taken a sports car out in such bad weather."

Espinosa spotted it almost immediately. He gulped and swiped at the snow caking his face. He shook his head at what he was seeing. Only Ted heard him say, "No one could have survived in that."

"Don't we have to ask permission before we take anything out of the truck?" Maggie asked.

"First we take it, then we ask. Possession is nine-tenths of the law," Ted said. He looked around to make sure no one was paying attention to him as he pushed at the tailgate of the big truck. He finally managed to pry it open. Quicker than lightning, they had the bags in hand, while Maggie crawled in the back and over the seats to search for the women's purses. She crawled back out, victorious.

The foursome trudged through the snow to the office, where a frantic, frazzled older woman, probably the owner's wife, was trying to do everything at once. She looked up at the reporters as she hung up the phone. "What?" she said loudly.

Dennis stepped forward and took charge. He went into his spiel, tears pooling in his eyes as he pointed to the ladies' bags. "I already identified their . . . their . . . remains at the morgue. Tell me what to sign." He fished around until he came up with his driver's license, his *Post* credentials, and a ten-year-old rumpled library card. "I'm taking their stuff — it's just clothes and stuff, but it's *their* clothes and stuff, and I want it. Do you have a problem with that, ma'am?" he asked, his voice husky with tears.

The woman's frazzled features softened. "No, Son, I don't. The police might, but that's their problem. Here, fill out this form and don't leave anything blank. Stand still so I can take your picture. All of you, if you're with this young man." The foursome dutifully lined up. The woman snapped off two pictures. She quickly scanned the form Dennis filled out and nodded her approval. She attached the Polaroid snapshots to the form with an oversize paper clip and she tossed the papers into an overflowing basket on the corner of her desk. "I'm sorry for your loss, Son. I've said that eight times already this evening. Be careful out there, I don't want to see your vehicle in here later on. Try and get behind a plow or a maintenance truck."

Back in the van, Ted had to do some fancy driving and maneuvering to get around all the tow trucks coming into and leaving the lot. He knew that at one point his back fender scraped against something, but he wasn't about to get out to see if there was any damage to the van. Inclement weather usually meant no responsibility for the reporter when the motor pool questioned the last person signed out on the van. They had what they had come for, so it was a plus all the way around.

"Where to now? Out to the farm or back to your place, Maggie?"

"The weather is too bad to try for Pinewood. Maybe in the morning. Let's go to my house, make a fire, and finish our dinner. This has turned out to be one hell of a day," she muttered under her breath.

"You can say that again," Dennis mumbled.

An hour and a half later, Ted did his best to pull alongside the curb in front of the house in Georgetown that he used to share with Maggie. The plow had already been through at least once, and snow was piled to the curb. The streets were already narrow as it was, so God alone knew what Ted would find in the morning when it was time to leave for work. He hated Georgetown when it snowed. He hated it when it rained, too, as the streets flooded.

The reporters piled out of the car. Somewhere down the street they heard a dog bark, a joyous sound, which probably meant the dog and a kid were playing in the snow. They raced over the piled-high snow and up the snow-filled steps to Maggie's stoop. They stomped their feet impatiently as Maggie did her best to fit the key in the lock in the darkness because she'd forgotten to turn on the outside light when they left the house earlier in the evening. They almost knocked each other out barreling through the door.

"It's turning to sleet now," Espinosa said. "That's not good."

Maggie turned the heat up. She issued orders like a general. "Ted, build up the fire. You know where the dry wood in the basement is. Dennis, warm up the food. Espinosa, start going through those bags, and someone call the farm and tell Myra and Annie what we've been doing. I'm going to put some warmer clothes on. Ted, you have a box of clothes in the guest-room closet if you guys want to change."

"You keep clothes here?" Dennis asked, his eyes round as saucers.

Ted raised his eyebrows. "Yeah," he

drawled. "You have a problem with that?"

"No! No!" There was so much he didn't know and so much he wished he didn't know. Dennis kicked off his shoes. "If you have any extra socks, I'd appreciate your lending them to me. If not, that's okay, I'll just put mine in the dryer. In fact, that's what I'm going to do, forget about the socks." He knew he was babbling, but he didn't care because he always babbled to himself when he was under stress.

In the laundry room, Dennis stripped off his socks and his khaki slacks and tossed them into the dryer. He danced around in his boxers, shivering as he waited for his clothes to warm up. It had been a hell of a day, he thought wearily. He wanted to cry but realized that wasn't very manly, so instead he squeezed his eyes shut and gritted his teeth. He struggled to remember his childhood prayers. He didn't pray often, but he did pray. Most people he knew only prayed when something was awry. He knew that because he'd once had a long discussion on stress and crisis with his college friends and a few of his instructors. He'd also read it somewhere and had wondered if it was true. Probably, he decided, if he was an example. He was sorry for that. He bowed his head and offered up a prayer for his pseudo-granny and -aunt.

When the dryer *pinged,* Dennis reached for his clothes. He couldn't ever remember anything feeling as good as when he donned his warm socks and pants. He heaved a mighty sigh. Now, he thought, I can take on the world. As well as Ted, Maggie, and Espinosa.

Dennis carried the warmed-up food into Maggie's family room in time to see a blazing fire and Espinosa ending his telephone call to the farm. Maggie plopped down on an oversize pillow right in front of the fire. She reached for her plate, looked at it, then shocked everyone by saying, "I'm not really that hungry." Maggie could eat 24/7 no matter the circumstances. Her colleagues blinked at her words.

Ted stirred the food on his plate, his eyes on the blazing fire. Espinosa sipped at his beer as he stared down at his plate. "Myra said we should call Nikki and tell her about the accident and that we have Sara's and Tress's belongings. I took the liberty of calling Nikki, and she said they were coming over. Guess they're here," he said, as the doorbell chimed. Maggie was up and running to the door. They all hugged as Maggie helped Nikki and Jack off with their snow-covered coats.

"Come in where it's warm; we have a good fire going. Are you hungry?" When she had no takers, she led her old friends into the family room, where she introduced Dennis to Nikki and Jack.

"This is just so hard to believe," Nikki said as she flopped down by the fire next to where Maggie had been sitting. "I talked to both Sara and Tressie earlier in the day. I've never met either one of them in person, but have had a lot of contact with the two of them these last few years. They were extremely private people. Very reclusive as well as private, and I honored that. Sara and Tressie were originally clients of Marcy Duval, an old member of the firm. She relocated to California four years ago because she decided that she really wanted to represent movie stars. As the owner of the firm, I inherited all of her clients. They seemed like nice ladies, shy and reclusive but ever so nice. It's such a shock.

"What I'm not getting is how you all know Sara and Tressie?"

"They got in touch with Myra and Annie. They wanted help from the Vigilantes. That's why we met up with them today out at Queen's Ridge. It was therapy day, and Myra and Annie took Lady and invited us to go with them."

"Why did you talk to them today?" Maggie asked. "Or is that attorney-client privilege? We . . . actually Dennis identified the . . . the bodies, then we went to the impound lot and got their belongings. Should we turn them over to you? We aren't sure what we should do."

Nikki nodded, then shrugged. "Sara and Tressie appointed me as their Personal Representative. That means I am the executor of their estates. I'll take care of it. Both women had wills. It was drawn up so that whoever passed on first, the estate would go to the survivor, but since they both expired at the same time, the estate will go to whomever they named as heir. They both agreed. Right now, I'm not comfortable discussing the will. We can do that later in the week after I review it and go through whatever they had with them. They did give me instructions today when we spoke. Again, I'm not comfortable discussing this right now. I will say that never in a million years did I think those two ladies would require the help of the Vigilantes. Which, I guess, just goes to prove that still waters run deep."

Nikki took a deep breath and rushed on. "So you guys are getting ready for a new mission? And it involves my clients. Past tense." Her voice was so wistful sounding, everyone in the room grew quiet and stared at the beautiful young lawyer. Even her husband, Jack, stared at her.

"You miss the adrenaline rush, is that what you're saying?" Maggie grinned.

"That's one way of putting it. I do miss all the excitement, the planning, then the execution. I miss seeing all of you whenever a new mission involved you."

"Help me clean up here, Nikki," Maggie said, getting up to gather up all the dinner plates. She almost laughed out loud when she saw Dennis curled up by the fire, sound asleep.

Nikki hopped up and followed Maggie into the kitchen.

"Girl talk, and it doesn't include us. Or they're getting ready to cook up something that doesn't include us. Women are sneaky," Jack said, authority ringing in his voice.

"Yeah." Ted groaned.

"You all going to the farm for Thanksgiving?" Jack asked, his thoughts on his wife and the wistfulness he'd heard in her voice.

In the kitchen with the door closed, silverware and dishes rattling, Maggie hissed, "Spit it out, girlfriend."

Nikki didn't bother to pretend she didn't know what Maggie was talking about.

"I got it from a reliable source that Jack is being considered for a federal judgeship. He doesn't even know it yet, and I can't say anything."

"That's great! Oh," she said at the expression on Nikki's face. "It's not great, is that what you're saying?"

Nikki lowered her voice to a harsh whisper. "Think, Maggie, how can it be great when he's married to me, one of the Vigilantes? He's not happy at the firm — he's not a defense lawyer; he's a prosecutor. He just joined my firm when things went nuclear. He's a fine defense lawyer, but he hates it. His heart just isn't in it. I can't be certain, but I think Annie and Myra and even Martine might have pushed this along. You know how things work in this town. It's not what you know, it's *who* you know."

Maggie added soap to the dispenser and turned on the dishwasher. "You don't want him to get the appointment, is that what you're saying?"

"Yes and no. I don't think he'd be happy sitting on the bench. Yeah, it's a cushy job — life tenure, great offices, all the staff he could want, lots of perks. He'd suffocate. He might be tempted to take the job if he's offered it, but the vetting process will drive him nuts. Then, after a few months, he'd be right back where he is now, unhappy as all get out."

Maggie sat down on one of the kitchen chairs and stared up at her friend. "Then what's the answer, Nikki? How can this be made right?"

"Finding a way for him to leave the firm thinking it's his idea and going back to being a prosecutor. A part of me thinks he knows what I just told you. Think about it. If I got downwind of it, surely he has, too, and he isn't saying anything just like I'm not saying anything. I hate secrets, I really do."

Maggie nodded to show she knew where Nikki was coming from. "Tell me why Sara Overton called you today, Nikki," Maggie said.

"I can't, Maggie. It is attorney-client privilege, and I take that oath seriously."

Maggie nodded. She understood completely. She explained then about Dennis West and what they'd gone through at the morgue and the impound lot. "He's going to be a great reporter. He's got it all: the gut burning, the passion, and the compassion. He asked for an advance on his salary so he could personally bury those two ladies. Ted called Annie, and she okayed it. She said he could pay the paper back ten dollars a week, and that's going to take him years to pay off, but he's okay with that. That should tell you what kind of guy he is. He adores Ted, and Ted has taken him under his wing. You'll like him when you get to know him."

"I'm sure I will. Is he going to be at the farm for Thanksgiving?"

"He said he was. His parents travel a lot since they retired. We're his family now, according to him. What about the others? Have you talked to them?"

"Kathryn called this morning. She said she and Bert are coming, and they're bringing Jack Sparrow with them. Alexis is on board. I spoke to Yoko a few days ago, and she said that she and Harry will be there. I've called Isabelle a few times, but she hasn't called me back. I'm pretty sure that both she and Abner will make it. It'll be like old times." Maggie could hear the wistfulness in Nikki's voice again.

"You really miss it, don't you?" Maggie said quietly.

"I really do, but don't tell Jack that. But you know what, I think he misses it, too."

"Well, I for one love it!" Maggie said exuberantly. "I can't wait to dive into this new mission."

Nikki smiled. "We gotta go. We didn't finish our own shoveling. The darn snowblower isn't working right. Jack was supposed to get it serviced, but he forgot. I'll keep you guys posted, and if we don't talk again, we'll see you at the farm on Thanksgiving."

"This isn't right. I live two doors away from you, and I hardly ever see you and Jack," Maggie grumbled.

Nikki laughed. "That's because we're up and out by five thirty and don't get home till eight or nine at night. That's what I mean, Maggie. What kind of life is this?"

"The one you chose, Nikki," Maggie said softly.

Chapter Eight

The nor'easter that crippled the entire Eastern Seaboard lasted seventy-two hours and left behind twenty-seven inches of snow, hospitals filled to overflowing, and exhausted police and fire departments. The sheer number of stranded cars covered in snow taxed sanitation departments in ways previously unheard of. It took three days after the snow ended for highway departments to plow, sand, and salt the roads because many of them had depleted their own supplies during the first twenty-four hours and had to wait for the roads to be cleared so they could accept supplies delivered from neighboring Southern communities.

The day before Thanksgiving, television stations finally gave the anxiety-ridden populace the all clear for road travel, only to have the snow start up again, which resulted in hazardous road conditions combined with bumper-to-bumper traffic to any and all points. As one anchor put it, there was simply nowhere else to dump the snow. He along with his colleagues from rival stations stressed caution on the roads and wished everyone a happy Thanksgiving as he reminded residents that there was much to be thankful for. One disgruntled listener called in to the anchor and asked if he would be good enough to deliver a turkey to his family since no one could get to the stores, and even if they could, delivery trucks hadn't been able to get through to deliver said turkeys. Never mind the trimmings, the caller said. No one was surprised when the caller was cut off in midsentence.

In the end, the storm that was over, then started up again, was said to be the worst ever since weather records had been kept.

Maggie, her expression fierce, started banging pots and pans to wake up her guests. Six days of staring at each other had left tempers short. They all had cabin fever and couldn't wait to travel to Pinewood and a Thanksgiving dinner with all the trimmings. Charles had been texting the gang, assuring them he had a thirty-pound turkey, plum pudding, sweet potatoes with little marshmallows, fresh cranberries, his special chestnut/raisin stuffing, along with giblet gravy and a host of other side dishes. Charles continued to text that he was making pumpkin, mince, and pecan pies for his guests' delectation. His last e-mail said he would be serving *real* whipped cream on his pies.

Ted poured coffee for everyone. "You're going to need to go to the store, Maggie. We ate you out of house and home. If I never eat another can of tuna or Spam, it will be okay with me. And I never want to eat another cracker again either. I'm starved."

"Think positive," Espinosa said. "We all lost a few pounds."

"Which we will put back on after that fabulous-sounding dinner," Dennis said, crunching down on the last of some dry cornflakes.

"I think we should get this show on the road and head for Pinewood. It's going to take us *hours* to get there. I'll go insane if we stay here another hour. If we're lucky, Charles will have some canapés we can stuff ourselves with until dinner. C'mon, let's go. Why are you still sitting there?" Maggie said.

"Because we're tired," Ted said wearily. "We had to shovel with our hands when that rickety shovel of yours broke. I got enough of a workout to last me for months. I am one big pain. Even my hair hurts."

"Boo hoo," Maggie said as she slipped into her heavy jacket. "We're good to go here. Coffeepot is off, TV off, fire banked. Heat is set back to sixty-five degrees. Let's *GO!*"

The normal forty-minute drive to Pinewood took the reporters precisely three hours and twenty minutes from Georgetown to the electronic gates at Pinewood.

"I think we're the first ones here," Maggie said as she bolted from the van and ran through the snow to the farmhouse. After the initial hugs and kisses, Maggie whirled around and swooned at the wonderful scents wafting all about the kitchen. The dogs started to bark as the boys barreled through the door, Annie right behind them. More hugs and kisses followed by sharp barking and growling as the dogs vied for attention.

"This is so exciting," Myra said happily. "Everyone is coming, *everyone,*" she repeated. "We were so worried that the weather conditions would interfere. Someone up there is watching over us. We have so much to be thankful for. Nellie and Elias were coming on snowmobiles, but they just canceled. Pearl is on the way. The girls are all inbound, their ETA was twenty minutes at the last text. They should be here any time now."

"It's cold out there," Annie said. "The temperature gauge in my car said it was twenty-nine degrees, and by the time I got here, it had fallen to twenty-seven. They said it might start to sleet later in the day. That will not be good. We might all be spending the night here."

"That's fine. We certainly have enough beds and food to last an army a whole year. Just ask Charles. He believes in being prepared," Myra said as she eyed a jittery Dennis, who seemed to have an itch all over his body.

"But . . . that can't happen. We . . . I . . . scheduled Ms. Overton and Tressie's service for Saturday. I already canceled it twice when the first storm hit; I can't do it again."

The kitchen went silent. It was Annie who finally broke the silence. "Look, Dennis, it's all right. I don't mean this to sound callous, but the ladies are in no hurry. I believe the term they use in situations like this is, 'they're on ice.' Meaning the bodies are still in the morgue. When I checked yesterday, they still had not been sent to the funeral home. I thought you said you were going to have them cremated. Did you change your mind, Son?"

Dennis stopped fidgeting long enough to walk around the table to the door, where Ted and Espinosa were standing. He opened the door, then stepped aside and whispered to Annie, "I am having them cremated because then I can take charge of . . . of their remains. They have no one. If I did a burial, who would visit the graves? No one, that's who. Even if I wanted to, life gets in the way, and I'd put it off. That's not right and not fair to those ladies."

Annie reached out and hugged Dennis. "What you're doing is a wonderful thing. And you're right about the burial. It will be okay. Let's not dwell on this today, okay?"

Dennis nodded as he moved off to join the guys in the family room, where a fire was roaring in the fireplace. The dogs were yipping their pleasure at a houseful of company, which translated to belly rubs and ear tickles as well as a special dinner. But instead of turkey, Charles fixed chicken to go with all the trimmings, just for the dogs.

Ten minutes later, all the guests had arrived. The old timbers of Pinewood literally vibrated with the goodwill, laughter, and conversation, and there was even some singing by Lotus Lily and Little Jack, as Yoko, Harry, Lizzie, and Cosmo, the proud parents, beamed at the way the two children got on with each other and the dogs. Kathryn led Murphy into the room just as Harry brought Cooper into the fray. Within seconds, it was obvious to everyone that Lady was top dog and welcomed the two outsiders to her brood. She was lady enough to lead the two newcomers over to the corner, where two baskets of toys and blankets were waiting for them. Glorious yips of pleasure ensued as the dogs cavorted all over the place to everyone's delight, especially the two children's.

Myra nudged Annie. "Doncha love it, Annie? All our chicks are with us and under the same roof."

"I do, Myra, I do." Annie's eyes were misty as she clutched Myra's arm. "Do you think *our girls* are here? Don't lie to me, okay?"

Myra nodded. "They're here. Trust me."

"Okay."

And then, as usual with most family gatherings, the women separated and headed for the kitchen while the men stayed in the family room with the kids and the dogs and a football game playing on the big-screen HDTV. Charles buzzed in and out of the room with trays of canapés, drinks, and the latest weather report, which was that it was sleeting outside. He wiggled his eyebrows and warned that, more than likely, they would all be spending the night.

Bert Navarro and Jack Sparrow were concentrating on the game being played out on the TV while the reporters muttered and mumbled little tidbits among themselves about the case they were working on. Jack Emery led Harry Wong to a little anteroom off the family room and motioned for him to take a seat. Harry's eyebrows shot up at this strange happening. "What's up?"

Jack flopped down on a chair opposite Harry's, his eye on the doorway. "Listen, Harry, I need to talk to you, and this probably is not the place to do it, but we're here, so listen up."

"Why do I have the feeling I'm not going to like what you're going to say?"

"Probably because you're spot on. Look, we're friends, right? That means we stick together, and it also means that if I know something you should know, I have a duty to tell you. Even if I shouldn't tell you. Do you agree, and do you feel the same way? Don't go hostile on me. Please be serious, Harry."

"Yeah. What, Jack? You're making me nervous here."

Jack leaned forward and lowered his voice to a whisper. "You agree with me that women stick together, and you can't pry them apart. More so than guys, agreed?" Harry nodded. "If Nik finds out I told you any of this, she'll kick my ass all the way to hell and back. She caught me eavesdropping on a conversation she was having with Yoko. She made me swear not to say anything. I swore, and I'm about to break my word, so that should tell you how serious this is. You following me here, Harry?"

Harry froze in position. He shot Jack a ferocious look that sent shivers up his spine. "You gonna make me pull your lungs out of your ears or what? Talk, Jack."

Jack swallowed hard, knowing Harry's martial-arts prowess. "Just remember, Harry, I'm just the messenger and your best friend. I think of you as a brother, my only brother. You're gonna remember that, right?"

"Not if you don't start flapping your gums. I told you to talk to me. Start before I rip out your tongue. After which, I'll go for your lungs."

"Okay, okay. You know how obsessed you are with Lily. I mean, you are over the top with her. Everyone sees it. You'd breathe for that little girl if you could."

"So. That's what fathers are for, you dumbass."

Jack didn't like the way that sounded.

"Well, Yoko has had it with you. You aren't giving her a chance to be a mother. You don't let her make any decisions in regard to Lily. She really hates that you sleep in Lily's room so you can anticipate whatever needs she has. She said you won't even let her cry. Babies and little kids need to cry, so their lungs can stretch. Even I know that and I'm not a father, but I can read. So, who's really the dumbass here, Harry?"

"Who told you that?" Harry hissed.

"Yoko told Nikki, and I heard them talking. Aren't you listening? Your wife wants Nikki to represent her. She's thinking about divorcing you. That means you don't have a prayer. You won't know what hit you. You know how those women do things. They might even kill you, Harry, because you're messing with motherhood. Those women do not, I repeat, do not care about fatherhood. Make sure you understand that. Don't go nuclear on me now, and while you're at it, think about this. They could have blindsided you if I hadn't given you a heads-up. You should be thanking me, pal. Wait, there's one more thing. Yoko said Lily is a spoiled brat, and you don't discipline her. She said she is going to get kicked out of play school because she's such a brat."

Harry leaned back in his chair and closed

his eyes. For one horrified moment, Jack thought Harry had died on the spot. He couldn't remember when he had ever been this nervous. Ten full minutes later, he almost fell out of his chair when Harry's eyes snapped open. Jack didn't know what he expected, but Harry's response definitely wasn't it.

"I love that little girl more than life itself. I don't know how to turn that off. Yoko doesn't . . . she likes to . . . never mind. What should I do, Jack?"

Harry pleading? Harry asking for advice? Jack felt himself tensing up. "Harry, I didn't get that far in my thinking. I just wanted to warn you. Hell, I don't know. I don't have any kids. I'm not the person to ask. Undo what you did . . . are doing, I guess. Lily's kind of young to be kicked out of play school, isn't she? Yoko said you sit outside the school while Lily's in there. The school and the other parents don't like that. The teachers don't like it either that Lily beats up all the little boys. They said they spoke to you about it, and you said she was protecting herself. Are you saying there are bullies in play school? I'm sorry, pal, but I can't buy into that."

"So what you're saying, Jack, is you

wouldn't have done any of the things I've done."

"Hell no, Harry. Nik wouldn't let me pull something like that. She'd slap me upside the head if I ever moved into her motherhood territory. I'm still trying to figure out how you got away with that."

Harry looked like he was going to cry. "Maybe because I said Yoko wasn't a good mother and that I would take over. I said that, Jack. Yoko would let Lily cry; she didn't change her diaper as often as she should have. Lily got a rash. I learned a lot from Espinosa that time we took all those babies to Maggie's house. Her bottom was beet red. After that, Yoko didn't do anything; she left it up to me. She didn't have enough breast milk, so Lily had to go on a formula. She, Yoko, thought she was failing the baby. That's what started this . . . obsessiveness. Yoko walked away from Lily. What the hell was I supposed to do? It's Yoko's guilt that has brought us to this point in time. For God's sake, Jack, what would you have done?

"I tried to explain how things like that happen, but Yoko didn't want to hear it. Lily wants me to take care of her. I swear, Jack, I try to get her to go to Yoko, but she starts crying and wants me to pick her up and hug her."

"No kid ever died from crying, Harry. What about play school?"

"Yoko said she needed to be around other kids, to get social skills. Lily hates it. They said she cried the whole three hours in the beginning. Then she turned aggressive. I stayed outside because I kept thinking they would want me to come in and take her out. Okay, okay, that was wrong. I guess. Tell me what to do?"

"Harry, I don't know. I think this is something for Myra and Annie. Later, after dinner, take them to the side and talk. We're probably all going to be spending the night, so you'll have plenty of time. Just remember this. You did it, you own it. Don't go making excuses, just ask how to fix the situation. Throw yourself on their mercy, but always remember, Myra and Annie rule the Vigilantes. For some reason, I don't think either Yoko or Nik have spoken to them about it."

Harry closed his eyes and sighed heavily. "Okay, I'll do that." His voice was tortured when he whispered, "It isn't too late, is it, Jack?"

"You know what, Harry, it's never too late if your thoughts and actions are pure. I know that sounds kind of profound, but I happen to believe it." Harry nodded.

"Harry, do you think you can turn this all off for a few minutes? I've got a problem of my own, and I need to talk to you guys. I need some help myself."

"Sure, Jack, what's the problem?"

"C'mon, I want you all to hear this at one time. And I don't want the girls hearing or . . . suspecting I'm asking. . . . It's serious, Harry."

"Then let's get to it. Is it bad?"

Jack suddenly felt like a tremendous weight had just been lifted from his shoulders. Harry, best friend, stand-in brother, always gave him hope. "Bad? Depends on your point of view. It's my life."

"Crap."

Jack settled himself before he whistled softly to get everyone's attention. He looked around at those he called the newbies to Pinewood: Abner Tookus, Isabelle's husband; Jack Sparrow, Bert Navarro's right hand in Vegas; and Dennis West. The only one missing was Charles, but that was okay since Charles was joined at the hip with Myra and couldn't keep a secret from his wife. Everyone knew that.

Jack Sparrow, Bert's right hand, looked questioningly at Jack, and said, "Spit it out,

Jack." Jack blinked. Sparrow was fitting right in. He looked over at Cosmo Cricket, who winked at him.

Jack looked nervously at the kitchen door. Dennis correctly interpreted the look and scampered to the swinging door that led into the kitchen. Oh boy, he was suddenly part of something *big;* he could feel it in his bones. "I'll let you know if it looks like they're going to invade us. *GO,* big guy!"

Jack leaned into the group, and said, "I think you all know I hate being a defense attorney. God, I hate it. I really do. I'm a prosecutor. I don't know how I let Nikki talk me into joining the firm. Plus, I'm the only male in the whole damn place. Rumor has it I'm up for a nomination to become a federal judge. I don't want that either."

The men listened and stared at Jack. "Well, what *do* you want?" Cosmo Cricket asked.

Jack hunched closer, his voice dropping so the others had to strain to hear. "You know what I want? What I really want? I want yesterday. I want what we all had when we were going against everything we believed in to right wrongs no one else could. There, I said it. Well, isn't someone going to say something?"

"Then take the bull by the horns and do

something about it," Sparrow said forcefully.

Yep, Sparrow was fitting right in, Jack thought.

Bert raised his hand. "Let me make sure I have this right. You want to . . . what . . . go back to being an auxiliary Vigilante? But the girls retired. Well, with the exception of Myra and Annie. And we all know how that's working. Martine bowed out. Nellie is . . ." Bert looked at his right hand, wondering how to say what he was thinking.

"It's okay, Bert, you can say it. Nellie spends all her time taking care of her husband because she loves him. He needs her help, is the way I understand it," Sparrow said simply.

"Right, right, Sparrow. That leaves Pearl, who is doing a bang-up job with her underground railroad. We can't fault her for that. So that brings us back to Myra and Annie, and as much as I hate to say this, they are not getting any younger. They can't continue the way they've been going alone. Either they shut down, which I don't see happening, or this is made to order for all of us. I'm *IN,* if that's what you're asking me."

"Me, too!" Dennis chirped from his sentinel position at the swinging door. He didn't even stop to wonder what being *IN* was all about.

"Okay," Harry said.

"I'm liking how this is sounding," Ted and Espinosa said at the same time.

"If you need me, I'm yours," Abner Tookus said.

Jack looked at Abner, and said, "No paydays on this, no oceanfront properties as a payout. You sure you're okay with that?" Abner smiled and nodded.

Jack Sparrow looked up at Bert, his boss, and grinned. "I'm yours for the asking."

Cosmo Cricket laughed out loud. "I was always jealous of Elizabeth and the girls and what they did. If this means I can all of a sudden be a part of it, you can count on me for whatever good I can do."

Jack bit down on his lower lip. He knew he needed to say something but couldn't find the words. It was Dennis who saved the day by starting to sing, "Over the river and through the woods, here come the girls . . ."

In a nanosecond, the TV volume was turned up as Isabelle and Alexis entered the room with trays of canapés. Both women looked around, but it was Isabelle who said, "You guys are up to something, right?"

"Yeah, right," Ted said, pointing to the big-screen TV. "We were moaning and groaning because that guy, wearing number 7, just got himself taken out of the game. Ooh, I do love spring rolls."

Isabelle shot a look at Abner, who returned the stare with a smile on his face.

When the door closed behind the two women, Jack whispered, hissing, "No more talk till later. They're sneaky. It's a given that at least four of them are behind the door."

"Three!" Dennis said in return as he squinted through the crack at the side of the door.

"Charles, my darling, I think as a good host you need to join the men in the living room. We can handle things here in the kitchen."

"Surely you jest, my dear. After all the work I've put into this dinner, I cannot in good conscience allow you to —"

"Screw it up, is that what you were going to say, Charles?" Annie snapped. Charles shrugged, an uneasy feeling settling between his shoulder blades.

Myra smiled up at him so sweetly, Charles felt his insides start to curdle. "I don't think you understood, dear. It wasn't a suggestion, it was . . ."

Charles beelined for the door. Dennis would have gotten a faceful of door had he not stepped aside nimbly at just the right moment.

Charles managed to squeeze himself onto the sofa between Cosmo Cricket and Jack Sparrow, which was no small feat. "Whatever you lads are up to, I do not want to know. They sent me in here to *spy.* Just so you know."

The guys nodded as one.

"So, who's winning?" Charles asked brightly.

"We have no clue," Ted said. Espinosa cackled.

"Tell me," Charles said in a hushed voice, "am I going to like whatever it is you are all planning, or, as Isabelle said, are up to?"

"Nope!" Jack said. "Well, maybe, but I seriously doubt it."

"Maybe," Harry said.

"Six of one and half a dozen of the other," Bert said.

Dennis had everyone's attention when he said, "I think it depends on where your loyalty lies, with *them* or with us . . . lads."

"Oh, Lord love a duck! So that's the way it's going to be. I have to choose up sides? I don't think I can do that, lads."

"Does that mean all that crap you've been

feeding us all these years about your being some superspy for Her Majesty can't work for you now?" Ted demanded.

The group verbally ganged up on Charles until he was putty in their hands, with the promise that they would all meet up in the War Room after the women were asleep.

If Charles had a tail, it would have been between his legs when he made his way back to the kitchen thirty minutes later.

"Can we trust him?" Dennis demanded. When there was no response to his question, Dennis sat down on the floor to play with the dogs.

"Who is that kid?" Abner whispered to Ted.

Ted bristled. "He's my protégé. That's who he is. If you don't like that answer, then go with he's our new secret weapon."

"Hey, I was just asking. He's got a set on him for a young kid. I like that."

"That he does. Plus, he's a damn fine reporter," Ted drawled.

Chapter Nine

Charles squared his shoulders when he faced the gaggle of women, who stopped talking when he entered the kitchen. "I'm sorry, ladies, but it's time for you all to leave my kitchen so I can get this scrumptious Thanksgiving dinner on the table. No, no, I do not need any help. I do want to thank you for packing up the dinner for Nellie and Elias and the guards, as well as Elias's nurses." He looked up at the clock and continued, "Someone should be here shortly to pick it up. Shoo!" he said, waving his hands about. As one, the women scattered and headed for the family room to join their menfolk.

Charles stood in front of the stove, which was under the kitchen window. He stared out at the stormy day as sleet slapped against the windows, making a *rat-a-tat* sound that set his nerves on edge. He didn't like sleet, and he didn't like snow. He liked warm breezes and bright sunshine. He frowned, an uneasy feeling settling between his shoulder blades. A premonition. The feeling had nothing to do with what was going on inside the walls of Pinewood. That he could handle. No, this was an ugly, ominous feeling that something, somewhere, was awry. Something that was going to affect him in some way. He knew it as sure as he knew he had to take another breath in order to stay alive.

He looked down at the pan on the stove. He needed to add the thickening to what would be a delectable giblet gravy. He whirled and almost fell over when he heard the sweet voice of his spirit daughter.

"Don't fret, Daddy. In the end, everything will be all right."

"Sweetheart," Charles managed to say as he dropped the wooden spoon into the gravy pan. He didn't care. "What will be all right?"

"You know. What you're worrying about. I don't want you to worry, Daddy. It's going to burn if you don't stir it."

A second later, he felt something touch his cheek. He gripped the edge of the stove and was surprised to feel a burning sensation on his fingertips. He jerked away and looked around, but the kitchen was the same as it had been, the gravy at the boiling point, the wooden spoon swirling around in the mix. He fished it out and reached for another one.

He was right: something was wrong. His spirit daughter only appeared to him and Myra when things went off the straight and narrow. What? His heart felt heavy.

Charles worked by rote then. He finished the gravy, then filled the bowls with his famous chestnut stuffing, his special mashed potatoes, the delicious cranberry compote, the different vegetables, and the various chutneys that he adored. He looked down when he felt Lady nudge his leg. "You sense it too, don't you, girl?" He bent over and took the dog's beautiful face in his hands. "Whatever it is, we'll handle it, right, Lady?" The golden retriever pressed even closer. Charles swallowed hard. "That bad, eh?" The golden whined and licked at Charles's hand. "Okay, then, I'm depending on you." He hugged the big dog. Tightly. And didn't want to let her go. Lady was normal. Lady was love. Lady was loyalty. Lady was family. Something burned behind his eyelids when he straightened up and went to the sink to wash his hands.

Charles stared out the window as he washed and dried his hands. Whatever was wrong was out there, beyond his grasp and sight. He didn't know how long he'd been standing at the window until he heard young Dennis ask if he could help carry some of the food to the table.

Charles shook his head to clear his thoughts. "Yes, yes, of course. It's always such a challenge to get all the food on the table while it's still hot. That's why I use chafing dishes. It will go faster if you load everything on the serving cart and just wheel it in. I'll carry the platter with the turkey."

"It smells heavenly. I've been dreaming of this dinner for days. We actually ran out of food at Maggie's, where we were all staying. We were down to dry cornflakes and crackers before we left this morning. I plan to eat until I can't move."

Charles chuckled as he elbowed the swinging door so he could get through with the huge serving platter. "Dinnertime," he called loudly.

There was a mad scramble as the guests went directly to the beautifully set table that held Myra's family china, crystal, and silverware. "Just sit anywhere, we don't have a seating plan," Myra called out happily.

In the end, Charles sat at the head of the table with Annie on his left and Myra on his right. Chairs shuffled as everyone oohed and aahed over the array of delicious-smelling food. Charles held up his carving knife and fork, a wicked gleam in his eye. Jack Emery took his seat closest to the kitchen door so he could carry the various wine bottles to the table. He poured generously, to everyone's delight. All eyes were on Charles and the carving knife as it slid into the scrumptious-looking bird.

Dennis, seated immediately to Annie's left, heard it first and froze in place. It was a sound he'd never heard before other than on television. He looked around; the others seemed oblivious, except for Annie, who he saw stiffen in her seat. He watched as Myra started to pass the various bowls from the serving cart down the length of the table. The sound was louder now. *Whump. Whump. Whump.* He felt rather than saw Annie swing her legs to the side. She was going to move. To check out the sound? He felt the fine hairs on the back of his neck move. He looked around again. Everything seemed normal, the others were filling their plates, talking to each other, and laughing. Vague, jumbled voices could be heard wafting in from the TV in the family room. Jack had just gone through the swinging door to the kitchen with an empty wine bottle. The noise was so loud now, the house shook. *Whump. Whump. Whump.* A helicopter. Here at Pinewood. On Thanksgiving. During a storm.

Dennis thought he was in a time warp as everyone at the table stopped, raised their heads, and listened. Charles tilted his head, and said, "I imagine that's Nellie's people coming on the snowmobiles for their Thanksgiving dinner. It's all ready on the counter in the warming bags."

Jack was just coming through the door and took his seat next to Nikki. Charles said, "Jack, you're nearest the door. Can you do the send-off?"

"Sure, no problem," Jack said, getting back up off the chair and heading out to the kitchen.

Snowmobiles, my ass, Dennis thought. Snowmobiles whined and growled. He should know; he'd ridden on enough of them. He knew the sound of helicopter blades even if his knowledge came from TV. Annie's uneasiness was palpable.

The dining room went as silent as the air outside. Everyone started talking at once as they continued to pass the bowls of food around the table. Charles announced that Myra would say grace, then they could eat. The table's occupants clasped their hands as one before they bowed their heads and prayed along with Myra as she offered up the Thanksgiving prayer. Without Jack, who still had not returned, at the table.

Dennis raised his head just as Annie slid off her chair and made her way out of the room by way of the family room. His eyes narrowed just as Jack opened the swinging door and said, "Ah . . . Charles, I think you need to, ah, come out here. Like, *NOW!*"

Everyone at the table froze, including Charles, who had just speared a succulent slice of turkey on his fork. "I didn't forget anything; it's all in the warm bags. They just have to warm it up for ten minutes. I wrote the instructions on the bags." The slice of turkey found its way to his mouth.

Dennis didn't like the way Jack sounded when he then said, "You need to come *NOW,* SIR MALCOLM!" Who the heck is SIR MALCOLM? He saw out of the corner of his eyes how Myra gripped her pearls with both hands. He'd heard about those pearls. He was off his seat and tracking Annie in a nanosecond. When he was within an inch of her, he blanched and almost fainted when he saw her rummage in her purse. He saw a gun in one hand and something else in her other hand.

"Shhhh," she said. She went back to her

purse and came up with a Taser, which she handed to Dennis. "Be quiet and just do what I tell you."

"Is that real? I mean, does it shoot bullets?"

Annie shot the young reporter a disgusted glance. "What do you think? It's the same one I used when we met your granny and auntie. Listen, Dennis, what are the chances you can get out the front door to see —"

"The markings on the helicopter? I knew that sound wasn't a snowmobile. Good. Good. I can do it."

"Then do it and don't make any noise. Hurry, Dennis." The kid was one sharp cookie. She made a mental note to give him a raise.

Annie leaned against the wall, her insides shaking, her legs trembling. But the hand holding the gun was steady as a rock. She thought about Myra and knew she was dying inside, knowing as she knew, because Charles had told them early on, that a day like this might come.

Sir Malcolm Sutcliff, superspy in his other life, childhood friend of the Queen of England. Sent here by the Queen and given a new life and a new identity when his cover had been blown. But it all came with the promise that his allegiance would always be to her and not his adopted country. Annie wasn't sure, but she rather imagined that Charles had signed off in his own blood. She'd discussed it with Myra at length, and Myra had agreed with her.

Annie inched closer to the short hallway that would take her to the kitchen. She had a clear view of two men in the kitchen whose appearance shrieked MI6. Her Majesty's Secret Service. Only Charles and Jack were in the kitchen with them; the swinging door leading to the dining room was closed.

Annie felt the coldness and knew young Dennis was back, soaking wet and dripping ice off his hair. His teeth chattered when he said, "It says MARINE ONE. That's the *president's helicopter*! The engine's running. That means they're burning fuel. I guess they don't care, and they don't care that it's Thanksgiving either."

Annie didn't take her eyes off the figures in the kitchen. "There's an afghan on the back of the sofa. Wrap it around yourself until you can change your clothes. Hurry, Dennis." Dennis hurried and returned with a pink afghan wrapped tightly around his shoulders, but he was still shivering.

"Okay, Son, it's just you and me. You have the Taser? It's not going to do us any good in your pocket. Remember, in order for it to work, you need to get as close as possible and just pull the trigger. Aim for whichever one is closest. Don't pay attention to Charles or Jack. You got it?"

Dennis nodded. "Are we . . . ah . . . going to take those goons out?" Despite his trembling lips and his shivering body, Annie could hear the excitement ringing in his voice. She liked this kid, she really did.

"Whatever it takes. Okay, here we go."

Annie kicked open the door and assumed a shooter's stance, the gun rock steady in a two-handed grip. "Stop right there, gentlemen! Hands in the air! Do as I say. *NOW!*"

The pink afghan dragging on the floor, Dennis advanced, the Taser straight out in front of him. His hands were shaking so badly he didn't know if he'd hit the refrigerator, the ceiling, or one of the burly men who were observing him through narrowed eyes. "You heard the lady, hands in the air!" he squawked.

"Easy, laddie, easy."

"Don't call me laddie," Dennis snapped. "I told you, do what the lady said, or you're going to find yourself with about eighteen thousand volts of electricity running out your butt."

"We're here on Her Majesty's orders. We're here to fetch Sir Malcolm and take him home to England. Now stand aside and let us do what we came here to do."

"That's Marine One out there in the pasture. What does the president have to do with this?" Dennis asked, worry etching his face as he tried to figure out exactly what Annie wanted him to do. He wished she'd say something.

"Stand down, gentlemen," Annie said, her eyes narrowing till it looked like she was squinting. "I think I should tell you I can take you both out. Two shots, center mass, and Her Majesty is short two agents. What's it going to be?"

"We have our orders. Your president graciously cooperated with us by allowing transportation in this hideous weather. Your president is cooperating with our government. We are allies," one of the agents said in a condescending tone.

Annie bristled. "Well, guess what, Mr. Super Agent, I have here in my hand something that trumps anything you might have. Dennis has the same thing. So, unless Charles — or Sir Malcolm as you refer to him — says he wants to go with you, I advise you to stand down. I won't tell you again."

"Ms. de Silva is an excellent shot, lads. Best to do what she says," Charles said.

"Yeah, do what she says," Dennis blustered, the hands holding the Taser shaking like leaves in a windstorm.

"Someone tell me what's going on here?" Annie ordered.

Jack, bug-eyed, nodded. He wondered how no one in the dining room had tried to enter the kitchen to see what was going on. Like Harry. He willed him to come to his aid but knew it wasn't going to happen.

The taller of the two agents took a step forward. Dennis perceived his movement as a definite threat and fired the Taser. The man gasped and sank to the floor, just as Annie fired her gun and blew out the second agent's kneecap. And then all hell broke loose as Jack was pushed away from the swinging door and the men and women from the dining room streamed forward, the dogs howling and yelping.

Charles threw up his hands and roared, "Everyone! Just take it easy! Listen to me!"

Dennis wrapped the pink afghan as tightly as he could around his pudgy body. His eyes were big as saucers as he stared at both men on the floor. He was shocked when he saw Charles help the agent he'd Tasered.

Charles looked around. "I have to go, Annie. But first I have to . . . I have to speak to Myra. I'm going to need some help getting that one" — he pointed to the man nursing his wounded knee — "out to the helicopter."

"I don't think there's anyone here who is going to help you, Charles," Annie said quietly.

"You bastard!" the agent said to Dennis.

"Takes one to know one!" Dennis shot back. "Give me any more lip, and I'll be more than happy to do it again!" he said bravely, now that all the guests had his back, pushing and shoving as they demanded answers to what was going on. Out of the corner of his eye he saw Espinosa snapping pictures. Front-page news. This would certainly upstage Black Friday and the shopping frenzy that had the entire country in a tizzy every year.

Hate-filled eyes focused on Annie and the gun in her hand. "You!" the agent gasped. "You'll pay for this!"

Annie waved her gold shield. "I very seriously doubt it, *laddie*!"

"*Now* you get here!" Jack said to Harry as he shouldered his way through the crowd to get to Jack. "I was willing you to come out here. Why didn't you? You should have paid attention, and none of this would have happened."

"*You willed me!* Is that what you said?

What? You think I'm some kind of mind reader? Don't answer that. What the hell is going on here?"

"I wish I knew, Harry. These guys are from MI6, Charles's old stomping ground. They came here to pick him up and take him somewhere. They arrived in Marine One, the president's helicopter. It's out in the pasture. That's the noise we heard. This is just a guess on my part, but I don't think Charles wants to go, but he's going to go anyway. British duty and all that. You know, that stiff-upper-lip crap the Brits are famous for. You should have seen Annie plug that guy. And the kid shot off the Taser while his hands were shaking so badly I thought the dart was going to hit the ceiling. The bruiser dropped like a noodle."

"Why?" Harry asked.

Jack shook his head. "I have no clue."

That's when they heard the high-pitched whine of a snowmobile. Moments later two Secret Service men, the men Nellie and Elias referred to as their protectors, approached the back door. They took in the scene and in an instant their hands went to their hips. Harry moved, but Annie was faster. She fired off two warning shots that took off half the doorframe. The agents stopped in their tracks.

"Nice and easy, gentlemen. Come in and join the party. Tread lightly," Annie warned. She turned to Charles, her eyes cold and hard. The love and affection she felt for Charles in the past were gone. "You might want to say something about now, *Sir Malcolm.*" The venom in her voice was not missed by anyone in the kitchen.

"Charles," Myra cried, pushing forward. It was such a pitiful cry, Charles whirled around. He bent over to whisper something in Myra's ear, but she wanted none of whatever he was going to say. She pushed him away. His shoulders slumped.

Charles took charge then the way he'd done numerous times in the past. He issued orders like a field general, orders that were instantly obeyed. He reached for his down jacket, which hung on a rack next to the half-destroyed doorframe. Then he turned around, and said, "I'm terribly sorry to have ruined everyone's Thanksgiving dinner. I have to leave now. I have no other choice at the moment. I'll . . . I'll carry my memories of you all with me forever." Then he left with the British and Secret Service agents. Myra sobbed against Nikki's shoulder.

"Kill them all, Harry," Jack hissed.

"I don't think this is the right time," Harry hissed back. "Thank God Little Jack and

Lily are still napping. He's actually going, so it must be serious, whatever *it* is. He's not taking a thing with him. That alone tells you this is extra-serious. Take note, Jack, that's a lot of serious firepower he's got going on there. Think about it: MI6, Marine One. That's as high as you can go."

Annie marched over to the door and kicked it shut. It flew back open with a torrent of sleet rushing inward. She kicked it again, then bellowed to someone to fix the door. Ted grabbed a kitchen chair and propped it up under the doorknob. It was a lousy temporary fix, and he said so. "But it will have to do for now."

Myra sobbed louder.

"Dennis, dear, go upstairs and get into dry clothes before you catch a cold," Annie said. "You did well, young man. I'm proud of you. Be quiet, though, so you don't wake the children." Dennis, beaming from ear to ear, scampered off. These people were just so exciting to be around. He couldn't help wondering what they would do for an encore.

"Nikki, stay with Myra. Girls, let's see about heating up all this food so as to not let it go to waste. Charles worked very hard to make this meal. Just to spite him, I think we should eat hearty and enjoy his endeavor.

Chop chop, everyone!" Annie said in a voice so controlled and cold that it could have chilled milk.

CHAPTER TEN

Warming the Thanksgiving dinner proved to be a wasted effort. Myra excused herself and ran up the back staircase. Annie looked around at the others, but she said nothing. Instead, she followed her dearest friend in the whole world up the back staircase.

The other girls rose as one and started to clear the table and pack up the dinner that no one had eaten. The boys scrubbed the pots and loaded the dishwasher. The children sat on the floor near the laundry room cuddling with the dogs, who had suddenly gone quiet.

Nikki looked around and said, "I think we should leave. The sleet has turned to rain, so the roads will be okay. Myra . . . Myra . . . won't want us here. Please, don't any of you argue with me. Jack, warm up the car, okay?"

No one argued. Dennis said he had a question.

"What?" Nikki barked.

"What about all this food?"

Nikki shrugged.

"Take whatever you want," Isabelle said to them as her hands flapped in the air to indicate all the covered dishes lining the countertop. "Annie will figure out something, I'm sure."

Ten minutes later, the kitchen was empty and quiet except for Nikki, who was the last one to leave. The dogs clustered around Nikki's legs. She crooned to them and patted each one on the head. "Go to Myra, guys." She looked at the chair propped under the kitchen door. She would have to leave by the front door. Satisfied that the situation was contained for the moment, she waved good-bye to the dogs. She waited for them to run up the back staircase before she let herself out the front door.

Sliding into the car, where Jack was sitting behind the wheel, she started to cry. "I don't believe he . . . he just up and left. He just left, Jack! How could he do that to Myra, to us? You don't do things like that. You just don't. Myra . . . did you see that awful look on her face? Of course you did," she said, answering her own question. "How could you have missed it? How could anyone have missed it."

"Maybe we shouldn't have left. Maybe she'll need us. We could turn around and go back, Nik. Just tell me what you want me to do."

"We're doing the right thing. Myra has Annie, who knows the whole story. Annie is who she needs at the moment. They'll feed off each other, and that is exactly what Myra needs right now. We would all just be in the way."

"What do you think it is, Nik? What could be so important that Charles didn't think twice about leaving his wife? We — actually, Annie and the kid — had them dead in our sights. With all of us, we could have taken them out."

"And then what? Charles said he was willing to go with those agents. That was the beginning and the end of it right there. And those guys didn't seem fazed with the gold shields or the fact that Charles had one, too. Whatever is going down — and we will probably never really get the whole story — is happening on the other side of the pond. That's just my opinion, for whatever it's worth," Nikki said.

"It sounded to me like he wasn't coming back. Remember how he said he would carry memories of all of us with him? Myra was standing right beside me, and when he said that, she crumpled against me. I can tell you that's how she took it, too. He cut all of us loose."

Nikki fished around in her purse for a pack of tissues. She wiped at her eyes but continued to cry. "I think that's how we all took it."

"Do you think we should get in touch with the others? I know we're meeting up for breakfast at Sally's Diner tomorrow morning, but I mean tonight, to hash this out? Maybe there is something we can do."

"Jack! Charles went willingly. I repeat, willingly. Whatever is going on is obviously more important than Myra and all of us. Morning will be time enough."

"Like he and he alone is going to save the British Empire from evildoers! Come on, Nik! The last time he left, he had a reason — his son. A son he claimed that he did not know he had. Myra forgave him that time. She even went to England to be at his side. But this time it's different. This time, Charles had a choice. He's a United States citizen. You said you and Barbara attended the ceremony and told me how proud he was that day. Aside from that one trip to England in regard to his son, he has never left our shores. He told me that himself. We're talking well over thirty years here,

Nik. What the hell could be so damn important that he'd hightail it out of here the way he did?"

"I don't know, Jack. I just don't know. I don't think Myra knows either. That's why it is going to be so hard for her to accept this."

"I wonder what the two of them are doing right now." There was no need for Nikki to ask what two of them he was talking about. She just cried harder into the wad of tissues clutched in her hand.

What the two of them, meaning Myra and Annie, were doing was staring at each other. At least that's what Annie thought they were doing until she waved her hand in front of Myra's face. When Myra didn't blink, Annie's heart skipped a beat. "Earth to Myra," she said, shaking her old friend's shoulder. Myra was so loose she felt like a rag doll under Annie's hands. Annie shook her again and said in a low, menacing voice, "Don't do this to me, Myra. Don't you dare! You're looking at that black hole again. I know you are. I feel it. The one you told me about when Barbara died. Don't go near it. Please, Myra, step back. I'm here, we're all here. Well, that might not be true. I think everyone left, but you can count on me. Step back, Myra. That's a damn order!"

Myra stirred. "I heard you the first time, Annie. There's no need to shout."

Annie grew so light headed she thought she was going to black out. "Do you want to go downstairs and get some dinner?"

"That would be lovely. I am rather hungry. I heard them all leaving. I should have made myself go down and say good-bye."

"It would be nice if you'd call them at some point this evening. You know as well as I do that they're worried sick about you. As am I."

"Why? Do you think I'm that unstable, that wimpy? So my husband leaves me! So what? He did it before, but I understood that. It had to do with his son, and children always come first. You and I both know that. But there are no children this time around. He left me, Annie. That's the bottom line. He had a choice, and he chose to leave. He's a U.S. citizen. He did not have to go, Annie.

"How many times did we talk about this in past years? Too many," Myra said, answering her own question. "I knew the day would come when he'd leave. I knew it. Charles said no, he would never leave me, but I never quite believed him, and look where we are. What's that saying, Annie?

Am I chopped liver or something?"

Annie shrugged. "We have all the time in the world to figure it out. Tomorrow is another day. I say we go downstairs and get something to eat. It did look like a feast to me when it was all spread out on the table. I hope that boy doesn't get pneumonia."

Myra was on her feet and leading the way to the back staircase. She was almost to the top when she turned and called over her shoulder, "I need you to help me do something first."

The two women marched back to Myra's bedroom, where she started yanking at the bedcovers. "These have to go. I want them out of here. Like now!" Annie understood perfectly.

Thirty minutes later the bed was made with brand-new linens, the pillows replaced with pillows from one of the guest rooms. Charles's side of the closet was now empty, as were his dresser drawers. A huge pile of clothing and bed linens sat in the middle of the floor. Both women glared at it.

"I say we pitch it all out the window. We can worry about it later, after the spring thaw."

"That works for me," Myra said as she raised the window. Arctic air rushed into the room. The flames in the fireplace danced and swirled as the cold air circled the room.

"You know what else, Annie? I called on my spirit daughter. Barbara always comes to me when I need her the most. She took her good old sweet time, and do you know what she said? She said . . . I didn't really need her. Just like that, and she was gone. Do you believe that?"

Annie just rolled her eyes as she tossed a pile of clothing out the window.

When the room was bare of Charles's belongings, Myra closed the window. Both women raced to the fireplace to warm themselves. "How do you feel now? The truth, Myra."

Myra looked around the room. The bed was neatly made the way it had been neatly made before the women stripped it. The closet doors were shut, so they looked the same. Charles's glasses and the book he'd been reading on the little table by his chair, the only real indication that anyone besides Myra had inhabited the room, were gone. "A bit like chopped liver, I guess."

"You need to get over that feeling real quick. You are not chopped liver, you were never chopped liver, nor will you ever be chopped liver. You will always be my best friend, my true best friend. I wouldn't know what to do without you in my life, Myra.

We've been together — perhaps not physically — since we were digging in the ground with our play shovels, convinced we were going to find gold or dig our way to China. It seems like a lifetime ago."

"Sometimes it seems like it was yesterday, and we were having tea parties on the veranda on rainy days. Memories for the most part can be quite wonderful. Even the not-so-good ones. They make us who we are. Yes or no, Annie?"

"Absolutely. Oh dear, will you look at all this food. I guess the fridge is full and that's why all this stuff is still out here on the counter." Annie opened the fridge to make her point. "So, do we pile a little of everything on our plates and chow down after I heat it up?"

Myra swallowed hard. "I say we go right to the dessert and worry about all of this tomorrow. This moment in time calls for sweets and a tumblerful of bourbon. What do you say, Annie?"

"I'm your gal. You dish out the dessert, and I'll pour. I'm going to add some more logs to this fireplace. I just love it that you have a fireplace in the kitchen. Mama had one in our old house. Do you remember how in the winter she'd set up a little table so we could draw pictures and drink hot cocoa? Remember that, Myra?"

"I do. The good old days. Right now we need to start thinking about making some new days. We have a case to consider."

"Yes, we do. I have a few ideas. Before I forget, I will pay to have your doorway fixed. I really did a number on it. I'll call someone tomorrow. Okay?"

"Sure."

Both women sat down on a pile of cushions by the fireplace. The dogs got up and came over and settled themselves between the two old friends. "See this, Annie. This is *true love.* No matter what, these animals love us unconditionally. Not to mention they are dying to get to those plates with our dessert." She laughed then, and at that moment, Annie knew Myra was A-OK.

They drank steadily until the bottle of Jack Daniel's Black was empty. They giggled, they laughed, and they shed a tear or two, tears that the dogs licked away. And then they slept, the sounds of their gentle snoring filling the room.

When the fire died down, Lady got up and signaled to her pups to follow her to the laundry room. She put her paws on the top of the dryer so that the pile of folded towels waiting to be taken upstairs would topple over. One by one, the dogs dragged the towels back to the fireplace, where they tucked in the two ladies from head to toe. She nosed the pups, and one by one, they formed a circle. Her head on her paws, Lady kept her eyes on the broken door.

Their world was safe and secure. For now.

Myra stirred when she felt something nudge her shoulder. She opened one eye and smiled at Lady, who was doing her best to pull away the towels so she could lick her mistress's chin. Time to go out, was the message. Myra opened her other eye, then quickly closed them against the blazing light in the kitchen. Outside, the world was a winter wonderland. The rain must have changed to snow while she was sleeping. And it was still snowing. She struggled to get up, with Lady trying to help. The pups barked, knowing they were going for a romp in that delicious white stuff that coated the world. Annie moved and groaned.

"Time to get up, Annie. You aren't going to believe this, but it started to snow while we were sleeping, and it hasn't stopped yet. You build up the fire, and I'll let the dogs out and make the coffee."

"What time is it?" Annie asked groggily.

Myra peered at the clock on the range. "Ten minutes past eight. Why, do you have someplace you have to be?"

"No," Annie snapped as she tossed several huge oak logs on the fire. She watched the dying embers grab hold of the dry wood. The dried-out wood snapped, crackled, and popped, showering the inside of the fireplace like a Fourth of July fireworks display. "Did you get up during the night and cover us?"

"No, I thought you did it. Must have been Lady. That dog is so tuned in to me. I bet you a dollar she guarded the back door all night long, too. How do you feel, Annie?"

"Like I drank half a bottle of bourbon. How do you feel?"

"The same way. Coffee will fix us both right up, along with a few aspirin. Once we shower, we'll be able to take on the world. And Manny Macklin. We have to make Mr. Macklin our top priority. But first we have to feed the dogs when they come in. After we dry them off, of course. Oh, that is a beautiful fire, Annie."

"You're certainly chipper this morning. For someone on the edge of that black hole, you certainly did a total 180, or is that a 160? Oh, who cares," Annie grumbled as she poured herself a cup of coffee.

Lady slammed against the door, and the chair underneath it moved so that she and the pups barreled into the kitchen, covered in snow. They danced and twirled, yelped and squealed as they slipped all over the slick floor. Annie and Myra both rushed for the towels to dry them off. If the dogs had been cats, they would have been purring at the not-so-gentle rubdown.

In the refrigerator were five extra plates full of the Thanksgiving dinner Charles had made for the dogs: chicken with all the trimmings. Myra heated them in the microwave, then set the plates on the floor. The dogs wolfed their food and settled themselves on the cushions by the fire. Time for a nap. Myra smiled indulgently. "It's like having five little kids, but less work."

Annie nodded as she pressed numbers onto her BlackBerry. She stated her business, discussed payment, and ended the call. "That Handyman Mike I've used from time to time will be here at eleven o'clock to fix the door. He's bringing all the materials with him. I'm sort of thinking maybe I should try and gouge out the bullets. What do you think, Myra?" she asked fretfully.

"I'm thinking that might be a good idea. But we have time for that. Let's just drink our coffee and enjoy it. Three or four aspirin, Annie?"

"Four," Annie said smartly. "Should we call the kids?"

"Yes, but not yet. After we shower and get ready for the day. Let's just sit here until our hangovers ease up. Annie, did you pick up on anything strange yesterday, and by strange I mean before . . . before the *main event*?"

"You mean like Jack's huddling with Harry, and Yoko suddenly in charge of Lily, and Jack and the other *men* huddling and whispering? Yep!"

"How can we find out what went on?"

"Don't you mean which one will squeal on the others?"

Myra cleared her throat. "That's one way of putting it. So, which one?"

"The newbie. Dennis is his name. I like that kid. I'm going to give him a raise."

"That's nice. What if he won't give it up?"

"Then I won't give him a raise," Annie snapped. Myra made a sound that could have been laughter. Annie wasn't sure. Whatever it was, she was assured that her best friend in the whole world was back among the living and not teetering over that black hole she'd been perched on just hours ago. She rather thought that the day was off to a good start.

"How are you going to get him to squeal?" Myra asked curiously.

"I'll think of something. But not right this

second. I have an idea, Myra. After we take care of Manny Macklin, let's go to Vegas for Christmas. I'll shut down the casino, kick out all the guests, and all of us will have the run of the casino and hotel. We can take Lady, the pups, and everyone else's dogs, and whoop it up till our hearts are content. You up for a walk on the wild side?"

Myra didn't know if she was or not, but she gave a thumbs-up. Hearing her name mentioned, Lady opened one eye and offered up a soft woof before going back to sleep.

Annie grinned. "Guess that means she's up for it. I have another idea. The adults can party at night — Christmas Eve — and on Christmas Day we can host underprivileged children from all over the state. I bet if we call on Rena Gold — you remember how Rena helped us on one of our missions — she could get the ball rolling. Tons of presents, a service of some kind, with different pastors and priests, along with donations. We could even do an animal one, too."

"Annie, that's a great idea. You're going to lose a lot of money shutting down the casino for twenty-four hours, though."

"There is that, but think of all the happiness we can create. I know you won't want to be here at the farm on Christmas because of the memories. A Vegas Christmas is about as far as you can get from a Pinewood Christmas. I'll pay all the staff so they don't lose out. We might get so much good press, our revenues will double when we reopen the doors. Lizzie and Cosmo can work on the sidelines to help Rena. Should we do it, Myra?"

"Yes! Yes! Yes! I think it's a great idea." Myra massaged her temples. Thank God the horrendous headache she woke up with was all but gone.

"Good. I'm so glad that you agree. I'll get right on it. I do love to delegate. More coffee?"

Myra held her cup out for a refill. "I don't want you worrying about me, Annie. Yesterday was a . . . shock, a bitter one. Part of me always knew this was going to happen someday. I always wondered what I would do if it happened. Now I know. The answer is, I can't do anything but get on with my life and do the best I can. Do I like it? No, I don't. Will I get over it? Probably not. Will I falter and sink into depression? Not likely, but if you see that happening, give me a swift kick. And, of course, the last question is whether I need a man in my life to make me whole. And the answer is no, a thousand times no!"

"Well said, my friend. We're survivors, Myra. We've had full and rich lives, most of it good, but we've had some down-and-dirty bad times, too. And yet, here we are. And here we shall remain."

Myra reached across the table to grasp Annie's hand. No words were necessary between the two women.

When the coffeepot was empty, Myra stood up and said she'd shower first while Annie started to put her Christmas plans into motion. When she returned to the kitchen, she'd call the girls to let them see she was okay. And then it was on to Manny Macklin.

At the landing on the back staircase, Myra stared out at the winter wonderland. It was so beautiful it took her breath away. It was all so pure and clean. Tears filled her eyes, but she brushed them away. She straightened her shoulders and climbed the rest of the stairs. Her steps were brisk as she made her way to her bedroom and the master bath.

Charles Martin, aka Sir Malcolm Sutcliff, was just someone she used to know. She bit down on her lower lip and switched her thoughts to Manny Macklin.

Chapter Eleven

"Why do I feel like I'm in a cocoon?" Annie demanded as she tossed her pen across the kitchen table to make some kind of point.

"Because," Myra said, raising her eyes from her laptop and pointing outside, "we *are* in a cocoon. There has to be at least a foot and a half of new snow out there. If you want my opinion, it's eerie. Now, Annie, having said that, do you agree or not that there is nothing we can do about it? Turn on the TV; at least that will give us some extra noise." Annie got up and obliged.

Both women leaned forward to listen to a curly-haired blonde, dressed in what looked like an ermine parka, chortle about all the snow and what it was doing to the Black Friday shopping frenzy that was just going to devastate every retailer on the Eastern Seaboard.

"I'm just surprised we haven't lost power,"

Myra said, getting up to pour more coffee into her cup.

Annie reached for the pot, rinsed it, and made fresh coffee — more to have something to do than anything else. "Did you come up with anything new?"

"You mean on the current Mrs. Macklin? She's just another bimbo. Thirty years younger, nipped, tucked, enhanced, and shellacked like the others. Spends her days and his money going to clubs, luncheons, and fancy stores. They've been married for three years and never seem to see each other. She stays in New York. He's all over the map. Her name was Jane Lincoln, twice divorced, no children. She was a hairdresser. Guess she coiffed Manny's hair at some point. Her current job seems to be spending her husband's money. Nice gig if you can get it."

Myra stared, transfixed, at the coffee dripping into the pot. Annie didn't know if she'd heard her or not. "Don't go there, Myra. Come on, talk to me."

Myra whirled around. "I was not thinking about Charles. I was just wondering who the beneficiary of our deceased clients is. I didn't come across a copy of their will in the folders they gave us. You didn't see one, did you?"

"No. But Nikki's firm represents . . . represented them. This is just a wild guess on my part, but I would imagine they left the bulk of it to charity, mainly the Salvation Army since that's the organization they were most loyal to. The people who helped them along the way. Do you think it's important for us to know that?"

"Well, yes, in a way. You don't think they'd leave anything to Macklin out of guilt or soft feelings, do you?"

Annie peered over the top of her reading glasses, which were perched high on her nose. "Surely you jest, Myra. They contacted us to *punish* him. Why on earth would they leave him anything?"

"Guilt!"

Annie poured coffee that she really didn't want into her cup. "The short answer is no. Nikki will tell us when she can. We're not going to be able to get to town for their memorial service tomorrow. Young Dennis is going to be upset."

"Maybe he'll reschedule it. I'm sure Nikki wants to attend. The others left on the red-eye to return to Vegas. There's just us."

"Well, there's nothing we can do about that either," Annie grumbled as she sat back down at the table. "We need to make a plan, Myra. But first we need to talk to Abner so we know what we're doing here. We might have to create a legend for ourselves if we plan on a face to face. How smart do you think that guy really is?"

Myra propped her chin in the palm of her hand. "Well, Annie, he was smart enough to pull off his Ponzi scheme up to this point without getting caught. He's been at it for more than twenty years and must have amassed a fortune. I'm thinking there might be cracks in his system. I don't have anything to base that statement on, just my gut feeling. Right now, this is how I see it. We have to find the first wife. Next to talking to Sara and Tressie, I think she's the one who can help us the most."

"I agree. If Abner can't find her, then we might as well give up. I don't know how else we can get to Macklin. The last article I read a while back said he's like a phantom — he's here, he's there, impossible to nail down. We missed our chance yesterday, but Dennis said Pauline, the receptionist, called to cancel his pot roast dinner once again, because she has the flu. She told him that Macklin canceled his Santa appearance yesterday. Said he was — the term she used was — *stuck somewhere.* She also said that was a first for him; he had never missed one till this year. So we didn't actually miss cornering him. I'm just wondering if this is part of his M.O. — you know, being on the move all the time — or if this is something new. And if it's the latter, then like I said, he's aware of the cracks. I wish Abner would get back to us already."

"There's nothing wrong with calling Abner for an update."

That was all Annie needed to hear. She had her cell phone in her hand and was punching out numbers in a nanosecond.

Myra carried her coffee cup over to the newly repaired back door and stared out at the blinding whiteness. Everything looked so beautiful, so pure, so chaste, so innocent. She crossed her fingers on her left hand and smiled to herself. *Life is what you make of it,* she told herself. No guarantees along the way. Her shoulders started to sag, but Lady nosed her leg as much as to say, no, no, no. Imperceptibly, Myra felt her shoulders lift. She looked down at her beloved companion. "You want to go out?" Lady backed away and trotted into the laundry room, where there were pee pads by the door for days like this.

"Woo hoo!" Annie shouted as she broke the connection and slipped her cell into the pocket of her sweatpants. "We have information!"

"So share it," Myra said, excitement ringing in her voice.

"We have a name and an address for Manny Macklin's first wife, Mary. She changed her last name to Carmichael. She lives about ten miles outside of Washington. Seems she had a half brother, different fathers. That was the holdup in finding her. She took his last name. She lives a quiet life, doesn't have a full-time job but does volunteer her services at her local church, and there does not appear to have been any contact with the family she walked away from. She cut all ties when she departed. At least, that is what Abner thinks. He's going to send us a fax with all the information."

Myra clapped her hands. "Good. Now we have a starting point. Did he say anything else?"

Annie grimaced. "The short answer is no. I guess you can say he failed." At Myra's look of horror, Annie hastened to explain. "He didn't actually fail. He said he didn't come up with anything because there was nothing to find. According to Abner, Emanuel Macklin is a Neanderthal. He does everything the old-fashioned way. He deals with telephone calls, and the investment statements he sends out to his clients every month are done on a typewriter using —

are you ready for this? — carbon paper. No computer trail.

"Going on nothing more than a hunch and his gut feeling, Abner said he went trawling and learned that his fortune is on the move. Millions and millions are moving at the speed of light. Abner said it was too complicated to explain over the phone. You aren't going to believe this, but that bastard opened up accounts in Lichtenstein in the names of *Marie Palmer* and *Sally Dumont* and *Mary Richardson.* So he probably does not know that instead of going back to her maiden name, Mary adopted her half brother's. Fifty million in each one. As in our dead clients, Sara and Tressie, and the ex-wife. The last time he moved the money was the Monday before Thanksgiving. Abner thinks he's getting ready to take it on the lam."

"Oh my! That means we're going to have to work fast, then. Do you think our dumping our accounts had anything to do with this?"

Annie shoved her glasses higher on her nose and fixed Myra with a hard stare. "Well, he did it a few days *after* our visit to Queen's Ridge. We dumped our investments at that time. So, yes, I think it's a very good chance we had a lot to do with it. He's faxing that stuff, too."

"Where do you think he'll go?"

"Abner said he has real estate all over the world. Some really fancy digs in exotic locations, others just houses in regular neighborhoods. In other words, safe houses where he can just blend in. He has almost a billion when you combine all his real estate, and not a single property is in his name. Most properties are in the names of Mary Richardson, Marie Palmer, and Sally Dumont. There isn't even a single property in the name of either of his kids. Tell me that guy isn't a skank! Now, all these years later, he's still using those two ladies and his ex-wife. What a guy!"

"Does he have any partners?"

Annie shrugged. "Abner didn't say, so I'd say no. Except for his son and daughter. They're on the books. Skeleton office staff. Mostly elderly people who have been with him for a long time. Six in all. Do they know? I don't know, Myra."

"That almost has to mean he's a one-man operation. He really uses carbon paper? I didn't know they still made carbon paper. Abner is right, the man is a Neanderthal. With the exception of his two children, no one else appears on the radar screen. I suppose he thought it was safer that way. Too many hands in the pie would not be a safe option. Go it alone, and if anything goes awry, you have no one to blame but yourself. It also means no one can squeal or tip off the SEC. I don't think I will ever be able to understand how he could amass the fortune he did, pay off all those clients those high returns, and get away with it for so long. Didn't we say over twenty years, or something like that?"

"Think about it, Myra. The man would have had to work at something like that almost 24/7, and he must have a phenomenal memory to keep it all straight. Do you think he keeps two sets of books? We're going to need those books. I'm going to go down to the War Room to see if Abner's faxes came through. While I'm doing that, why don't you make us some breakfast, something beside toast and jam, okay?"

"How does a turkey omelet sound?"

Annie just rolled her eyes.

Myra walked over to the back door and stared outside. Déjà vu. She'd just done this a little while ago but still marveled at the pristine outdoors. The scenery hadn't changed one iota since she'd stood at the door earlier. Her thoughts were different now, though. They were across the pond with her husband. She felt her eyes start to burn. She clenched her fists at her sides and squeezed her eyes shut.

"Why, Charles, why did you do this?" she whispered over and over to herself. When she couldn't come up with an answer, she sighed mightily and made her way over to the refrigerator. She had orders to make an omelet, and an omelet was what she was going to do. She sniffed at what she perceived to be the injustice of it all.

CHAPTER TWELVE

Emanuel Macklin paced frantically around his palatial home in Olympic Ridge, his son's recent unbelievable words still ringing in his ears. According to Adam, after all these years, his ex-wife Mary had surfaced. Surfaced with a vengeance, according to Adam. Blessed with a phenomenal memory all his life, Manny, as he was known to his friends, peers, and the media as well, recalled every syllable of the words his son had left on Manny's voice mail.

> Mom called. I couldn't believe it, but she sounded just the way she used to sound. It wasn't a social call, Pop. She told me in no uncertain terms that if I didn't rectify an account for someone named Peter and Nan Anders, she was going to the SEC. She gave me till noon to hand deliver a check for the previous balance in the account plus a two-hundred-thousand-dollar

bonus for having tried to defraud them.

She meant business, Pop. I tried calling you, but you didn't answer. You really need to start answering your phone. Before you say anything, Pop, she didn't give me a choice. She meant business, and she let me know there was no wiggle room. I did what she said, and the working account is now down to $103.64. I asked her who the guy was, and she said a friend. Then she hung up on me. I have the guy's address if you think we should go talk to him, but something tells me we should let sleeping dogs lie. I say we just bite the bullet and hope that Mom keeps her word since we paid up.

A worm of fear crawled around inside Manny's belly. He needed to call his son. Needed to have a long talk with him. Adam was cracking. He could sense it, see it, feel it. His son had almost lost it a week ago when two major investors dumped their accounts. Not just two accounts but two major, multimillion-dollar accounts, one of which had only recently been opened. Right on top of another megamillion-dollar account several months earlier. High rollers. The kind who talked to other high rollers like themselves. More cracks. The whispers were starting, he could sense that, too. The economy was in the toilet. Investors didn't want to hear that. All they wanted was the 20-percent return on their investment that he'd promised. The high rollers wouldn't cut him an ounce of slack. It was the little investor, the mom-and-pop investor with two kids in college, who took it on the chin. Because they pinched their pennies, they kept watch on the economy and understood that investing was a gamble. They also didn't complain when they were getting dicey returns. They might grumble at the downturn, but he'd stake his life on the fact that none of them would go to the SEC. If they even knew what the SEC was.

Maybe it was time to set the wheels in motion. Go to ground. Something Adam had been advising for over a year now. He'd refused to take his son's advice back then, instead setting about to recruit new investors, and he'd succeeded in getting the teachers' union to sign on. The sudden influx of megadoses of money had enabled him to carry on for the past six months. But he was back now to robbing Peter to pay Paul. Keeping the high rollers happy was the name of the game.

Macklin brightened momentarily when he thought about the velvet-lined box nestled in the bottom of his golf bag. The contents of that particular box alone could set him up in the lap of luxury for the rest of his life. And the best part was, no one knew a thing about it. A fortune in diamonds he'd been squirreling away for over fifteen years. And he knew just how to get them out of the country, too.

Then his mood darkened. Mary. How in the name of God had she come back into their lives? Mary knew exactly what was going on. Always had, or so he thought, but Mary was loyal. She would never betray him or her children. Instead, she had just walked away. No one had been more surprised than he was when she had just disappeared and never blew the whistle on him. He tried to bring a vision of his ex-wife front and center, but the truth was, he couldn't. All he could remember was that she kept a clean house and was a good cook. She had never made demands, didn't enjoy living like the rich and famous. Mary was a gentle, loving, sweet soul without a mean bone in her body. He hadn't been devastated when she left. All it meant to him was that he had to hire a full-time live-in housekeeper to see to his and his children's needs.

Over the years, the kids had asked him to try to find her. He'd pretended to but never did a thing to find his ex-wife. He dummied up investigative reports showing he'd tried to no avail. After that, Mary's name was never mentioned again — until just the other day.

Manny stared out at the snow. He had to get out of here before he went crazy. The question was how? Dog sled? He didn't have one. Four-wheel drive? He didn't have that either. Limo? Impossible. Damnation, he was stuck until the roads were cleared. Possibly twenty-four hours before he could get out of here and into town to talk to his son. By that time, he'd be stark raving mad.

In times of stress, the only thing that could calm him was to go through his beloved ledgers. With that thought in mind, he heaved his bulk around and headed for the small elevator that would take him to the third floor, where he kept a fully equipped office of which one section was a private living area with an entertainment center. Hell, he could live up there for months if he had to. He might starve, but he could live in this one gigantic room that ran the whole length of his ten-thousand-square-foot home. Once he went through all his snacks and soft drinks, there was every possibility that he might well starve.

The special closet with the latest high-tech

security alarm he'd installed himself after the house was built beckoned him. There was a special floor-to-ceiling bookshelf that he'd crafted himself as well as installing the hydraulics that would slide the shelves to the side so he could access his secret closet. Inside were shelves and shelves of ledgers, from the day Macklin Investments was just a gleam in his eye. He felt himself relax almost immediately as he reached out to press an ornate curlicue he'd added to the trim on the bookshelves. The monster creation slid soundlessly down the wall on its well-oiled track, which was all but invisible to the naked eye.

This, then, was his special place, his port in the storm, so to speak. It was the only place where he could think, plot, and scheme. The place where the long lines of dollar signs made him feel invincible.

He reached for a double set of books and carried them over to his favorite reading chair. But first he opened a can of Diet Dr Pepper. For some reason, when he held and read his ledgers, his throat always went dry.

Manny perched his reading glasses on his nose and leaned back as he let his gaze sweep the room. It looked just like any business office except that it had two of everything so that on the rare occasions when his son came all the way out here, the two of them could work side by side. Two computers, two fax machines. Two landlines. Two paper shredders. Everything was operational but the computers. While they were hooked up, they were rarely used. The only things done on both computers were household expenses, mortgage payments, tax payments, mundane things everyone these days committed to their computers. There was no smut, no searches on anything to come back and haunt him. No way in hell was he ever going to put anything of importance on a computer. Only a fool would do something like that, and he was no fool. No siree, he was the darling of Wall Street, the Magician who made financial dreams come true. Definitely not a fool.

Adam had tried to convince him that converting everything to DVDs was the way to go if they had to cut and run. He had pointed to the shelves of ledgers, and said, "Pop, how do you plan on carrying those out of here? And what do you plan to do with the thousands of boxes of carbon copies that are stacked to the ceiling in storage?"

He knew that Adam was right, but he simply could not bring himself to do what his son wanted him to do. Now he wondered if Adam hadn't done it anyway. His insides started to rumble at the thought. Maybe it was time to destroy all those copies. But how?

Manny closed his eyes. He knew deep in his gut that he was never going to reach his imaginary goal line of being called The God of Wall Street. The cracks and the whispers were a warning. And, of course, he had to think about Mary. Should he act, or was it already too late?

He set the ledgers aside and got up. He really needed to do something about his weight. He really did. He started to pace, his thoughts all over the map. There was something wrong somewhere. He swore then as his thoughts took him way back in time to the orphanage, where he'd spent so many happy days with Marie and Sally. He'd had his whole life ahead of him back then. He thought of the promises he'd made to the two little girls he'd protected. Wherever they were, he wondered if they ever thought of him the way he thought of them. He could truthfully say a day didn't go by when he didn't think of little Marie and his special feelings for her. If he had any regrets in life, they were about Marie. How he'd loved that little slip of a girl who looked up at him with her big blue eyes. She was so trusting, and he could see in her adoring gaze that she felt about him the same way that he felt about her. But they were too young back then to do anything about those feelings.

He thought about the years he'd searched for her when he didn't have the money he needed to hire private detectives. Then, later, when he did have the money, their trail had gone cold. The realization that he was never going to see his two old friends again was the hardest thing he'd ever had to accept in his life.

Manny stopped in front of the closet and stared at what he called his life, the stacks and stacks of ledgers. Maybe he should burn them. Even he was smart enough to know there was no safe place where he could hide or bury them. As much as he hated to admit it, Adam was right. They should have put all the information on disks, then destroyed the ledgers. Impossible now. He reached for the Dr Pepper and drained it in one long gulp. He tossed the can into a decorative trash can and popped another one.

The allure and the comfort he usually got from his ledgers was gone. He slapped the two ledgers he was holding onto the shelf and closed the doors before pressing the curlicue to reset the bookshelves. He needed to *think.*

Manny paced then, faster and faster because the walls were starting to close in on him. How could he get rid of the ledgers? How? The faster he paced, the faster his thoughts ricocheted inside his head. He could call a packing company, have them boxed up. No, no. Then they would know what it was. He would have to box them up himself. Maybe crate them, then call a freight company to pick them up and ship them . . . where? Someplace far away. He did have a private Gulfstream. But the pilot would be forced to tell that he flew cargo at his behest to somewhere in the world. Was there a way around that? He was smart enough to know he couldn't trust anyone but himself. There was a time when he'd sworn he could trust his children, but not anymore. Both of them would sing like canaries at the first mention of prison.

There was a solution to everything. He just needed to find it. A solution without a paper trail. What he needed was a magician. What he really needed to do was to calm down and think logically. Easier said than done.

Manny walked over to his lavatory and stood in front of the mirror. He really did look like Santa Claus. He really did. Maybe it was time to shed all the excess hair and some of his weight. He'd look totally different. But did he really want to look different? He was vain enough to like all the complimentary things the media said about him, how benevolent he was, how he played Santa and talked about his philanthropy, which was known far and wide. Who was he kidding, he *loved* it when they paid tribute to him.

If he had to run, how would he do in some third-world country? Not well, he thought. Maybe he could get rid of the hair, the beard, the girth, and have plastic surgery in some far-off place where no one knew him. He'd create a new identity and live happily ever after. But that wasn't going to happen either, and he knew it.

Well, goddamn it, he had to do something, and sooner rather than later. He looked outside the lavatory window and cursed the snow, his son, his daughter, the faceless Peter and Nan Anders, and his ex-wife Mary. *I need to get out of here.* And then he had an idea.

Manny walked over to the phone and dialed 911. Earlier, he'd heard that the only vehicles permitted on the roads were emergency vehicles and ambulances. He made his voice sound hoarse, filled with pain, and managed to gasp the words, "I need help. Send an ambulance." He whispered the address, then slammed the phone down and raced to the elevator, which took him to the first-floor foyer. There, he unlocked the door and curled into a ball on a thick, beautiful, one-of-a-kind Persian rug. As soon as the EMS people got him to the hospital, he would have a miraculous turnaround. Of course, he would send a magnificent donation in thanks. He didn't give one iota of thought to the fact that he would be using an ambulance someone might actually need to stay alive.

Brilliant, absolutely brilliant.

It was because he was so brilliant, he knew, that he got the big bucks.

Chapter Thirteen

Dennis West straightened his tie and shrugged his shoulders so that his suit jacket fell into place. He looked around at the guests in the little chapel. Four; five if he counted himself. Maggie, Ted, Espinosa, and Nikki Quinn. He was surprised to see the lawyer and wondered how she'd gotten here, but then he remembered this chapel was only a block away from where she and Maggie lived — the main reason he'd chosen it in the first place when Maggie pointed it out to him.

He didn't like the smell in this little chapel in front of the mortuary. The scent of flowers and incense was making him light headed. The minister caught his eye and nodded, which meant the service he'd arranged for was about to get under way. He looked around and sat down, his hands clenched into a tight ball in his lap. He listened and wondered how this strange minister knew so much about the two women he was talking about. Maybe Nikki Quinn had told him. She was, after all, Sara and Tressie's attorney. Yes, that must be it. How could she not know personal details about her clients?

The voice droned on and on, a steady monotone of goodness. And then it was over. His hand was being shaken, and the portly man disappeared through a side door. Another man entered the room, the mortician, in his somber-looking dark suit, pristine white shirt, and plain tie. His hand was shaken too. And then, in a hushed voice, the man, whose name was Cedric Davidson, asked if Dennis wanted to take the deceased with him or come back later in the week. Dennis looked over at a sideboard, where two urns stood side by side. He swallowed hard and said later in the week would work better for him. Mr. Davidson nodded agreeably and withdrew through the same door the minister had left by.

"Dennis, do you think you could come with me for a few minutes? I spoke to Mr. Davidson earlier, and he said we could use one of the small offices. I need to speak with you about . . . about Sara and Tressie. You guys don't mind waiting a few minutes, do you?" Nikki asked, addressing the three newspaper people. They all shrugged, moved to the back of the chapel, and sat down, their eyes on the two urns on the sideboard.

"What's up?" Dennis asked curiously, as Nikki closed the office door. "You aren't worried about paying for this, are you? I already paid, and I have the receipt."

"No, no, not at all. Perhaps I should have waited and made an actual appointment, but I knew I would be here and you would be here, so this just seemed logical to me. Especially with our current weather, and they say more snow is coming. Relax, Dennis, you look nervous. The reason I asked you in here to talk privately is, I want to read you Ms. Overton's and Ms. Weber's wills. Sara and Tressie, as you knew them."

"Oh, that's okay, Nikki. It was just an honorary kind of thing. Them being my granny and aunt, I mean. It was nice at the moment, but I don't think I should hear about their wills. Isn't that private?"

"Actually, Dennis, I would have called you to come to the office if you hadn't scheduled this memorial service. If you'll just take a seat, this won't take long."

Dennis, a frown building on his forehead, sat back and laced his fingers together. His thoughts were on the two urns in the other room and where he was going to put them when he took them home once the weather cleared. Was he supposed to display them, or did one put them in a closet, never to be looked at again? Neither of the options sounded right. Clearly, he was going to have to research this a little further. He couldn't help but wonder what his sleep would be like at night if he took the ladies home with him.

"Dennis, did you hear what I just said?" Nikki asked gently.

"Yes. You said they were of sound mind when they made their wills."

"I mean after I said that?"

"I'm sorry. I was wondering . . . I guess I was woolgathering. My mother always says that when I don't pay attention."

"The ladies, your honorary grandmother and aunt, left you their entire estate aside from some charitable bequests."

Dennis blinked; and then he blinked again. He grew so light headed that he slid off the chair he was sitting on. He shook his head to clear it. "Did you just say what I think you said?"

"I did, and it's all right here," Nikki said, tapping the will in the blue binder.

"But why? They don't . . . didn't even

know me."

"You paid for their . . . funeral arrangements. Not many people would do that. I should tell you that both women had a provision in their wills concerning their burial needs and costs. It is standard procedure in a last will and testament for the deceased to make provision for his or her remains. That's why I'm here. Well, one of the reasons. Under the circumstances, the estate will, of course, reimburse you."

"No. I don't want to be reimbursed. I did all this" — Dennis waved his arms about — "because it was the right thing to do."

Nikki smiled. She liked this young man. Annie was right — he was a gem. "It was a kind, generous thing you did. You might not know this, but Sara and Tressie told me that they got their start in life from a lady who left her estate to them. They told me they took care of her in the nursing home where she was living. They never forgot her kindness to them. That's why they left their estate to you. You are a very wealthy young man, Dennis. You're going to need some financial planners and some wise moneymen. When you're ready, I can help you with all that. For now, I'll take care of all the legalities, and you think about what you want to do in the future. Deal?"

"You're right. Sara did tell us about how they got their start, working at a nursing home, and how a lady they took care of left them her money. I think she said it was something like fifty thousand dollars, which was a lot in those days. How much, ah, money are you talking about here? When you need financial people and wise moneymen, it has to be over a thousand dollars, right? I suppose it might even be as much as fifty thousand dollars, like they inherited. I'm just not into those kinds of numbers."

Nikki couldn't keep herself from laughing out loud. "Dennis, let's just say that it's a little less than a billion. That's billion with a B. Believe it or not, they still own more than 50 percent of WELMED. At today's stock price, those shares are worth over $900 million. When everything else is taken into account, you come to just under $1 billion."

"I don't believe this. Why me? Why didn't they just leave it all to charity?"

"Look at it this way, Dennis. Neither Sara nor Tressie — and that's how I've always thought of them, not as Marie and Sally — were planning on dying the day they made their will. They actually had a will, they just changed it the day they passed on. I guess they saw something in you that made them do it. You now owe it to them to use it all wisely and for a greater good. Nothing has to change in your life unless you want it to change. You do understand that, right?"

Dennis didn't trust himself to speak so he just nodded.

"Unless you have some questions, I think we're done here."

Dennis shook his head. "Well, maybe one question. Is this a secret, or can I talk about it?"

"It's no secret, Dennis. You can tell anyone you want. Before long, when I file the will for probate, I'm sure every hawk on Wall Street and every reporter in the District will be wanting to talk to you. I don't think either Sara or Tressie would want you revealing their real identities. They worked very hard to remain anonymous."

"I understand. I won't tell anyone except the guys . . . You know."

"Good. Good. Okay, well, if you think of anything, anything at all, just call me. I'll say good-bye now, Dennis. I'm glad you picked this particular mortuary since I can walk home from here."

"Okay. Thanks. I think . . ." Dennis mumbled.

Back in the waiting room, Dennis stared at his colleagues. He flapped his arms like a wounded bird trying to get off the ground.

He tried to make his tongue work, but no words would come out of his mouth.

"What's wrong with you, Dennis?" Maggie demanded.

"Spit it out, kid!" Ted growled.

"Are you okay, Dennis? You look peaked," Espinosa said softly.

"Peaked?" Ted exploded. "What the hell is 'peaked,' with two syllables?"

"Shut up! Everyone just shut up! I'll tell you what's wrong with me, but first you have to shut up."

The room went silent. "Okay. My new granny and my new aunt left me their entire estate. I own most of WELMED. The estate is worth a little less than a billion dollars, that's a billion with a B. That's why I look like I look, and I'm babbling here like an idiot."

For the first time in their collective lives, the three intrepid newspeople were at a total loss for words. All they could do was stare at their colleague.

"Nikki read their wills to me. They changed them the day they . . . the day they died. Nikki said the reason they did it was because someone had done the same thing for them a long time ago. Of course, we already knew that, so what she said about the why of it did not come as a surprise.

But that they would actually do it, that is unbelievable.

"That's all I know. I have to . . . to meet up with some money people sometime soon to make decisions. Whatever it is you do when you inherit . . . a lot of money."

"I don't get it, kid. Why aren't you jumping up and down? All that money! You should be over the moon," Ted said.

Dennis squeezed his eyes shut so he wouldn't cry. "Maybe . . . maybe I would if this happened thirty years from now. I didn't want those ladies to die. I didn't . . . don't want to inherit their money. I'm just a kid, as you point out to me on a daily basis. I haven't even lived yet. I want to do it all the right way. Corny as this may sound, I want to work at something I love. I want to get married and have a mortgage and car payments. I want to save for college for my kids. I don't want all that money. I didn't do anything to earn it.

"So knock it off, okay? I don't want to hear any more of your bullshit either. If you want to fire me, go ahead; I'll just find a job somewhere else. And if it's all the same to you, I'll walk home."

"I'll walk with you, Dennis," Maggie said. She swatted Ted on the side of his head to make her point.

"Yeah, I can't wait to slog through the snow," Espinosa said. "If nothing else, we can pull each other out of the drifts."

"Wait a damn minute!" Ted bellowed. "What the hell did I say that was so wrong? Whatever it was, I'm sorry. Dennis, I would never disrespect you. I guess I was just as stunned as you are . . . were. I admire you. I really do. I wish . . . I wish I was more like you. That's not bullshit either. I can't fire you, only Annie can do that, and she thinks you're the *Post*'s secret weapon." He held out his hand, his face miserable.

Dennis nodded and grabbed Ted's hand. He pumped it up and down with gusto. "Just so you know, Ted, I'm not someone you can trifle with. I want you to remember that."

"You know what, ki— Dennis, I just figured that out. Breakfast's on me."

Chapter Fourteen

The show Emanuel Macklin put on for the EMS attendants in back of the ambulance was an Oscar-worthy performance. He gasped, he moaned, he groaned and muttered and mumbled as the young man monitored his vitals. Out of the corner of his eye, he could see the puzzlement on the attendant's face. Other than a possible elevated blood-pressure reading, he couldn't find anything wrong with him.

"We're here, Mr. Macklin. Steady now. We'll have you fixed up in no time."

Manny tried to sit up, waved off the attendant, then let out a belch that all but shook the ambulance. "Ah! That felt good! See, that was my problem! All that rich Thanksgiving food!" Such a lie. He'd had a Spam sandwich for Thanksgiving dinner.

"No, no, you can't get up, Mr. Macklin! Please."

Manny's legs were already over the side of

the gurney, and he was sitting upright. "I'm fine. I just had gas. Damn, that felt good. Thank you for getting me here. I appreciate it." In a nanosecond, he had his checkbook out of his breast pocket and was writing out a check. "Ten thousand should cover it, doncha think, young man? Thanks again." And he was out of the ambulance and running toward an SUV that had pulled up behind the ambulance.

"What the hell . . ."

"Where's the patient? I thought you guys radioed in a possible heart attack," a flustered nurse said as she looked around for the patient.

The attendant jerked his head in the direction of the SUV. "Just call it a miraculous recovery and let it go at that. The guy paid for the trip, so we're good to go here. Gotta run, a call is coming in."

The attendant looked around for the plump white-haired man and wasn't surprised to see him climbing into the SUV. Later, he would think about all that had happened, but now he had to get back on the road.

"Emanuel Macklin, sir. I'll pay you anything you want if you take me into town. Just name it."

Tom Furgeson looked at the man who had

climbed uninvited into his van. "Hey, who do you think you are? Get your ass outta my van."

"I'm just a guy who needs to get into town. I told you I'd pay you whatever you want. You're just sitting here, and this is a four-wheel drive, right?"

"I was just sitting here because I was waiting for my wife to get off her shift, but she said they were shorthanded, and she agreed to stay on for a few more hours. I was waiting for the ambulance to move so I could drive off. I'm not some damn chauffeur, and the roads are treacherous. You need to get out of my truck. Like now, mister. I'm going to park and wait inside until my wife goes off duty."

"How does a thousand dollars sound?" Macklin said, whipping out his checkbook.

"Buckle up, buddy! Where do you want to go?"

Macklin rattled off his office address as he buckled up. *It always comes down to money,* he thought smugly. *Money can buy anything. And I'm the living proof.*

Ninety minutes later, huffing and puffing, Macklin climbed two flights of stairs to his Washington office. He wasn't surprised to find the office empty. After all, it was Saturday. He turned on the lights and the heat and walked around. It was a rattrap, no doubt about it, but his business quarters were his stock-in-trade. The offices in New York were even worse. He was known for blathering on about overhead that didn't need to be passed on to his investors. Not to mention that he had a fifty-year lease with affordable rent. An office was an office. A place to toil from nine to five. He didn't need fine rugs, rich paneling, and custom-made furniture. And his investors loved the frugality he displayed, convinced that it contributed to the outsized returns they were earning when the dividend checks rolled in.

Macklin sat down on one of the old-fashioned swivel chairs. Wood, not Naugahyde or faux leather, but there was a beat-up flat cushion on the seat. Adam's chair. He looked around at the other chairs, which were pretty much the same, the gun-metal gray desks, lamps with green shades and hundred-watt lightbulbs. Everywhere he looked there was clutter. Piles of papers, statements, cartons filled to overflowing that had to be relocated, dust and grit everywhere. He knew for a fact that the two back rooms were filled to overflowing. Adam wanted to rent a warehouse, but Manny had vetoed that idea immediately. No way did he want his files and records someplace he couldn't get to in minutes.

Macklin looked around again and swiveled his chair so that he had a view outside the dirty windows. Now that he was *home,* he could think and plan. He allowed himself to relax until he was almost in a trance. A trance that was shattered when the phone rang. He debated about answering it. He finally picked it up and listened to a young-sounding voice ask if this was Macklin Investments.

"My name is Dennis West, sir. I'd like to set up an appointment to discuss investing an inheritance that just came my way."

Macklin sat up straighter in his chair as he fumbled for his standard first-time speech to prospective newbies. Say no, then the client begged you to take them on. It worked every time. "Actually, Mr. West, I'm not taking on any new clients. I like to keep to a small shop, so I can give my clients 100 percent of my attention. I can recommend someone if you like."

Dennis started to sputter. "I thought you were the best. That's what everyone told me. I need the best because I don't know a thing about investing, and my aunts don't know that much either. This is just too much money to give to someone I never heard of. I've heard of you."

Macklin sighed loudly, just loudly enough for Dennis to hear. "How much money are you talking about, Son?"

"I'm not sure. The lawyer told me it was in the hundreds of millions but not quite a billion. My granny left it all to me."

Emanuel Macklin thought he was going to have a coronary on the spot. His mouth went dry, and his hands started to shake. "I suppose I could make an exception. When do you want to meet? The weather is such a hindrance."

"I was thinking Monday morning. By then, the roads should be clear, and things will be back to normal. I can be at your office at nine."

"I have a better idea. Why don't we meet for breakfast on Monday morning. Remember, Son, I haven't committed to taking you on. I'm going to need some details. We might not be a good fit, but like I said, I can certainly recommend someone to help you. Shall we say the Knife & Fork at nine?"

"That will work," Dennis said, excitement ringing in his voice. "I'll see you on Monday then."

The moment Macklin broke the connection, the first thought that came to mind was *setup. Someone is out to set me up.* But then his greed took over and pushed that thought right out of his head. *Millions but not a billion.* Who was this young person? Dennis West. He looked over at the far corner and saw the computer that Adam used to keep track of office expenses and research. While he wasn't computer literate, he knew how to do a search on Google, a company, he would self-deprecatingly tell people, he had missed out on when it first went public. He fired up the ancient computer, which belonged in some museum for ancient computers, along with tape drives and floppy disks, and waited for it to boot up. He clicked on the Google button and typed in Dennis West's name.

A reporter. A good one. He had won a Pulitzer at a very young age. *Setup.* A chill ran down Macklin's arms. Then again, maybe not. He'd sounded sincere, but then he himself had perfected sincerity.

Macklin thought back to the brief conversation. He'd played it just right. He hadn't been eager, had offered to turn him over to someone else. That was good. It wouldn't hurt to meet up with the young man to see if he was on the up and up. He prided himself on reading people. No green kid would be able to pull the wool over his eyes. Once he found out where his inheritance came from he could check that out and take it from there. *Setup. Hundreds of millions but not a billion.* If it was true, this was the stuff dreams were made of.

Macklin looked down at his watch. In about forty hours, give or take a few, he'd know for sure if he was being set up or not.

While Macklin leaned back in the old swivel chair to contemplate his navel, forty miles away as the crow flies Annie de Silva and Myra Rutledge high-fived one another the moment Myra clicked off the speakerphone.

"I told you that young man was a secret weapon, Myra. He pulled it off, he actually got through to Macklin and has an appointment with him. Right now, I'm happier than a witch in a broom factory. How about you?"

Myra smiled. "When Dennis called to tell us about his inheritance, I couldn't believe it. It makes sense; that's how Sara and Tressie told us all they got their start. How wonderful to return the favor to that young man. I hope he uses the fortune wisely. And how clever of him to come up with the solution to our problem. We are good to go, Annie. By Monday, the roads will be clear, and we'll be able to take Charles's Range Rover and drive into town. I know, I know the weatherman is predicting more snow, but with no major accumulation. The big decision we have to make is, should we go with Dennis to that meeting or let him handle it himself? What do you think, Annie?"

"I say we let that young man handle things. We could work with him later on the phone, prep him, that kind of thing. While he's meeting with Macklin, I think you and I should get a bead on things and meet up with the first Mrs. Macklin. Then we can meet with Dennis and see what we have and how best to proceed. We don't want to waste too much time since we're planning to do Christmas in Las Vegas."

"That sounds like a sterling plan. What's your thinking? Should we try calling Mrs. Macklin or surprise her?"

"Surprise is always good. That way, she won't be able to prepare a story in advance or blow us off. The element of surprise kind of leaves one a little vulnerable and prone to blurting out things they might think were best left unsaid."

"Surprise it is, then," Myra said. "I like the way you think, Annie."

Annie preened at the compliment and got up to look out the window at the winter wonderland. "I can't ever remember this much snow this early in the year. I wonder if it's an omen of some kind. The kind of omen we need to pay attention to. I don't mean to pretend that I'm psychic or anything, but I'm picking up all kinds of undercurrents. And not just undercurrents but *dark* undercurrents. I don't like the feeling, Myra." Annie shook herself like a wet shaggy dog to bring herself back to the present. "I think I'm just getting nervous in my old age." When Annie laughed, there was no joy in the sound.

"Then let's get to it. We have work to do and plans to make. Monday will be here before you know it." Myra held up her hand for sudden silence. "Do you hear that?"

"I do." Annie ran to the door and peered out. "Ah, it's Mr. Choo with his sons and his snow-blowers. That means we'll be able to navigate by the end of the day. Do you want me to tell him to clear the way to the barn since that's where Charles's Range Rover is parked?"

"No, he knows what to do. Come on, Annie, we need to hunker down here and make plans. It's definite, then — we're going to go to see Mrs. Macklin first, right?"

"I think so. Always start at the beginning. Isn't that what Charles always told us? Oh Myra, I'm sorry, I didn't mean . . ."

"It's all right, Annie, and you're right,

Charles always said to start at the beginning, so that's what we're going to do."

Myra excused herself and went upstairs. She went into her bathroom and scrubbed her face until she thought the skin was going to peel off. She blinked as she stared at her reflection.

Who was this person with the glassy eyes and shiny red face staring back at her? A woman whose husband had just left her. For the second time. That's who was staring back at her. Her clenched fists banged down on the tile vanity as her foot lashed out to kick at the cabinet underneath. She felt the pain, but it was almost a welcome pain compared to the mental anguish she'd been going through.

She wanted to cry, but there were no more tears left. Myra had cried rivers for days now in the darkness of her room and under the covers when Annie had gone to bed or off somewhere to sit quietly.

Someone else in the world was more important to Charles than she was. How could that be? She'd thought all these years that he was her lifeline, her rock. And she to him. To be sure, they tiffed with each other from time to time, but at the end of the day, they were always on the same page. Not anymore. Maybe never again.

Myra turned and sat down on the edge of the bathtub. She dropped her head into her hands and let the tears flow.

"Mummie, don't cry. It's going to be all right, truly it is. I tried to tell you that when Daddy left. I told you that you didn't need me. And you didn't need me because everything will be all right. That's what I told Daddy, too."

Myra brought her head up with a jerk. She knew she wouldn't see her spirit daughter, but she could hear her. "No, darling girl, it isn't going to be all right. If it were going to be all right, I would feel something. I don't feel anything except a terrible loss. I feel empty, betrayed by my own husband. How can that ever be all right?"

"Oh Mummie, it will. Can't you trust me on this? Daddy would never knowingly or willingly do anything to hurt you. But sometimes certain loyalties have to be addressed at a precise moment in time. Sometimes there are no other choices or options. Please, Mummie, try to understand. I can't bear seeing you cry and being unhappy. Please, Mummie."

Myra wiped her eyes on the sleeve of her robe. She'd never been able to deny her daughter anything, in life or in death. Finally, she said, "Tell me what you want me to do," she whispered.

"Have faith, Mummie. Have faith."

Myra felt something brush against her cheek. She knew her spirit daughter was kissing her cheek. Fresh tears flowed down her cheeks. "Take care of your daddy," she finally managed to say through her sobs. When she left to go downstairs for her war council with Annie, she was starting to feel some hope about the future.

Monday morning arrived with gray skies and the promise of light snow throughout the day. Myra rolled her eyes as she filled dog dishes and water bowls. She handed out rawhide chews for the dogs and gave the animals her standard pep talk, the one she always gave when she was going to be gone for more than a few hours. The dogs wagged their tails as much as to say, okay, we get it, we'll behave.

Annie elected to drive while Myra programmed the GPS. "According to this, under normal circumstances the trip should take us ninety minutes. I'll go out on a limb here and say we should arrive at our destination in two hours and twenty minutes. It's seven o'clock now. I say that, barring any problems, we'll get there around nine thirty. Let's just hope that Mrs. Macklin is home and will talk to us," Myra said.

"Why wouldn't she talk to us? We aren't

the least bit scary. Women tend to relate to other women."

"About most things, yes, I would agree. But we're talking about her ex-husband as well as her children. Women are loyal to family. Think about it, Myra. The woman never said boo all these years. There are no public records concerning her anywhere. That means she wanted to disappear, get lost, and put distance between her and her family. No woman walks away from her children. A husband, yes. Not kids. Even though the son was in college and the daughter was in her last year of high school, they're still her flesh and blood. We might have to really finesse her."

The two women chatted then about the girls and the boys, as they referred to their little family. When they exhausted that topic, they switched to the dogs, their latest antics, then moved on to Christmas in Las Vegas.

The robotic voice on the GPS interrupted the women's conversation. Annie slowed down and turned the corner. "Bet this is a pretty little street in the spring and summer. All those big old shade trees. I think this is what they call an established neighborhood. I think it's the fourth house, Annie. The one with the green shutters. No cars in the driveway, but it's clean. Actually, look around, the whole street looks like it's been plowed, then groomed. Neat as a pin. Neighbors working with neighbors would be my opinion."

"And our plan is . . ." Annie said, getting out of the car.

"We don't have a plan, Annie, remember? We said we were going to wing it and take our cues from Mrs. Macklin." Myra looked down at her watch. "I wonder how our secret weapon is doing? I really thought he would have sent a text by now. You don't think Macklin suspects anything, do you?"

"If I were him, I would definitely be suspicious. I think the man lives in fear and looks over his shoulder constantly, so yes, I think he will be suspicious of young Dennis. But in the end, I am confident that his greed will win out. Okay, here goes," Annie said as she jammed her finger against the doorbell. Inside they could hear the melodious chime.

The door opened to reveal a pleasant-looking woman with rosy cheeks and gray hair. A big fat cat circled her feet. "Can I help you?" Her voice was as pleasant as she looked, Myra thought.

"I hope so, Mrs. Macklin." Myra felt a stab of uneasiness at the look of shock on the woman's face. But she didn't deny the greeting.

"Do I know you? You look familiar somehow."

"I'm Myra Rutledge, and this is my friend, Annie de Silva. No, we've never met. We need to talk to you."

Mary's shoulders stiffened. "About what?"

"Your ex-husband," Annie said coolly. "It's rather cold out here, do you mind inviting us in? We won't take up too much of your time. And we certainly mean you no harm."

Mary backed up a few steps, the cat staying with her. "I'm sorry, of course, come in where it's warm. I just made coffee, and I just took a walnut streusel out of the oven. Would you like some?"

"I would dearly love some," Myra said. Annie nodded.

Mary Macklin Carmichael led them through beautifully decorated, comfortable rooms that led into one of the cheeriest kitchens either woman had ever seen. They expressed their admiration.

"I love cozy and comfortable. My half brother lived here, and when he passed away, he left me the house. It used to be dark and gloomy, but I do love color, so I did it all a little at a time." All this was said as she laid out china plates and cloth napkins, which had to be washed and ironed. She poured coffee into pretty china cups with violets on the sides of the cups. She sliced into the warm walnut coffee cake and set it on matching plates. It was a ritual of some kind, Annie was sure.

Myra noticed that their hostess didn't pour coffee for herself or serve herself some of the fragrant cake. Instead, she bent over and picked up the fluffy cat and held it on her lap, stroking its soft fur.

"Why do I have this feeling that I know you? Are you sure we've never met?"

"We'll make it easy on you, Mrs. Macklin."

"Please don't call me that. I'm Mary Carmichael. Call me Mary."

"I'm sure you've seen our pictures in the paper at some point in time. The media call us 'the Vigilantes.' "

Mary's eyes popped wide. "Of course. I . . . ah . . . didn't know you were . . . still in business. Now I understand. You found out about Manny, is that it?"

"Yes, that's why we're here. He has to be stopped. Which brings us to the question, Why didn't you try to stop him? You were married to him?"

Mary licked her dry lips as she stared

around at her warm, cozy kitchen. "Back then, Manny was . . . just getting started in what he was doing. For a long time, I wasn't sure . . . I just suspected. All of a sudden, there was so much money. Manny said we needed to move to a bigger, more substantial house. He bought us new cars, and the furniture he ordered was specially made. We had chandeliers from Bavaria, I think. Suddenly we had a housekeeper, and Manny had a chauffeur. Adam was in college. Manny bought him a sports car. Ava was in her last year of high school. They took to all the new money like ducks to water. They couldn't get enough, and Manny never said no to anything they wanted. It was like Christmas morning every day. Manny and I had separate bedrooms. I hated it. I'm a kitchen kind of person, but the housekeeper wouldn't let me into what she called her domain. I didn't know what to do with myself. My old friends distanced themselves from me. They couldn't relate to all the new money. I spent my days at the library or browsing through stores just to kill the hours."

"Did you ever try to talk to your husband?" Annie asked.

"I did, but he said that his work was his business and my business was to run the house and take care of the kids. That was such a joke I laughed. Then the blowup came, and Manny took the kids' side. They were complaining that I was plain, that I needed to fix myself up, buy some decent clothes so I wouldn't embarrass their father when we went out with clients. I looked at Manny, and he just shrugged. I knew right then that things would never get better. Manny was on the way to becoming the financial wizard that he has the reputation of being these days. They all stormed out of the house, and I was left alone. I went into Manny's office and looked at his books. He kept two sets. That alone told me all I needed to know. I couldn't believe what he was doing. I didn't *want* to believe it. All I could think about was the disdain I saw on the faces of my family, especially of the children I had helped to raise. I thought about calling someone but didn't know who to call. I thought about the FBI, but that seemed kind of stupid since this was a financial thing. I really didn't know about the SEC back then. I know I should have done something, but the bottom line is that I didn't do anything. I just put my coat on and left. I took my purse, and that was it. I made my way to my half brother's house, and he took me in.

"Eventually, instead of taking back my maiden name, Richardson, I changed my name to his, which is Carmichael. And I stayed here and took care of him until he died. He arranged for my divorce, and that was the end of that chapter in my life. I've never seen or talked to my husband or children since that day I walked away.

"Well, that's not quite true. I spoke to my son the other day when my neighbor showed me his monthly statement, and it said there was no money left in his account, that he had been wiped out. I was so furious I called Adam, and I . . . threatened him. I gave him twelve hours to make good on Pete's account and to add another two hundred thousand dollars for screwing it all up. He did it, too."

"Just like that, he did what you said?" Myra asked, surprise ringing in her voice.

"Well, I did threaten him with the SEC and everyone else I could think about. Pete's wife has MS, and the bills are out of sight; he needed that money. Manny just bled him dry. Once Pete had the check, I sent him to the man who had handled my brother's investments. That's all I can tell you. What are you going to do?" Her voice displayed such anxiety that Annie felt sorry for the little woman sitting across from her, stroking her cat.

"Take care of him," Annie said in a voice that was so cold, Mary shivered. "Did you follow your husband's career over the years as he became the financial wizard? The man is a household name."

"No. I closed that door of my life. If I did see something, I ignored it. It was too distressing. I had to get on with my life. It was all I could do. Until my neighbor came over and showed me his investment statement. Then it all came back in a flood. I acted because that's what you do when someone needs your help. I'm not sorry either. Do you think they're going to say I blackmailed them? Oh Lord, am I in some sort of trouble?"

"No. No. Not at all," Myra said soothingly.

"Tell us about your husband. Everything you can remember, anything that can help us to hold him accountable."

"When I first met him, I was working in a bakery. He came in for donuts. I think he lived on donuts in those days. Eventually, he asked me out. I called them moneyless dates. Walks, picnics, hours spent in parks. Beach days. He told me about his life in the orphanage. He told me about Marie and Sally. His two best friends. He said he was their protector. I suspected he had strong feelings for the one named Marie. He said they got separated, and he was never able to find them once they left to make their own way in the world. I always had the feeling, even though Manny denied it, that I was a Marie substitute. While he was with me, he wasn't really with me. He was always mentally somewhere else. That feeling never changed in all the years we were married. Today, with the benefit of hindsight, I would say Manny is a psychopath. He worships money, but I guess you already know that."

"Where does he keep his records? We read so many crazy reports about him. Some say it's all done by hand, that he doesn't believe in computers. That he is a hands-on manager for his investors. The articles say he has no partners, just his son and daughter working for him. That's so hard to believe. Actually, I pretty much think it's impossible for him to be a one-man, even a three-person operation if you count the two children."

Mary stopped stroking the cat and waved her arms about. "I have no idea. He kept ledgers, the old-fashioned kind that shop owners used in the old days. Huge, old, hard-covered ledgers. He just kept them on a shelf in his home office. The entries were all handwritten. Why?"

"We need them," Annie said bluntly.

"Manny is very crafty. I'm sure he's got them hidden somewhere. Maybe where he lives. Have you spoken to his . . . other wives?"

"Not yet. But we will. If you didn't know anything, it's doubtful the other wives will either. He doesn't even live with his current wife. Seems she lives in New York and he lives around here at Olympic Ridge. His crown jewel, which is worth billions. In one of the articles he said he was more proud of what he called his creation than he was his investment company."

Mary nodded. "How did you . . . who told you about Manny? Did something happen?"

"Two very special ladies who invested with him came to us for help. They asked us to stop him before he ruins any more lives. We agreed to step in to help."

Mary's eyes narrowed as she leaned forward. "Those two special ladies . . . would their names by any chance be Marie Palmer and Sally Dumont?"

"Yes."

"Manny tried for years to find them. He hired so many private detectives, but they could never find the two girls. Did you know Manny's name was Billy Bailey?"

"Yes, Marie and Sally told us that. They became very wealthy, and they did so legally. They're dead now. They were killed in an automobile accident last week. Actually, it was the very day we met with them. They were hit head-on by a truck. They were supposed to leave for Europe the following day. They hired us, but they didn't want Billy or Manny to know they were his whistleblowers. Even though they are gone, we have to honor the commitment we made to them. We're trusting you to honor that same commitment. Otherwise, this is not going to work. By the same token, I suppose that you could be held accountable because *you knew* what was going on and did nothing to stop it. Do we understand each other, Mary?"

"Oh, that's so sad. When Manny finds out, he will be devastated. I do understand, believe me, I do. I give you my word that I won't say or do anything you don't want me to. There is one thing. I don't know if it means anything or not, but I'll let you be the judge. Back when Manny first started making serious money, after we moved into the big new house and got the new cars, Manny left his checkbook on the vanity in the bathroom. I looked in it. I don't know why, I just did. The entries started in January and ended in June, so I guess it was June when I saw what I saw, which was an entry marked RENT. I don't know what he was renting. But the amount was five thousand five hundred dollars and he wrote checks from January through June. There was no name as to who the check was made out to. The register just said RENT. I know for a fact it was not the rent for the New York office or the office he keeps in the District. The rent on those were paid by the company. It was an LLC. At the time, I didn't know what that was, but I know now. The entries for whatever he was renting were in the checkbook for Manny's personal checking account. If you need a year, I'd be guessing, but I think around 1995 or close to that. I don't know if banks keep records that long or not. I once heard him talking on the phone about feeder funds, hedge funds. It was Greek to me. But he had something going on in England, too, and I thought that was strange. He made two trips over there around the same time. Meaning right after the big house and the new cars."

"That's very interesting. We'll see what, if anything, we can come up with. I want you to think. Where do you think your husband would store his ledgers? Without those, we can't do anything. We're told he does everything the old-fashioned way, that everything is done by hand. Obviously, he doesn't believe in electronics. He's careful about leaving a trail."

"Yes, Manny is like that. The only thing I can tell you is that he would not want to be far from wherever they're stored. To me, that means his home. I don't even know where he lives these days. Maybe in that place they call his crown jewel. Years ago, I think, he lived in New York with one of his wives. But I think it was last year, maybe the year before, I saw his picture on the cover of a business magazine. There was a big article about that complex he built. I think the article said he lived in one of the houses there. My memory isn't what it used to be, but I think that's right. More coffee?"

"No, I'm good," Annie said. Myra nodded agreement.

"When we leave here, are you going to get in touch with your husband or son to tell them we're on the case? If you do that, a lot of people are going to get hurt. People like your friend Pete and his wife. Will you promise us not to alert them? And remember what we said about your being found culpable."

"You have my word. Manny is very wily, so you are not going to have an easy time of it. He's always one step ahead of everyone else. He never turns it off. Never."

"We're not exactly slouches ourselves. I think Mr. Macklin may have met his match in us. We never give up."

"What will happen to him?"

Annie laughed. "You don't want to know."

Myra smiled. "Clarify that question, Mary. What will happen to him if he's arrested or if we get to him first?"

Mary shook her head. "Forget I asked. From what I remember reading about the Vigilantes, I don't think I want to know. All I want is to be able to keep living here, to get through my days and be able to sleep at night. Truly, that is all I want."

Mary Macklin Carmichael shivered. The fluffy cat hissed and jumped off her lap.

"My children?"

Myra bit down on her lower lip. "In your opinion, are they as involved as their father?"

"I'm afraid so."

"Then you don't want to know. We really should be going now. Your coffee cake was delicious, and so was the coffee. We'll be in touch, if that's all right," Myra said.

"I'm sorry I wasn't more help."

"Actually, you were a big help. Like I said, we'll be in touch."

In the car, Annie turned to Myra. "Do we

believe her?"

"I think so. The only thing she might have regrets about are her kids and rightly so. She's a mother. But she's an honest woman."

"Only to a point," Annie said. "She never turned him in. In my eyes, that makes her just as guilty as her husband. The fact that she took herself out of the equation means squat. Look at what he's become. She had to know. I don't quite believe she lives in the bubble she would like us to believe she lives in."

"Point taken," Myra said. "We were there for almost two hours, and Dennis still hasn't sent us a text or called. Maybe by the time we get back into town. I would hate to go all the way back to the farm and not meet up with him."

"See those snow flurries?" Annie said. "Are you sure you don't want to head straight out to the farm? We can always call Dennis to check in from the farm. I don't know about you, Myra, but right now I'm happier than a witch in a broom factory."

Myra grinned from ear to ear. "I kind of feel like the fox in the henhouse myself right about now. Let's see what the weather looks like when we get to town. And then we can decide what we should do."

"Yes, ma'am," Annie said, and stomped on the gas pedal.

Chapter Fifteen

Dennis West leaned back in the comfortable captain's chair he was sitting on. He hoped he was conveying a blasé attitude. He wished now he'd taken some acting classes when he was in college. He'd known the moment he sat down at the table that he was going to be played by a master. He did his best not to laugh. If only the guys could see him now. All the advice Myra, Annie, Maggie, Ted, and Espinosa had given him last night swirled around inside his head. He was confident he was pulling it off. He glanced down at his watch. Ninety minutes for a simple breakfast was not the norm. However, with the bad weather, the little diner that he loved was almost empty of customers, so it was okay to dawdle.

The first hour had been spent getting acquainted and speaking of mundane things: the weather, this hole-in-the-wall eatery, which served the best breakfasts in the District. It wasn't until the second coffee refill that Macklin had finally turned the conversation around to why they were here. Dennis leaned forward so he wouldn't miss a word. He hoped he was successfully conveying the image of a young, dumb guy with no financial savvy. He knew in his gut that the man sitting across from him was trying just as hard to convey to him that he didn't need his business and was just sitting here to kill time on a Monday morning.

The fancy phone sitting on the table like an obscene eye chirped constantly. He pretended not to see Macklin glance at it each time it chirped. That alone told him how important this meeting was even though the man sitting across from him mostly looked bored.

"How do you stand that?" Dennis said, pointing to the chirping phone.

"It's a way of life. When I sign on a client I tell them they can reach me 24/7. How could I do less? My clients trust me with their futures, so I have to be available. Sometimes it's just offering encouragement when the markets go south. I would do the same for you if you were a client. I just wish more counselors operated the way I do. I pride myself on returning all calls within an hour. I can turn it off if it annoys you."

"No, that's okay. I just hope I never get so important that I live 24/7 tied to a phone." Dennis let his gaze go to his watch again. "I understand that you aren't taking on any new clients, Mr. Macklin. You made that clear on the phone on Saturday, so what I *don't* understand is why we are wasting each other's time. And like I told you, I can't make a decision anyway until my two aunts give me the okay."

Macklin's voice was like warm syrup. "Are they financially wise? Do they understand the market?"

Dennis laughed. Actually he giggled. "Well, they are good cooks and go to the *market* every day, but that's not what you meant, is it? No, they are not financially wise, but they do know how to stretch money and live on budgets. I would never make a decision without talking to them first because I value their wise counsel. They have lived long lives and had many life experiences. Life experiences mean more than anything you or anyone else can come up with. I depend on them, and they depend on me. My parents are retired and travel the country and are not available all the time. I could have arranged a meeting with them, but you said you weren't taking on new clients, so I didn't say anything to them about this meeting. I realize this is just a courtesy meeting, and I do thank you for that. So, who is this other financial wizard you mentioned on the phone that you're willing to recommend?"

Macklin sipped at his coffee and dabbed his lips with a napkin. "Ah, yes: Ruben. I called him before I left the house this morning, but he informed me he isn't taking on any new clients either. One of his partners retired, and they haven't hired anyone new to replace him. That means he and his other two partners are swamped. I know that's hard to believe in this miserable economy, but it's a fact. I suppose I could make an exception and work with you till Ruben gets up and running at full speed. I hate to see a young investor go blindly into the financial world with no backup. It's a feeding frenzy out there."

"I don't like changing horses in midstream, Mr. Macklin. My daddy always said that, and if that way of thinking was good enough for my daddy, then it's good enough for me. I'm not in any hurry. I just found out about this massive inheritance on Saturday."

The warm, syrupy voice got warmer. "Again, who was it that passed on and left you the inheritance you spoke of? Did I understand you to say it was your grandmother? Did I get that right?"

"It was my grandmother and one of my aunts. They were together when they were killed in a car accident. The memorial service was this past Saturday, as was the reading of the will. I inherited a company called WELMED and, of course, all Granny and Auntie's personal holdings."

Macklin thought his head was going to explode right off his neck. This country bumpkin was the answer to all his prayers, and he had just fallen into his lap during one of his darkest hours. He leaned forward, and in a soft, comforting voice that was his stock-in-trade, said, "Money is not the answer to anything when a loved one passes on, and in your case, two of your loved ones. Please, accept my condolences. If there's anything I can do, just ask. I'll help you any way I can. You didn't say, Dennis, but I assume you have no grandfather. If you need a stand-in, please consider me."

Dennis forced a sickly smile. If he didn't know what he knew about the man sitting across from him, he would have signed on the dotted line. The guy was good.

He removed his glasses and wiped at his eyes with his napkin. Two could play this game, he thought smugly. "That's very nice of you to say, Mr. Macklin. Thank you."

The syrupy voice was now so thick, you could cut it with a knife. Dennis felt his insides cringe. "We all need someone at one time or another. I see you looking at your watch. Do you have somewhere you need to be?"

"I'm meeting up with my aunts. We have some decisions to make about . . . about a lot of things. And I do have a job. My colleagues are waiting for me also. This darn weather has managed to foul everything up."

"Well, not quite everything. You and I got to meet each other. Having said that, young man, how do you want to leave it?"

With my foot up your ass, Dennis thought to himself. "I'll call you. Should I call the number I called on Saturday or do you have a cell phone?" He pointed to the cell phone on the table, which was still chirping.

Macklin pulled a business card out of his side pocket and slid it across the table. Dennis reciprocated.

Worms of fear crawled around Macklin's stomach. This bumpkin was getting away from him. He could sense it. He had to do something fast, or he was dead in the water. "I have an idea, young man. Why don't you arrange a meeting with your aunts, so I can explain things to them in simple, everyday terms? I would be more than happy to help you. This way, your aunts can be up to speed and in a better position to guide you. In the end, you might decide to just let your inheritance stay as is. I'm sure that would not be a bad thing, but I do think I could get you a better return on your investments than what you have now. But at this moment, that's not the important thing. What's important is that you have peace of mind, knowing your future will be well taken care of by people who care about you as a person. You won't be just a number on a bank statement but a real flesh-and-blood person."

Dennis pretended to think. "Well . . . I don't know. My aunts are simple people. They aren't big on dining out. Going to an office would . . . I think intimidate them. I just don't know. Maybe a social setting . . . your kitchen perhaps?" Dennis threw his hands in the air to show he was perplexed.

"My *kitchen*?" Macklin said in a strangled voice. "Did you say my kitchen?"

"Yeah, kitchen. You have a kitchen, don't you? Everyone has a kitchen. My aunts are kitchen people. That's where they conduct all their business. Like men conduct business on the golf course. They're partial to meat loaf and mashed potatoes. Hey, what can I say? If you could arrange that, they might — I say might — be receptive to meeting with you. Listen, Mr. Macklin, I really have to go. My aunts don't like to be kept waiting. They get ornery when that happens. Thanks for taking the time to meet with me. I'll call you." Dennis slipped into his Redskins jacket, jammed a wool hat down on his head, and turned to leave. He whipped around and held out his hand. Macklin, still in a state of shock, reached for it as he tried to figure out how the tables had turned so suddenly.

Setup, his mind shrieked. Maybe not. *Kitchens. Meat loaf. Mashed potatoes.* He hadn't sat in a kitchen in like forever. The last time he'd eaten meat loaf and mashed potatoes was when his first wife Mary made it twice a week to stretch her food budget when the kids were little. Son of a bitch!

Macklin continued to sit at the table. He raised his hand to signal the waitress for more coffee.

Outside, Dennis, a grin on his face, jammed his hands into his pockets, hunkered down into the Redskins jacket, and started walking the three blocks to a Cajun restaurant where he was to meet Annie and Myra. Snow flurries and gusty winds whipped at him head-on. He felt his cell phone vibrate in his pocket. He stopped, backed up against a brick wall, and looked at the text message. "Oh shit!" he muttered. He read the words twice before he sent a return message. **Change location. Am meeting Myra and Annie at the same place in five minutes.**

The return message was sent back instantly. **Too late, we are here. We'll be in the back.** "Oh shit," Dennis said again. "I wasn't cut out for this cloak-and-dagger stuff," he muttered as he made his way into the spicy-smelling eatery. It was a small restaurant, but there was a room in the back that was reserved for special celebrations and large parties. That was where Ted and the guys were sitting. For now, though, the outer room was only half full. He spotted Myra and Annie immediately. He did his best not to let his gaze roam toward the back room, where the guys were meeting up to discuss what he thought of as Jack Emery's harebrained idea.

Annie waved. Dennis offered up what he hoped was a cocky grin as he made his way to the booth where the two women were sitting. Thank God they didn't have a view of the back room.

"Well?" Annie said the moment Dennis shed his jacket. He countered with a "Well" of his own. "You go first, Dennis. We ordered for you: a lobster po' boy with all the fixings. And a strawberry milk shake."

"Great, great!" How he was going to eat the monster sandwich was beyond him. He hadn't even digested the pancakes and sausages he'd just eaten.

"Okay, okay. Mr. Macklin tried to play me. I let him think he was succeeding. He said the guy he was planning on turning me over to wasn't taking on any new clients because one of his senior partners had retired, and they're swamped, even in this economy. But out of the goodness of his heart, such a generous man is Mr. Macklin, he was willing to take me on at least temporarily; and then maybe he could turn me over to this guy named Ruben when he was back up and running. I didn't buy it for a minute. I played dumb and said I couldn't make a decision until my two aunts gave their approval. Believe me when I tell you the man was salivating when I told him I had inherited a controlling interest in WELMED. He had his cell phone on the table, and it chirped constantly. I mean constantly. He said he is available to his clients 24/7. To his credit, he looked at who was texting or calling, but he didn't answer.

"The man is easy to like. He makes you

think you're special and that he really cares about you. By the way, do you like meat loaf and mashed potatoes?"

Annie grimaced. "I can take it or leave it alone."

"Charles has a wonderful recipe for meat loaf. He uses ground chuck, veal, and pork with a lot of chopped onions, celery, and tiny crisp bacon bits. Then he puts two strips of bacon on top of the meat loaf so the juice from the bacon drips into the loaf. The gravy is out of this world. It really is a delicious dinner. Why are you asking, Dennis?"

Dennis explained about the kitchen meeting and his story of the meat loaf. If nothing else, it got a laugh out of both Myra and Annie.

"How long do you think it will take him to extend an invitation to his home for dinner, dear?" Myra asked.

"I'm thinking by Thursday. Today is Monday. Between now and then, he has to figure out how to make a meat loaf." Dennis laughed at his own wit, then sobered when neither woman joined in his laughter. "Will you go to dinner when he issues the invitation?"

"Of course. It's the only way to get to him. You're the conduit," Myra said. "You did good, young man. I'm proud of you." Annie nodded.

"What happened when you met with the first Mrs. Macklin?" Dennis looked down at the huge sandwich sitting in front of him, which was loaded with delicious chunks of delectable lobster. He loved lobster. Lobster was his favorite food in the whole world, but right now he knew he couldn't take a bite of it. He guzzled the milk shake instead and would take the loaded sandwich to go.

"She's a sweet, simple lady. A good person. She lives a quiet life. If she has any regrets, it was hard to see what they are. She told us Manny Macklin worships money. She thinks he's a psychopath. She said back when she was married to him, he kept two sets of books, and she said he would never commit anything to a computer or leave a paper trail. He does everything by hand and keeps all the details in his head. She feels like he corrupted her two kids. Last week was the first time she's spoken to her son since the day she left, what she referred to as a lifetime ago. Seems that her neighbor's account with Macklin Investments was wiped out. She took it personal and intervened, and the account was paid off in spades and cashed out. She stepped out of her comfort zone to do that for her neighbor. She said she threatened her son personally. The man's wife has MS, and they need the money. She threatened to go to the SEC if the firm didn't make good. She would go to the wall for a friend and neighbor, but she didn't do a thing to stop what her husband, and then her children, were doing. That bothers me. I suppose she might still have feelings for her ex-husband or some misguided sense of loyalty. Whatever it is or was, she hasn't done anything to bring down her husband's nefarious enterprise.

"Oh, and one other thing that might or might not be important: she said he had some mysterious rental that she can't account for. We'll get Abner on it and see what he can come up with."

"Do you think she will alert her son or her ex-husband that you were there raising questions?" Dennis asked.

Annie shook her head. "I don't think so. Myra and I talked about it on the way over here after we left her home. She's made a new life for herself, and I don't think she is going to put that in harm's way. We did point out to her — nicely, of course — that she could be held culpable because she knew, or at the very least suspected, what her husband was doing and did nothing to stop him. She'll keep quiet and just go on as she has in the past. Manny Macklin is someone she used to know. It's that simple. As for her children . . . if they did wrong, she will think they have to be punished. She won't lose any sleep over it. That's my take on it, and it goes without saying I could be wrong, but I don't think I am."

"I agree with Annie 100 percent. Mrs. Macklin, who took her half brother's last name, Carmichael, did tell us something interesting. She said her ex-husband talked early in their marriage about his two friends from the orphanage. She said she always thought he had special feelings for the little one, meaning Marie or Ms. Sara Overton as we knew her, your new granny, Dennis."

"Well, then, where does that leave us?"

"Waiting for our invitation to dinner," Annie said, laughing.

CHAPTER SIXTEEN

The minute Myra and Annie were out of sight, Dennis whirled around and ran back to the Cajun restaurant. He stiff-armed his way into the restaurant and raced to the back room, where the guys were chowing down on po' boys.

"We ordered for you, kid," Ted said. "Sit!"

Dennis sat and looked at a mixed shrimp and lobster po' boy. If this kept up, he'd be eating po' boys for the rest of the week.

"Talk, kid, while we eat. We'll fill you in with what we have when we're done eating. By the way, how's the weather out there?"

"Snowing. Just flurries right now. Okay, here we go . . ."

"Perfect timing," Jack said ten minutes later as he wadded up his napkin. Dennis gulped, sighed heavily, and leaned back in his chair.

Jack finished the beer in his bottle. He set it down with a loud *thump.* "Weird as this is going to sound, we also have something to report. It dovetails nicely with what you just told us, and I'm going to go out on a limb here and suggest — I say suggest — it might have something to do with Charles's going off to Merry Old England like a bat out of hell. Who wants to go first?"

Abner waved a lazy hand. "I'm up. First things first. I was all alone for the past three days because . . . Isabelle flew to England. She's been hired to build a whole community just outside London. She's being given the opportunity to create a whole city. She says this will put her at the top of the pack and definitely on the map. I'm telling you this because I want you to know why I lived on the computer for seventy-two hours, and it's why and how I came up with the information I plan on sharing with you."

Ted held up his hand. "Hold the results till we all share our last seventy-two hours because, as Jack said, it all dovetails. Joe and I," he said, pointing to Espinosa, "were on the horn all weekend with calls from sources and snitches. It was hard to run some of them down, but we did our best, and let me be the first to tell you the dark stuff is about to hit the fan."

Jack waved his arm for attention. "Bert called me and told me that things are heating up with the Fibbies. They're on to Macklin but are going to play it close to the vest. Jack Sparrow is on his way here on Bert's orders, and Bert gave me an inside tip, which is that Mr. Sparrow does not like to be called Jack. He prefers to be called Jay. So, all of you, make a note of that for the future. It makes it simpler, anyway, since two Jacks can be confusing. Remember that Sparrow has an in with the good guys in the FBI since we got him cleared. He also has a few old grudges to settle."

Harry smiled and said, "I just came for lunch. And to listen. But I can tell you how the FBI got involved." Harry laughed when he saw that he had everyone's attention. He loved it when he was able to make Jack's jaw drop.

"And . . ." Dennis demanded.

"Saturday night was the homicide playoff at the dojo. That's when all the precincts go up against each other. Every detective in the District participated. They were like a swarm of pissed-off bees. They went at each other like nothing I've ever seen from those guys. Come to find out the reason they were so pissed was that their pension fund is in the Dumpster because the fund was invested with Macklin Investments. They had their union rep go to the FBI and file a complaint. So that must be what Bert was talking about and why he sent Sparrow back here. At least that's my take on it."

"Where does all of that leave us?" Ted asked.

"Back with me," Abner said.

"Let's hear it," Harry said.

"First things first. I won't even pretend I'm in the same . . . league as you guys when it comes to . . . to what it is you all do. What I'm going to volunteer now to you all is my opinion. *My opinion* based on being married to Isabelle and skirting the edges of . . . her other, ah, job. Back in September, right after Labor Day, she got a letter from the Architectural Board asking her if she wanted to bid on a job in England. Nothing else at that time. She thought about it and decided she didn't want to move to England even if it was on a temporary basis. She wrote back a week later and declined. A few days later, she got another letter, and this time there were specs included along with the proposal, and they intrigued her. They asked her to reconsider. So she did.

"At the end of September, she got a prepaid first-class plane ticket to fly to England for a meeting. She was told there were six other contenders. She went, was interviewed, and came home convinced that she was out of the running. The other architects were all well-known and had more notches in their belts. She said she felt like the poor relation at the grand ball, that kind of thing.

"Then, ten days later, she got another prepaid airline ticket and was told they wanted her to come for a second interview. She was a little excited but was going to decline. I actually talked her into going, so she went.

"When she came back, she said she wasn't allowed to talk about anything, that she and all the other architects had to sign a confidentiality agreement not to discuss anything that went on. She signed it and honored it. I don't know a thing for sure. But Isabelle changed right there. By the way, she got the job. She's the top gun. The project will allow her two assistants. Kind of like lawyers when they go to trial, one sits first chair, second chair, that kind of thing. Are you guys following me here?"

"Well, yeah, but what does any of that have to do with what we're discussing?" Ted demanded.

"Well, for one thing, Charles Martin was the one who was responsible for getting Isabelle's license restored after the Vigilantes sort of disbanded. I'm sure you all know that. Isabelle told me over the years how tight Charles was with the Queen. Then, at Thanksgiving, Charles just up and leaves, with no explanation whatsoever. I might not be the sharpest tool in the shed, but something isn't ringing right in my ears as of now."

"Where are you going with this, Abner?" Jack demanded.

"I think Isabelle's new employers are the Queen and her husband, Prince Philip. I think they are the ones building the new-age city and using their personal funds to do it. Perhaps not them personally but their money people. Funds the money people invested with Manny Macklin. I don't have a clue what it would cost to build a new-age city, but my guess would be billions, with a B. Think about it, guys. Charles, the Queen's childhood buddy, is suddenly whisked back to England. Isabelle flew over there on a chartered flight a month ahead of schedule. Charles. Isabelle. What the hell would you think, Jack?"

"Holy shit!" was what Jack had to say. The others at the table echoed his outburst.

Abner held up his hand. "Hold on here, don't get carried away. I said that's just my opinion. However, it makes sense. You guys tell me if you think it has any teeth."

"I think 'fangs' might be a better term," Ted said.

"Are you telling us you can't get your wife to confide in you?" Dennis asked, his face red with excitement and outrage at what he was hearing.

"That's exactly what I'm telling you," Abner said. "Weren't you listening? My wife signed a confidentiality agreement, one she intends to honor. I have to respect and honor that."

"But she's your wife!" Dennis sputtered. "I thought spouses didn't keep secrets from each other. This is like . . . learning there's no Santa Claus."

"Lawyers don't reveal their clients' secrets and problems to their spouses, so why should this surprise you, Dennis," Abner said irritably.

"Do you think Isabelle confided in the sisters? They were huddling at Thanksgiving in the kitchen," Jack observed. "I hate to say this, but with those girls, husbands don't really count for too much. They have a special bond we guys can never ever crack. I think we all know that, right." Jack's voice had a degree of frustration in his tone.

"I don't know. It wouldn't surprise me if she did," Abner admitted.

"Well, I know one thing. If Charles is

involved in this, Myra will not allow any of us to touch it with a ten-foot pole. She's viewing Charles's going AWOL, without so much as a by-your-leave, as the ultimate personal betrayal. And I can't say that I blame her either. Is it any wonder that the girls are as close as they are, closer even than with their husbands? If anything, Myra will want to go after Charles and let the devil take the hindmost, or whatever the hell that saying is," Jack mumbled. "This is going to take on a life of its own and grow legs."

"This is not good. Definitely not good," Espinosa chimed in.

"Where's Maggie in all of this?" Jack asked suspiciously.

"Cleaning house, buying snow equipment, and stocking the larder. Why?" Ted asked.

"Does she know what you were doing over the weekend? You did say you guys stayed at her house to help out because of the weather."

"Nah. She was busy. We were all doing our own thing. What's up with all these Maggie questions anyway?" Ted demanded.

"Did you sleep?" Jack barked.

"Of course I slept. Oh shit!"

"Then she knows," Harry said solemnly.

"Yep, she knows," Jack said. "She's probably outside spying on us as we speak, or she's with Myra and Annie."

"I told you not to sleep," Espinosa groused.

"Where does that leave us?" Dennis asked nervously.

"That's a good question, and one whose answer is not on the tip of my tongue," Jack said. "What do we do here? Do we band with Myra and Annie, pool all of our information, and go after that skunk Macklin? Or do we leave it to the SEC and the FBI? I think I can safely say that Myra and Annie are working toward a snatch and grab. What do you think, Dennis?"

All eyes zeroed in on the cub reporter. "The snatch and grab would get my vote."

"By the way," Abner said, "there have been at least a dozen complaints filed with the SEC about Macklin over the years. Complaints that never got off the ground. Someone even went so far as to show the impossibility under any scenario of his returning 20 percent to his investors year after year, in up markets and down markets.

"But no one at the SEC would step in given his reputation as the man with the magic touch who cared so much about his investors, big and little. But someone or some ones outside the SEC were and probably still are watching him. He was just too smart, always two steps ahead of everyone else. Until now."

"Something is bothering me. If what Abner is saying is true, and I tend to agree that it is, why would the Queen and Prince Philip order Charles back to England? Wouldn't he be more help over here? I think we must be missing something," Jack stated.

"I was able to go back five years," Abner said, "and I discovered that Macklin opened a branch office in London. While it was separate from Macklin Investments, he had remote cameras set up that allowed his people to monitor things in New York and here in DC. There are twenty-some employees in London. Here in the States, he would have the world believe he was a one-man operation, three if you count his two kids. Yet in England, he needs more than twenty. It doesn't make sense.

"True, it's been reported that the London office handles his personal investments. I'm sorry, but I'm not buying that. I think his personal investments were really the Queen and Prince Philip's money. Their Royal Highnesses would want to keep their money on their side of the pond, and Macklin would keep his on this side. That part makes sense to me since we're talking about at least a cool billion dollars, possibly more. My take on this, and I could be wrong, is that Macklin somehow snowed the royals and convinced them to build this new-age city that would rival his crown jewel, otherwise known as Olympic Ridge, here in the States. In all the articles I sifted through, that alone seems to be what Macklin is most proud of. It's right up there with being called the Wizard of Wall Street. Olympic Ridge is something you can see with the naked eye. Investment returns and statements . . . are not something people wave around to be seen. Talked about, yes, so being the Wizard of Wall Street is all well and good, but I think that to his way of thinking, it comes in no better than a distant second to Olympic Ridge.

"One other thing. Do you think the royals know about the Vigilantes and that Charles was the backbone of them? Because if they do know, then that is all the more reason to keep him here and enlist the aid of the sisters. Anyone got any ideas?"

"Only that the waitress is eyeing us and wants us to leave. People are waiting for our table," Dennis said.

"The kid's right," Jack said. "We can move on down the street to the Squire's Pub and continue this conversation, or we can split up and think about this and meet up tomorrow. Let's take a vote. Lunch is on Dennis since he just came into a fortune." Jack placed the bills under the salt-shaker.

"I vote to adjourn to the Squire's Pub," Ted said. "I sent Tom Murphy a text to fill in for me. Espinosa has Chuck Harris standing in for him. No news other than snow, so the two of us are good to go. Dennis goes wherever we go. What about you, Jack?"

"I had appointments with only two clients today, and both canceled because of the weather, so I'm good."

"Harry?"

"Same here; my classes were canceled."

"Abner?"

"Being self-employed gives me all the leeway I want. Let's hit the pub and do some serious talking."

The waitress smiled tightly when she saw her party get up to leave. The smile took on real meaning when she saw her tip. She waved good-bye.

It was still flurrying when the group hit the sidewalk. "We'll be frozen by the time we walk three blocks since we're walking into the wind. A nice hot toddy will fix us right up, don't you think?" Ted said.

"I'll just have hot chocolate with those

little marshmallows," Dennis said. "You guys go ahead and drink, and I'll be the designated driver. And I can take notes."

"Sounds like a plan to me," Jack said as he took off at a trot, Harry abreast of him.

Dennis huffed and puffed as he struggled to keep up. He felt giddy that he was included in what was about to be, he knew in his gut, a life-altering mission of some kind.

Not only that, but he was going to get to pay the bill with his brand-new *Post* expense credit card. How neat was that? Pretty darn neat, he decided. He was almost positive he was now officially one of the guys.

CHAPTER SEVENTEEN

Adam Macklin looked at the old-fashioned clock hanging on the wall. He was two hours late. The first time he'd been late in years and years. Normally, he was at his desk at the crack of dawn. He grimaced as he shrugged out of his heavy coat and muffler to hang them on a coat-tree by the office door. He carried his bagel, two containers of coffee, and a sticky bun over to his desk. He looked at the pile of mail sitting on the corner of his desk. Unopened mail that had accumulated over the past week. Right next to the pile of mail was a stack of pink phone-message slips. Calls that needed to be returned. Well, that wasn't going to happen anytime soon. At least not by him.

Adam tore into his bagel, which was loaded with scallion cream cheese, twice toasted, along with butter under the cheese. He propped his feet up on the scarred old desk and sipped at his coffee. The beginning of the end. Everything was coming to an end, even his relationship with Caroline. He regretted that his girlfriend had returned to her family in Alabama. She said the relationship was no longer working for her. He finished his bagel and ripped into the sticky bun. He let his mind wander backward in time to the days when his mother used to make pancakes in cartoon shapes for him and his sister. Sometimes they were action-figure pancakes, sometimes just shapes of things like trees and squirrels — anything that he and Ava liked. The butter was always soft, and the banana syrup always warm. He closed his eyes and could almost taste those pancakes. Then she'd bundle him and Ava up for school and hand them their lunches. They were the best lunches, the crust cut off the bread, a fat sugar cookie, and a bright, shiny red apple. Then she'd give them each a hug, tell them she loved them, and to have a good day. He could feel the warm hug. God, how he missed that.

Adam was wadding up the remnants of his breakfast when the door to the office opened. He looked up and wasn't surprised to see his father standing in the doorway. He looked like a huge white bear. Adam could feel his insides turn to jelly. He tossed the paper sack into the trash can, drained the last of the coffee, headed to the coat-rack, and shrugged into his heavy coat. He settled his backpack on his shoulders and then shrugged until the pack settled comfortably on his back. His entire life was inside the backpack.

"Where are you going, Adam?"

"Guess!" Adam snapped.

"I'm not in the mood for games."

"Me either. You might want to check the mail and those pink slips. It's over, Pop. There are a lot of people out there who are requesting an audience with you. Like, for instance, the FBI, the SEC, and those holy-terror lawyers of yours. Out of some misguided sense of loyalty, I've been telling people you're in England. You're on your own now. I'm done. In case you aren't getting it, we're dead. They just haven't embalmed us."

"We're not dead. I'm about to sign up WELMED. That will keep us going for years to come. You didn't answer my question. Where are you going?"

"I'm going to see Mom. I called Ava and I'm going to ask her if she wants to go with me. I'm going to pick her up at the airport. I called her to tell her to come here today. If she doesn't want to go with me, I'll drop her off here, and you two can decide what you're going to do until the embalming starts."

"Oh no, you are not. You are going to stay right here and take care of business."

"Wrong, Pop. And I don't give a good rat's ass about WELMED or anything else. And when things come crashing down, I'm going to man up and take my punishment. If I'm lucky, they might let me cut a deal. I hired my own lawyer. I can't speak for Ava, but if I were you, I'd definitely prepare myself for the worst."

"What the hell do you think your mother is going to do for you?"

Adam walked back into the room and towered over his father. They were so close he could smell his father's coffee breath. "I don't know, Pop. I'm hoping she'll give me a hug. I don't deserve anything more."

"So, just like that, you're bailing out?"

"Yep! You win a gold star for getting it. Congratulations."

"How can you do this to me?" Manny barked. "How?"

"It's really quite simple, Pop. I finally figured it all out. All I have to do is walk out the door and wait for whatever happens next." Adam whirled around and headed out the door. The last thing he heard was his father calling him an ungrateful bastard. Well, that, at least, was true. Probably one of the only things his father had said in years that was.

Manny Macklin stood as though rooted to the floor. He blinked. Then he shook his shaggy head. Was this a bad dream? Or had this really just happened? He yanked out his cell phone and punched in his daughter's number. When his call went straight to voice mail, he knew in his gut that his son had told him the truth.

Manny sat down in his son's chair and looked at the pile of mail and the stack of pink slips. He poked at them. Adam was right. He looked through the pink slips and saw six of them were from his lawyers. It was a place to start. He punched in the number, identified himself, and then waited for Asa Bellamy to come on the line.

Manny steeled himself for what was to come. "I'm in the middle of a deposition, Manny. I'll be tied up for the next two hours. When I walk out of here, I expect you to be sitting in my waiting room. If you aren't there, then you will need to engage a new firm to handle your affairs. Are we clear on this, Manny?"

Manny's first inclination was to bluster, but he knew that would get him nowhere.

"I'll be there, Asa."

Now what? Should he just walk out the door the way Adam had? Should he go back to Olympic Ridge and wait to be taken into custody? Or . . . did he hang in and close the WELMED deal? Or did he call his pilot and arrange for a flight to Europe?

Manny leaned back and closed his eyes as his mind whirled and twirled with scenario after scenario playing out behind his closed lids.

A long time later, he opened his eyes and looked up at the clock. Fifteen minutes past noon. His cell phone buzzed. He brought it to his ear and listened to Dennis West's voice. He sat up straighter. The answer to his dilemma. "Of course, young man, I think that will work. I look forward to it. You say you'll pick me up? Fine, fine. Tomorrow at six o'clock. Yes, yes, I understand I am to bring all the papers for you to sign should your aunts give their approval. By the way, young man, I need to thank you because I am not worth much in the kitchen. I don't think I could make an edible meat loaf if my life depended on it. Stay warm, young man."

Manny jammed his phone back into his pocket. He smacked his hands together in jubilation. Maybe he wouldn't need his pilot after all. He heaved himself up and out of the chair. He might as well head over to Asa's office. Sometimes, and this was one of those times, it would pay to be early.

The decibel level at the Squire's Pub wound down as the late lunch crowd departed the premises. Ensconced in one of the private rooms in the back, Jack held court. They were drinking coffee, cup after cup, and they were all wired to the hilt, Dennis thought. He'd thought they would be drinking beer, but no, they were here to come to terms with what had to be done. He was dizzy with the ideas he was hearing. He'd taken only one break, to call Myra and Annie and suggest they prepare dinner tomorrow night for one Mr. Emanuel Macklin. All he had to say was, "This way you get him in your clutches, and you won't have to stalk him and worry about what to do with him." Both women agreed instantly. When he returned to the private room and informed the group what he'd just done, he was slapped on the back and congratulated.

"Well, now, that takes us out of the locker room and puts us onto the playing field," Ted said. "Let's kick this around and see what we come up with. Abner, do you have anything else?"

"I can't remember what all I've said so far. If I covered this, stop me. Some of the foundations that invested with Macklin are going belly-up. This is really important. For every billion dollars in foundation investments, Macklin was on the hook for around $80 million a year. If he wasn't making real investments, he could make the principal last somewhere around fifteen to twenty years, depending upon what he was earning in treasury bonds. By going after the charities, Macklin could avoid some knee-jerk withdrawals and not get caught with his pants down.

"From what I can figure out, the guy has something like thirty-five hundred investors and close to twelve thousand separate accounts. I can't keep this all straight anymore. His clients include hedge funds, banks, universities, wealthy individuals, movie stars. That's where I got my information when I started hacking. Macklin has no personal electronic trail to follow. It's like you open a box to find another box inside, then another one, and after that still one more. If I'm going nuts doing what I'm doing, you have to ask yourself how the hell that guy was and is keeping it straight. I simply cannot fathom how he has kept this scheme going all these years and not gotten caught. It's not only mind numbing, it is unbelievable that anything like this could happen in the first place."

An hour later, the little group dispersed, each of them going his own separate way, their thoughts all on the same plane.

Adam Macklin stood leaning against the wall as deplaning passengers found their way down the concourse at Reagan National. He saw his sister immediately; she was hard to miss. She looked like a runway model in her designer coat trimmed in mink, spike-heeled boots, and a Chanel bag that cost what a family of three could live on for two months. At one time she had been pretty, but now she appeared like a mannequin that had been dipped in a vat of shellac.

The minute she came abreast of him, Ava began to speak without breaking stride. "What's with you, Adam? This is the last time I'm listening to you. Why do I always have to come here? Why can't you come to New York? What's so damn important that this meeting had to be face-to-face? Why couldn't you just call me on the telephone? What's got your knickers in a knot this time? Don't tell me you and Daddy are at it again. I don't want to hear it. Start talking,

Adam, or I'm going to turn around and leave," she said, as they walked outside to the short-term lot.

"Do you ever just talk, Ava? What happened to 'hello, Adam, how are you?' All you do is bitch, moan, and groan. And when you aren't doing that, you're complaining about something or other. Do you ever say anything nice or kind to anyone? Do you ever smile? Ooops, guess not, I forgot, the Botox won't allow it. By the way, you look like shit."

"Aren't you the little ray of sunshine this morning. If picking me up was such a chore — and might I remind you, you're the one who engineered this meeting — you could have sent a car service. Where's the car?"

"Two aisles over," Adam said through clenched teeth.

"You're still driving that hunk of junk? It has to be at least ten years old. Does it run?"

"It's twelve years old, and yes, it runs. Get in and shut up, Ava. Already I'm sick of listening to you."

"Does the heater work?"

"Of course it works. I keep the car maintained. And don't even think about lighting a cigarette."

"All right, all right. Now, will you please tell me what is so hellfire important that you made me come down to Washington? I'm sick of holding your hand, Adam. Let's get on with it."

"I quit this morning. I already told Pop when he came to the office earlier. I'm out. It's just you and him now."

Ava turned sideways on her seat so she could see her brother better. "Are you serious? Why?"

"You can't be that stupid, Ava. You know why. You guys can fight it out with the SEC and the FBI. Not me. They're closing in. I've been warning you both. Did you listen? No, you did not.

"When I told Pop this morning, all he could say was that he had this big deal cooking, that he was going to sign on WELMED. I do not care. You can't fix this. I'm going to turn myself in and admit to my part in this whole mess. It's over, Ava. It's all going to come crashing down."

"Are you crazy? Pop never said a word. Are you on some kind of dope or something? He would have told me," she said, but her expression clearly didn't match her words. Adam got a perverse sense of pleasure out of seeing the panic on his sister's face.

Adam took his eyes off the road long enough to look at his sister. For all her bluster, he could see the fear in her eyes.

"So when did Pop ever say a word about anything? He thinks he's God. He's the damn devil, Ava. And we were his disciples. Well, not anymore. I'm out. I'm dropping you off at the office, and after that, we're done. I only picked you up because I said I would, and I try never to break a promise."

"How damn noble of you, Adam. You have me spooked now. What brought all this on?" she asked tightly, as Adam expertly maneuvered the car out of the lot, onto an exit ramp, and out to the secondary road that would lead him to the main highway. It was still flurrying. God, would this winter ever end?

"Calls and letters from the SEC. Rumor has it the FBI is on Pop's trail. More than one disgruntled investor has filed complaints with them. They are finally beginning to take this seriously, Ava."

"Complaints have been coming in for years. What makes this time any different?"

"Pop has stopped paying the small investor. And you're the goddamn chief compliance officer. I had to stop answering the phones. Everyone was calling and threatening me. Me? Are you telling me you don't know what's going on? That's bullshit, Ava."

Ava inched her way over to the corner of

her seat and leaned against the passenger-side door. She closed her eyes, and the rest of the trip was made in silence.

Forty minutes later, Adam said, "Okay, we're here. Pop was in the office when I left to pick you up. I don't know if he's still there or not. If he left, call him. From here on in, you two are on your own."

"Where are you going, Adam? What will you do?" Adam heard the fear in his sister's voice, but he turned a deaf ear.

"For starters, I'm going to see Mom. After that, I'm going to wait for someone to come arrest me."

"Stop being so damn dramatic. Mom! Is that what you said? Where is she? How can you go to see her after she walked out on us? Where's your loyalty, you bastard?"

"Not with our father, that's for sure. I'm only telling you this in the interest of full disclosure. Something you need to think about when they come after you. At that point, it will be all about full disclosure. You need to start practicing now.

"As for Mom, has it never occurred to you that there are two sides to every story? We only ever heard one side, Pop's side. And he was anything but impartial on the topic of Mom's departure. And if his history with trophy wives number one, two, and three is any indication, I find no reason to believe that what he had to say about Mom was even close to the truth. To make a long story short, I think it's long past the time that we get her side of it."

"I can't believe what I'm hearing. After all this time, now — when you say things are going to get tough — you want to run to Mommy. What do you think she's going to do for you, Adam?"

Adam smiled. He repeated the same words to his sister that had so stunned his father. "I'm hoping she'll give me a hug." If he hadn't been watching his sister's face so intently he would have missed the way her face started to crumple. "Do you want to come with me?"

Ava sucked in her breath, got out of the car, whirled around, and stalked to the entrance of the building that housed the rat-trap offices of Macklin Investments.

"Guess that's a no," Adam muttered as a horn blared behind him. He pulled out into traffic. Next stop: his mother's house.

Adam turned on his GPS, which he had programmed earlier. It was a cheap, crappy, old Garmin unit he'd installed himself on his old car. But it didn't matter since it did the trick as far as he was concerned.

His thoughts were all over the map as he made his way to his mother's house. What would his sister do now? What was his father going to do? He cringed when he thought about the upcoming arrests, which were inevitable, and how his sister and father would handle things. Just last week, he'd read something on Page Six that said his father's latest trophy — read bimbo — had left for Argentina and would file for divorce. He wondered if his father even knew she'd left.

After the news snippet ran, she had called the office and said the same thing and asked Adam to give his father the message. It was in the pile of pink slips on his desk. Adam did not think it important enough to treat it any differently than all the other messages he had been bombarded with.

Then again, maybe his father had actually paid her to go. Her shelf life was probably up. And that led him to think about his own longtime girlfriend and his inability to commit to her. When she'd gone eyeball to eyeball with him, and said, "Admit it, Adam, I'm just a booty call," he knew it was over. They'd parted friends, and she had gone home to her parents in Alabama. He was glad now. Caroline was too nice to be involved in what was going to go down in the coming days. Better she be with her family. They'd never find her in the little town she'd grown up in. At least he hoped they wouldn't.

Adam could feel the nervousness creeping through his system. What if his mother wasn't home? What if she wouldn't let him in to talk to her? What would he do then?

Then I'll just sit outside until she does, he thought. *Even if I freeze to death.*

The robotic voice coming from the dashboard announced that he had arrived at his destination, jarring him out of his pessimistic thoughts. His intention had been to park on the street, but the snow was piled too high, taking up too much room on both sides of the street. Instead, he pulled into her driveway, which looked like it had been freshly shoveled and salted. He looked around before he cut off the engine.

His mother lived in what looked like a quiet neighborhood, with big trees that would be like giant umbrellas when they came into leaf in the spring. He closed his eyes for a moment as he visualized kids on bikes and roller skaters whizzing down the walkways, with dogs barking in their wake. Then they'd all go home to some kid's house, and a doting mother would pour lemonade and hand out cookies and maybe

Popsicles. Cherry Popsicles, his favorite from childhood. He wished he were a kid again. If he could just turn back the clock.

Adam took a deep breath and climbed out of the car. He pulled his heavy jacket close to his chin and, with his head down, ran across the driveway to a brick path that he just knew in the spring would be bordered in flowers. His mother had always loved flowers. The snow flurries had turned to sleet and were beating at him like tiny pinpricks.

His hand was shaking so badly, it took Adam three times before he hit the tiny button that would ring the bell inside. He didn't realize he was holding his breath until it exploded out of his mouth like a gunshot. He sucked in his breath again, his eyes on the doorknob. It was moving. In a second he was finally going to see his mother. He wanted to cry in relief. And then she was standing framed in the doorway, looking just the way he remembered.

"Addy! Is it really you?" His childhood nickname, a name only his mother called him. He felt weak at the sound of it.

Adam could barely make his tongue work. "It's me, Mom. Can I come in?"

"Good Lord, of course you can come in. It's freezing out there." And then she was hugging him and crying and he was crying. They clung to each other, wondering how this miracle had finally happened.

"Oh Addy, how did you find me?" Mary said, wiping her eyes on her apron.

"It doesn't matter. I found you; that's all that is important. I don't want you to think I never tried before. I did. Pop said he hired private detectives to try to locate you after you left, but that they came up blank. I know now he lied. Mom, I thought about you every single day of my life since you left. I'm in a boatload of trouble, Mom. But that's not why I'm here. I just wanted to see you."

Mary gave her son one more bone-crushing hug and kissed him on his cheeks. "Here, let me hang up your coat. Come along to the kitchen. I was just getting ready to have some lunch. Are you hungry?"

"Actually, I'm starved," Adam said as he trailed behind his mother. He was aware of a cheerful fire coming from a brick wall. He saw shelves of books; deep, comfortable furniture; lots of windows; and soft carpeting. Later, he hoped his mother would give him a tour of her house.

He was unprepared for the kitchen, and yet he should have known it would reflect his mother. He looked at everything and closed his eyes, burning the room into his memory. "This is really nice," he said, sitting down at an old oak table with claw feet. He was facing a huge bay window where luscious, healthy-looking ferns hung from a beam directly overhead.

"Turkey soup and turkey sandwiches. And apple pie. You know how it is with Thanksgiving turkeys. You eat off them for days. Today is my last day."

Adam frowned. "Thanksgiving? When was Thanksgiving?"

"Last Thursday, Addy."

"Guess I missed it. I was working. Well, not actually working. I was trying to . . . it doesn't matter. It smells good even if it is four days old. How are you, Mom?"

"Good now that you're here sitting at my table. I missed you, Addy. And Ava."

No more lies. "I picked her up at the airport. I told her I was coming here and asked if she wanted to come. She said no. Ava . . . Ava . . . she changed. All that money went to her head. I'm not sure you'd recognize her these days."

"It's all right, Addy. You're here. Now eat your soup and that nice sandwich. And then we can talk about what brought you here."

"How did this happen?" Adam said, waving his arm about.

"When I left, I had nowhere to go, so I came here. This was my brother Lowell's house. Lowell was my half brother and quite a bit older. We had the same mother but different fathers. He took me in; and then, a few years ago, Lowell got sick, and I took care of him. When he passed, he left all this to me. He was a good man. A shy man with few friends. I guess you could call him a recluse. I got him out and about, and we had a pleasant life until he passed. He made sure he provided for me because he knew I wouldn't take a penny from your father. Little by little over the years I changed the house from a bachelor's home to what you see now. Lowell loved it. He would sit here for hours at the kitchen table, doing his crossword puzzles. I still miss him."

Adam held out his bowl. "Can I have some more?"

"Is it that good?" Mary laughed.

"It is that good." Adam laughed, too. He couldn't remember when he'd laughed last. It felt good. "Do you work, Mom?"

"I work one day a week in a bakery in town. I help out at the church. I do a lot of volunteer work. It all works for me. I belong to a bridge club. I made a pleasant life for myself. At first it was hard. I missed you and Ava so much. That was my only regret when I left, but you were in college, and Ava was getting ready to leave for college. I had to leave, Addy. Once I . . . That's for another time. Let's just enjoy each other for the moment. Are you married? Do you have children?" she asked wistfully.

Adam shook his head. "No, I was married to the business and to Pop. I did have a girlfriend for a long time, but she got fed up with me a little while ago and dumped me since the relationship wasn't going anywhere. Returned to Alabama, where her parents live. It was for the best. Ava never got married, either. Pop, on the other hand, hit the altar a few more times, three to be exact. The last one called the office last week and said to tell Pop she was returning to Argentina and would file for divorce. I left him a note. I'm pretty sure he hasn't seen it yet."

Mary smiled, then laughed out loud. Adam threw back his head and joined her. Almost like old times.

Mary wiped at her eyes as she stared at her son. Yes, he was older, but he had the same clear blue eyes and long lashes girls would die for. His unruly dark hair was a little too long and just as curly. Strong jaw, beautiful smile. She remembered the braces he'd worn when he was younger and how he hated them. The beautiful smile was the result of those braces. He was tall, six foot two. She wasn't sure, but she thought he probably weighed as much as her neighbor Pete, which would be around 180. Her son. And she loved him. Would always love him. No matter what.

And here he was sitting at her kitchen table. It was something she'd thought she would never live to see. Her cup runneth over.

"Coffee and pie, Addy?"

"Absolutely. Do you still put the raisins and nuts in it?"

Mary nodded as she cut a thick wedge of pie. "Ice cream?" Adam nodded.

"Let's go into the family room and eat our dessert by the fire. I like having dessert in there with a fire going. I watch the news in the evening. We can talk instead of watching the midday news. Would you like that?"

"Yeah, Mom, I would."

"Oh my, would you look outside. It's snowing again. Earlier, it was just flurrying. You might have to stay over unless you absolutely have to be somewhere."

"Are you serious, Mom? Can I stay here? I was going to ask, but I figured I better wait to see how you felt after I told you what I came here for."

"Addy, you can stay here forever if you want. I would never turn you away. You should know that. In fact, you're about Lowell's size. I bought him a lot of new clothes before he passed that he never got to wear. They're all in garment bags in one of the guest rooms. I can outfit you from the skin out," Mary said happily.

Mother and son settled into two companion chairs in front of the fire. Within seconds Winnie came out of nowhere and leaped onto Adam's lap, to his delight. Now it was perfect, just perfect. The plump cat settled and began to purr loudly.

"You should be pleased with yourself, Addy. Winnie doesn't take to strangers. Guess she likes you. Of course, she is eyeing up that pie on your plate."

A pleasant hour passed until the coffee cups were drained and the plates empty. Mary collected them and set them on the hearth after adding two logs to the fire.

"Talk to me, Son. Tell me everything, and let's see what we can do to make it better."

Chapter Eighteen

"This is really nice, Mom," Adam said. "I always like a fire. Not that I've had time to sit in front of one very much. I'm having trouble believing I'm here and that we're talking and that you didn't tell me to get lost. I swear to God, Mom. I tried to find you. It was like you disappeared off the face of the earth. We lost so many years. I can't believe Pop did that. That's something, among a whole list of other things, that I will never forgive him for. I know that Ava feels the same way even if she won't admit it. She'll come around, Mom, you'll see."

Mary listened as her long-lost son rambled on, knowing it was just a nervous reaction to what he had come here to say. She hoped when it finally came her time to speak that she would have all the right words for her tormented son. She stared into the fire as Adam talked about his small garden apartment, his twelve-year-old car, and how he had never spent any of the money his father put into his brokerage account. "It was blood money," she heard him say. "I couldn't spend it. It's all there. I have my own account. Remember, Mom, when we were kids you opened accounts for each of us at school, and all my birthday money and Easter and Christmas money went in there. I kept the account when I worked summers and when I was in college. Then, when I graduated and went to work on Wall Street, I switched the account to a brokerage house and saved and invested just the way you taught us. Remember what you said? A rainy day will come, and you're going to need it. Well, Mom, the rainy day is here, and I am so glad I listened to you. I invested aggressively but wisely. I have over $2 million of my own *legal* money. And a large part of it is going to be used to pay a good lawyer. I'm just babbling here. Okay, here we go."

Mary folded her hands in her lap as she listened to her son detail his life from the moment his father had laid a guilt trip on him and forced him to go to work for him. She felt sick to her stomach at what she was hearing. She wished he would stop, wanted him to stop, but she couldn't make her tongue work.

The small, ornate clock on the mantel,

which Mary could see from her chair, said her son had been talking nonstop for almost two hours. Twice, she'd gotten up to add a log to the fire, but he'd barely noticed.

"That's it," he finally said. "I have an appointment with my lawyer tomorrow morning at 9:00. I'll have him make appointments with the SEC and the FBI. If we can't get in to talk to them tomorrow, then surely the day after, which is Wednesday. I don't want to drag my feet on this. I'm going to confess all of it. I helped, I did it, I own it. I tried to warn Ava. I don't know what she's going to do. She's always been about the money, so I'm not hopeful. I can't live with this anymore, Mom. I just can't."

This was so much worse than what she had expected, Mary thought. She couldn't pretend not to be upset. She was upset. She hated the way Adam was looking at her like she was going to pull a magic rabbit out of a nonexistent hat. All she could think of at the moment were trips to some federal prison once a week, taking baked goods and home-cooked food to her son if it was allowed. Maybe she would have to move, to be closer to the prison in which he was incarcerated. Her stomach heaved at the thought.

"Are you going to say something, Mom?"

Mary cleared her throat and stared for a moment into the fire, hoping for some insight. "You made mistakes. We all make mistakes in life, but the ones you made are a lot more serious than most. The fact that you're willing to stand up now and do the right thing will hopefully count in your favor. You do realize, don't you, that you will be a whistle-blower? That is not a bad thing. When you go to the FBI, I will go with you. I need to do some confessing of my own. I knew years and years ago, but I never did anything about it. I'm just as guilty as you are."

"Hell, Mom, that doesn't count. You just had suspicions. You had no way of knowing what Pop was really doing. You're off the hook on that, trust me."

"I knew enough to know there were two sets of books. The real set and the doctored-up set. I can read balance sheets, Addy. It's time for me to confess, too.

"Now, I have something to tell you. This morning, bright and early, before the snow started to really come down, I had two ladies visit me. They said they were hired by two other ladies, named Sara and Tressie. They were older ladies, much like me. They were very well-known a few years ago as the Vigilantes. I'm sure you heard or read about them. I'm not sure about this, but I am assuming they came out of retirement to, ah . . . take care of your father. I also gathered it would not be done in a way that observed the legal niceties, although neither woman came out and said that. I do believe they have a plan in place. They wanted whatever background I could give them, and I told them what I knew from those early days. They already knew about you and Ava."

Adam's eyes almost bugged out of his head at his mother's words. Then he shrugged. "Everything happens for a reason. Isn't that what you always said? My coming here right after them, not having a clue about their visit or what their plans are. My finally making the decision to blow the whistle. Kind of scary when you think about it. Did they give you any clue about whatever it is they plan to do?"

"No, but I got the impression it was going to be sooner rather than later. In other words, the ladies are on it. I have to say that I used to follow their activities, as did every living, breathing woman, and some men, I'm sure, while they were actively righting the wrongs of the world. I was transfixed by them. I even donated money to every cause they endorsed.

"Now I have a question for you. I told the ladies what I know about this, which is almost nothing. One time shortly after serious money started flowing into your father's bank account, I looked in his check register and saw six months of entries marked simply as RENT. I never said anything to your father or asked him any questions because I didn't want to admit that I had been snooping. Do you know anything about that? Back then, it was quite a bit of money. And it was in New York."

Adam shook his head. "Ava might know, but I sure don't. Pop has always been secretive, you know that better than I do. Sometimes, I think Ava has the skinny on everything; then there are other times I think she's in the dark about most of it. Secretive and frugal. The frugal part is all a facade. He dresses in polyester, wears cheap shoes, cheap shirts. Makes a point out of saying he buys his suits at JC Penney and his shoes at a discount store. He tells everyone he doesn't believe in frills and accoutrements. Yet I've seen rows of Savile Row suits in his closet, silk monogrammed shirts. Hermès ties, and John Lobb and Bruno Maglia shoes. I have no clue where he wears all that stuff. From start to finish, he's as phony as a three-dollar bill. If you want me to take a guess, I'd say that's where he houses his *other people,* his silent partners. By no stretch of the imagination can what he is doing be a one-man operation. Oh yeah, he touted Ava and me, but we were nothing more than glorified office help, even though Ava's title is chief compliance officer, for God's sake. What a joke. The only rule Macklin Investments ever complied with was the one that said that, by hook or by crook, Emanuel Macklin was to be made as rich as Croesus."

Mary just shook her head. "Addy, why did you wait so long? Why didn't you do something sooner?"

Adam shrugged. "That's the sixty-four-thousand-dollar question, Mom, isn't it? I don't know. The best I can come up with is, he's my father. I did what I could behind the scenes, trying to make things as difficult as I could for him and better for the investor, but he was always one or two steps ahead of me. If he even had a clue about what I was doing, he never let on. Sometimes it worked, but most other times, it didn't. Two years ago, when he got all fired up about his newest project, one across the pond, which had been in the works for years before that, it finally hit home. I'm sure you've read about that new-age city he wants to build someplace outside London. He says it will top his crown jewel. It was two years ago that he finally started raising the funds for it, and nothing has been done in the way of construction. He's collected billions from his investors, and rumor has it that the Queen of England and Prince Philip ponied up beaucoup bucks. Something is awry, but I don't know what it is."

"Addy, do you know what your father is worth these days?"

"Billions, Mom. That's billions with a B."

"With all you've told me and all that has been going on, aren't you fearful he'll abscond? Just disappear?"

"Not as long as there's another sucker standing in line, and he has one right now that he said will keep his investors happy for another few years. It's called WELMED. He's hoping to sign him up tomorrow. I think that's what he said."

"That kind of falls into place with what the ladies told me earlier this morning. Something is going to happen in the next day or so. At least that's the impression they left me with. I don't think I'm wrong about that, Addy. Maybe they're setting him up with the WELMED thing. Those ladies are not only wicked; they are wily. I can say in all confidence that your father is no match for them. They will clean his clock, and he will never know what hit him."

"One can only hope." Adam yawned, then yawned again.

"You look tired, Son. Come along, I'll show you to your room, and you can take a nap. When was the last time you had a good night's sleep?"

"Like forever ago. Are you sure you don't mind?"

"Good heavens, no, I do not mind. We can talk the night away. Come along, then. Winnie loves it when I nap during the day. I'm sure she'll keep you company. Is there anything special you'd like for dinner?"

At the landing on the staircase to the second floor, Mary parted the curtains. "Mercy, would you look at that snow coming down. Well, we don't have to be anywhere today, so we're safe and sound. My neighbor has a snowblower, and he'll clear everything up nice and tidy again. I'm sure you'll be able to get out to go to your lawyer's in the morning."

"Spaghetti. Or is that too much trouble? I used to love snow when I was a kid. You'd take us to Central Park, we'd get our mittens wet, and there was that time you pulled some old socks out of your bag, and we used them as mittens. I still remember that,"

Adam said, sadness ringing in his voice.

Good Lord, the boy remembered the socks. She'd forgotten about that until Adam had reminded her just now. "I do remember that. I do not mind one little bit," Mary said happily. "I love to cook. Meat sauce or meatballs?"

"Both," Adam said smartly. "Garlic bread?"

"Absolutely," Mary responded. Adam sighed.

Mary opened the door to a pretty room that was neither feminine nor manly. It was done in soft, neutral plaids, easy and pleasant on the eyes. The bed was a king-size four-poster with big, plump pillows. Creamy off-white curtains cut the glare from the mesmerizing white outside. Ankle-high carpeting hugged his ankles. "This room has its own bathroom. Everything you can possibly need is either in the closet, the dressers, or the bathroom. Rest, Adam. You have your head on straight now, and you are doing the right thing. I'll be right beside you every step of the way, for whatever good that will do you."

Adam swallowed hard and hugged his mother. The door closed softly behind her. He looked down to see the fat cat rubbing against his ankles and purring. He smiled and looked around. He could stay here forever. He eyed the deep, comfortable chair in the corner, with the reading lamp next to it. He didn't know how he knew, but he knew that the chair and lamp had belonged to his uncle Lowell. God, he was tired, but not so tired he didn't want to be a kid again for all of ten seconds. That's all it took for him to run across the room and leap up onto the four-poster. Winnie meowed as she leaped up right behind him. The moment Adam's head hit the pillow, he was sound asleep. It would, as he would say later to his mother, be the *bestest,* soundest, most welcoming sleep he'd had in years. Because that's what he used to say when he woke in the morning when he was a kid without a problem in the world.

While Adam Macklin was sleeping peacefully at his mother's house, his father was going toe to toe with his attorney. They were snapping and snarling at each other. Then each of them threatened the other. After that, three of the law firm's other senior partners were called in to the conference room, where more snapping and snarling took place, with Emanuel Macklin barking the words any lawyer hates to hear. "If I go down, I'll make damn sure you go down right along with me. I made each and every one of you bastards fucking rich. Don't even think about telling me I'm going to jail. Fix the damn SEC and the FBI. You told me a thousand times that this firm could fix anything. Well, put up or shut up, and you know I mean it. Rest assured," he repeated, his voice rising, "that if I go down, you go down, every last goddamn one of you. Move your asses, starting now, and do not — I repeat, Asa — do not ever threaten me again. If you do, you'll live to regret it. If you live at all. Are we clear on all this, gentlemen?"

Not one of the lawyers spoke, but they all nodded.

Macklin heaved himself out of his chair and stood up. There wasn't even a thought about shaking hands. He turned around and stomped out of the plush offices of his thousand-dollar-an-hour lawyers.

Confident that his orders would be obeyed with a successful outcome, Macklin took the elevator down and walked out to the lobby. His phone chirped in his pocket — Ava. He clicked it on and listened to his daughter's frightened voice telling him she was sitting in Adam's chair in Adam's office because Adam had quit and was going to blow the whistle on Macklin Investments.

"What are we going to do, Daddy? I'm scared. Where are you? Can you come here right now?"

Macklin sighed. His daughter the drama queen. He assured her he would get there as soon as he could, and if she cared to look outside, she would see that his arrival might be a tad delayed. He didn't bother listening to her wailing. Thank God there were taxis moving in the streets. He walked to the curb and held out his hand. A cab pulled up, and he stepped in.

Just one more set of problems. Well, he could control Ava. Ava was just as greedy as he was. She would do exactly what he told her to do and when he told her to do it. Ava loved money too much to ever go against him, unlike her do-gooder brother, Adam. Ungrateful son of a bitch that he was.

CHAPTER NINETEEN

Stifling a yawn, Annie entered Myra's kitchen, where Myra was already sitting at the table having her first cup of coffee of the morning. "I feel like I live here," she grumbled. "I should go home today to check on things."

"Why?" Myra asked.

"You know, to break up the monotony. Doing something different from watching snow fall. I see it's stopped." Annie yawned again to make her point.

"Probably during the night. You can't go home, Annie. Today is our big day. We have to make a meat loaf for our guest tonight. Have you ever made a meat loaf?"

Annie stifled yet another yawn. She looked at Myra as much as to say, you're joking, right? "I can't say that I have. Have you?"

"Never! Charles has a stack of cookbooks. I think we can figure it out. I already took the meat out of the freezer, and it is thawing in the sink. In the end, who cares how it comes out. The way I see it, we're just two cons trying to con the biggest con on Wall Street. In other words, the Wall Street Wizard."

Annie gulped at her coffee, hoping it would wake her up fully. "Want to go over our plan one more time to make sure we don't screw things up?"

"I don't think so. But we do need to decide if we're going to allow Dennis to stay for the . . . festivities. I say we send him home after he drops off our guest. What's your thinking on it, Annie?"

"Well, it is all about Dennis now, isn't it? I know he told Macklin that he wouldn't make any decision without our approval, so that does more or less put us in charge. In other words, I have mixed feelings. I'm not sure the boy will be okay with us . . . ah . . . sequestering said guest in the dungeon. Which then also brings up another problem of how we're going to get him down there on our own. Macklin is a big man, Myra. Those steps going down to the dungeon are pretty steep and narrow. We might have to call the boys to . . . help us. Which then opens another can of worms. To be more specific, we can't do it on our own and need to be put out to pasture. I resent that.

Deeply resent that even though the words just came out of my very own mouth."

"Then we won't go there, dear," Myra said. "Let's just send Dennis home and worry about it later. We have knockout drops we can put in a drink for Macklin in case he gets feisty. We can do this, Annie, I know we can."

"From your lips to God's ears, my friend. Are we having breakfast?"

"Only if you make it. I had a Pop-Tart. Strawberry with frosting. By the way, I finally threw out all things turkey that were in the refrigerator."

Annie reached for the box of assorted Pop-Tarts and pulled out a blueberry one, which she quickly crunched down on. She made a face. "Kind of like chewing on cardboard. I'm surprised no one has called us this morning."

"It's just seven o'clock, Annie. The day is just beginning. I have a feeling the day is going to heat up rapidly, and I'm not talking about the temperature outside.

"I know what you meant, Myra," Annie groused. "Two more hours, and Adam Macklin will be visiting his attorney. Do you think Mary will call us to say how things are going and what their game plan is?"

"I do. She's on our side, and she's torn

about her son, but in the end she will do the right thing. She just couldn't do it herself, but she's perfectly content with her ex being brought to justice.

"She's a good person, Annie. She really is. Just like Sara and Tressie. They wanted Macklin taken care of, but they couldn't bring themselves to do it directly. At least, that's how I see it. This whole thing is going to be hard on Mary, but she's a survivor like you and me. In the end, she'll be okay."

"Then I guess we just wait to see how that all plays out. Listen, while you take your shower, I am going to check out the financial news on the Net."

Myra nodded as she headed for the stairs, her thoughts all over the map as she thought about what lay ahead. "We can make this right, I know we can," she muttered over and over as she stripped down and entered the shower. Her thoughts went to England and Charles, and she hoped everything that needed to be done was being done and that he would be coming home soon. Her spirit daughter had told her that everything would be all right, and she had never lied to her before.

Downstairs, Annie was also muttering under her breath as she scrolled through the financial news and the headline news without finding anything relating to Emanuel Macklin. Like Myra, she muttered over and over, "We can do this. I know we can do this and get away with it."

An hour later and fifty miles away, Adam Macklin dressed himself in his Uncle Lowell's clothes. No one was more surprised than he was that everything fit perfectly. He felt comfortable and at ease.

It was hard for him to understand why he felt so good, so alive, so ready to deal with whatever life was going to throw his way. Going to a federal prison didn't frighten him as much today as it had yesterday when he woke up. How weird was that? Pretty damn weird, he decided. His shoulders felt lighter, as if a large burden had been removed; there was a spring in his step, and he couldn't wait to get on with it.

Downstairs, his mother was waiting for him. She was making breakfast. A home-cooked breakfast like those she used to cook for him and his sister. He knew it would be pancakes with warm butter and sweet banana syrup, his favorite. He also knew there would be crisp rashers of bacon because he could smell them and the coffee, the aromas wafting up the stairs. A great way to start the day. A new day, as his mother called it.

Adam stood in the doorway, watching his mother as she flipped the pancakes on the griddle. He could smell the syrup all the way across the pretty yellow kitchen.

"Morning, Mom."

Mary turned and smiled at her son. "How did you sleep, Son?"

"Like a baby. I didn't think I'd sleep at all, but I did. I don't know how to thank you, Mom."

"Oh Addy, I wish I could have helped you sooner. We lost so many years. Sit down, sweetie. I made pancakes and bacon." Mary slid a dinner plate loaded with a stack of fluffy pancakes in front of her son. The side dish of bacon went next to it, along with the warm butter and syrup. She filled his coffee cup and sat down across from him.

Adam looked at the stack of pancakes and knew he could never finish it all, but he did. He gobbled up the bacon and sneaked a few small pieces to Winnie, who had hopped onto his lap.

"I saw that." Mary laughed. "I do it all the time, too; that's why Winnie is so fat.

"The early weather report said the roads are bad but drivable. I backed Lowell's truck out of the garage. It's in excellent shape, and I drive it when the weather is bad. It has four-wheel drive, so you should be good to go. It's warming up right now. You need to allow yourself extra time. Are you sure, Addy, that you want to do this?"

"I'm sure, Mom. Thanks for a wonderful breakfast. It was like old times." Adam got up and hugged his mother. It was a fierce hug. Mary's hold on her son was just as fierce. "Scoot, now. Call me if you need me."

Adam chewed on his bottom lip. "Yeah. Yeah, I will. I don't know when I'll be home. Maybe they'll arrest me on the spot. If that happens, my attorney will call you. By the way, his name is Sam Andover. He's a personal friend of many years. He and I went to school together. You'd like him, Mom. He has a nice wife and five kids. Good guy."

Mary nodded as she watched Adam slip into his own jacket. She held out the scarf, and he wrapped it around his neck with a wild flourish.

And then her son was gone. She listened as Adam slipped the car into reverse. She was glad now that she had kept up with the maintenance on the truck. When she could no longer hear the truck's engine, Mary bowed her head and said a prayer that things would work out for him. Losing him a second time would be almost too much to bear.

With no plans for the day, Mary tidied up the kitchen as she half listened to the weatherman on the small television on the kitchen counter. She needed to think about what she should cook for dinner in case Adam returned home. Stuffed peppers. Adam had always liked stuffed peppers even though Ava hated them. Chicken parm. Both Adam and Ava liked it, but it was something Manny would never eat. Stew? Stuffed pork chops? In the end, she decided on the stuffed pork chops, twice-baked potatoes, and her special hot bacon and brussels sprouts for the vegetable. She'd make enough for Pete and Nan. Maybe a peach cobbler for dessert. She had plenty of peaches she'd frozen when they were in season because peaches were her favorite fruit. She felt relieved that her dinner menu was settled.

Mary set all the frozen foods to thaw on the counter. She couldn't cook until later, so she wondered what she was going to do in the meanwhile. Sit and think? Pray some more? Build up the fire and watch the morning talk shows? Or perhaps she should just go back to bed and hope for sleep since she'd been awake all night. All of the above? Maybe what she should do was build up the fire and just sit and think. About the past, the present, and the future. No matter how painful the reflections were.

So that's what Mary Macklin Carmichael did. She built up the fire, picked up Winnie, and settled herself into her favorite chair. Winnie's soft purring was like a soothing balm, and before Mary knew it, she was sound asleep.

As his mother dozed off, Adam finished explaining to his old friend about the trouble he was in.

Sam Andover was a short man as opposed to Adam, who was six foot two inches tall. Sam was round but light on his feet. He had a nimbus of gold curls on his head that he hated; clear, sharp, piercing blue eyes; and a beatific smile. He hated his deep dimples as much as he hated his blond curls. The only advantage of his looks was that opposing counsel almost always underrated him, a mistake they made only once.

Adam knew for a fact that Sam could have had a job with any of the big white-shoe firms upon graduation from law school, but he said he wanted a life and not just billable hours. He was in a two-man firm with all the business he and his partner could handle. The kind of business that allowed him to go home by six to have dinner with his family, a family he loved and adored.

"And you're just coming to me now? What's wrong with you, Adam? Didn't you trust me? You are in some serious shit here, my friend."

"And you think I don't know that? I do. That's why I'm here. So, let's go, I'm ready to turn myself in. Everything I have in the way of proof is in my backpack. I'm leaving it with you, along with my personal bank account. There's a check in there for you to take all the money in that account. The paperwork will prove that it is legitimate money. It's over $2 million, and you can use every penny of it defending me. So, can we go now?"

"Listen to me, you dumb schmuck. It doesn't work that way. And it will not cost you anything like the amount of money you are speaking about. Not for me or any other lawyer. All you pay an attorney for is the time they spend on your case. If it goes to trial, then it becomes expensive. But from what you are telling me, that seems unlikely since, in the worst case, you are ready to plead guilty. But talking about trials and jail is getting way ahead of ourselves.

"This is what happens. I go to them. I try to cut a deal. We might get lucky. I will try for immunity since you're blowing the whistle. I never saw anyone so hell-bent on going to prison. At least let me take a stab at it. I know some guys at the FBI, and I have two really good friends in enforcement at the SEC. I'm not saying I can pull off a miracle here, but at least let me try.

"And I don't want your damn money, Adam. I want to help you because you're my friend and godfather to two of my kids. I'm going to try to cut a deal, if only because I do not like the idea of my children's godfather being in jail. But you're not going to get off the hook. You need to know that going in, Adam. One way or another, there will be consequences for you. It's the *other* that I'm going to work on. Just tell me one thing. Why?"

"He was my father. At first I was blinded by all the money and what money could buy. From the very beginning, I could see how much money there was, but I knew that money is not the answer to happiness and my needs were always fairly modest. Sure, when we were in college, at least the last year or so, I lived high off the hog on my father's money. But I had no idea at that time where it came from. I had no reason to believe that he was dirty.

"When he finally got me involved with his work — his Ponzi scheme, it turned out —

I didn't spend any of the money he kept shoving my way. Yes, I took a decent salary for the work I did. But all the rest, I simply put into a separate account that I never touched, even if I had to pay taxes on the interest. And once I was there for a while, I found myself in too deep, and like I said, he was my father. But I can honestly say that I never benefited from the money he stole beyond what he paid me in salary. Hell, I'm driving a twelve-year-old pickup with a first-generation Garmin GPS I bought years ago."

"I guess I can understand that. To a point. This is your lucky day, pal. I'm free today, since a trial I had scheduled has been postponed because of the recent bad weather. I'm going to go see my buddies. I want you to go home and spend time with your mother. Can you do that?"

"But I thought —"

"Don't think, Adam. That's what I'm here for. That's why I get paid the big bucks. By the way, who is your father's attorney?"

"Asa Bellamy."

Sam laughed. And kept on laughing. "I kicked that guy's ass twice in court. And then I battled their firm all the way to the Supreme Court and won my case. Don't sweat those thousand-dollar-an-hour goons.

When they go up against the U.S. Justice Department, they will get blown away like a card table in a hurricane."

Adam just stood there with a stupid look on his face.

"What? What, you didn't think I knew how to kick ass and take names later? I do. But, and this is the important thing: You are not in an adversarial legal position with your father or his lawyers. If things go as I hope, you are a government witness against your father, and the only contact you have with his lawyers is when they take your deposition and cross-examine you during a trial."

"Okay, Sam, you're the boss. As long as you're sure." He hugged his old friend, then looked deep into his eyes. "I wish I was half the person you are. I mean that, Sam."

"I know you do, Adam. Now go on, get out of here, and let me figure out how I'm going to save your ass."

When the door closed behind Adam, Sam went through Adam's backpack. Everything was there, just as he had said it was. He stuffed the binders and the stapled stacks of forms back into Adam's backpack. Then he picked up the phone and called his friend, Fred Barry Isaacson, on his personal cell phone, knowing he'd answer it. Fred was meant to be a federal agent because, as he said, his initials spelled FBI. Fred was that rare person who had a heart even though he dealt with the underbelly of society.

"Sam, what's up?"

If you only knew. "Blue Goose in forty minutes."

"Ooh, you're scaring me, Sam. I'll be there."

And that was it.

The Blue Goose was a dirty dive in a dirty alley in a dirty section of the District. There was no sign on the establishment, just a faded picture of a blue goose. It was owned by a skinny ninety-year-old lady from Poughkeepsie who had made her fortune in bottled water that she sold for ten bucks a pop. While the Blue Goose sold food that was inedible and liquor that was watered down to the nth degree, it was reported by those in authority that the lady from Poughkeepsie was a multimillionaire. When people questioned how that was possible, it was explained that anyone entering the dive had to spend at least ten dollars. The lady from Poughkeepsie was happy to sell bottled water for ten bucks a pop, and her customers obliged. Most times, the bottles were never opened and just recycled.

The Blue Goose was known far and wide in Washington circles. It was the best-kept secret in town that everyone knew about. Congressmen, senators, cabinet members, judges, lawyers, and all manner of snitches met there at one time or another, duded out in baseball caps, wraparound dark glasses, and scuzzy jackets. No one ever looked up, not that there were any cameras; it was just the kind of place a person didn't want to be seen in. The Blue Goose was where business that couldn't bear scrutiny was conducted.

When you left the Blue Goose, you either felt the need for not one but two showers or, at the very least, a dip in the Tidal Basin.

The old lady from Poughkeepsie laughed all the way to the bank, the sack carrying her red book of guests tucked deep inside. There were those who said the red book was worth more than all the gold in Fort Knox.

Sam hated touching the greasy door handle on the equally greasy door, but there was no other way to enter the Blue Goose. He yanked at the bill of his baseball cap, settled his Ray-Bans more firmly on his nose, bit the bullet, and opened the door. The dump was full of people whispering to one another, water bottles all over the place. Sam had his ten-dollar bill in hand, accepted the cold bottle, and looked around for his friend. It was hard to look around without calling attention to himself. When he felt a light touch on his arm, he moved off with Fred toward the back of the long, narrow room.

Fred Barry Isaacson, Mr. FBI himself, was tall and broad shouldered. He had a narrow waist and a runner's legs. He wore a buzz cut that was starting to go gray at the temples. His face was chiseled, and his nose was a study in broken bones. He had a lopsided grin that could lull you into a nice quiet frame of mind or cause terror to run through your veins. "Get to it, Sam. I don't want to spend one more minute in this shit-hole than I have to. Talk. Now!"

Sam obliged. When he wound down, he broke the rule and looked up at the stupefied expression on Fred's face.

"Are you going through some life crisis, Sam? Is Patty cheating on you? What the hell are you telling me?"

"Well, Mr. Super Agent Isaacson, what I'm trying to tell you is to believe in me, help me out here, and you stand a shot at going up the food chain to maybe Director of the FBI. What I'm about to give you will put you right on top."

"You're crazy. Who said I wanted to be the Director of the FBI anyway?"

"You did, you big jerk. More than once, as a matter of fact. Granted, you were drunk, but when someone is drunk, they say things they mean."

"The answer is no. *NO!* Don't give me that crap again that this is a hypothetical. Who is your damn client? I want to know."

Sam's plump chest puffed out. His dimples deepened. "Sorry. It's hypothetical until you agree to my terms. Take it or leave it, Mr. FBI."

"Stop calling me that, Sam. I could haul your ass, right now, across to the Hoover Building and hold your ass for seventy-two hours. I can lose your paperwork and keep holding you until I find it. Think about that, *Pudgy*!"

Sam knew he had him right then. He could feel it in his bones. Fred never called him Pudgy until he was ready to cave. "Try it! I'll just put in a call to Lizzie Fox to hop right up here to help defend me. You really want to go there, Fred?"

Fred was so wired up, he actually removed the cap from the water bottle. Crap. He set it down on a fly-crusted table. He knew Sam would do just what he said. He'd learned the hard way a long time ago that the pudgy lawyer never made idle threats. The director was going to piss green at the mention of the legendary lawyer Lizzie Fox. That alone would put him in Sam's corner. Still, he had to posture and bluff to save face. "Don't push me, Sam."

Sam ignored him. "This is what you're going to do. You're going back to your office, you're going to run everything I told you past your section chief, who will then run it past his boss, who will carry it to the assistant director, who will beat feet to the director's office, who will then get back to you and you to me. By four this afternoon or the deal is off the table. Capisce?"

"I'm not doing that! There is no way in hell I'm doing that. You think your client should get immunity! What the hell planet are you living on, Sam? After all he's done, you want a walk! Man, you are one sick puppy."

"I didn't say he was guilt free. He is guilty. But he never actually took any of the money that was illegally generated. What was thrown to him is still in a separate account. And, yes, he even paid taxes on the account's earnings, so do not go there. I just don't want prison time for him. You can give him a hundred years of community service, make him give speeches to college students on the greed and wicked ways of Wall Street. Give him house arrest for twenty years, I don't care. No prison time. You take all the illegal money — he hasn't spent a cent of it, as I told you. And he has $2 million in money he earned honestly from investing with his own capital. He's blowing the whistle, so you can nab the big Kahuna. And then you get to be director down the road. Remember, he knows where all the bodies are buried. Well, maybe not all of them, but I think it's safe to say quite a few. And if the consequences of his actions do not include forfeiting his own money, you get to save half of the fee you would have to pay him as a whistleblower.

"Don't even think about going there, Fred. I know you guys pay off whistle-blowers, but my guy is willing to forgo half the fee, which is probably in the tens of millions, if he can keep his own honestly acquired money. How else is he going to live out the rest of his life, which will be ruined once he talks? He won't be able to get a job anywhere — you know it, and I know it. So, how much is the fee for something like this? I can find out on my own if you're too shy to tell me. Like I said, win-win!"

"Win, my ass! It's $7 million," Fred said through clenched teeth, "so by taking only half in exchange for keeping his own $2 million, he leaves $1.5 million on the table. And if I don't do what you want?"

"Then you and your fellow agents can spend the next five years chasing your tails trying to run the others into the ground. Think about all that bad publicity, to which I will personally be contributing. Four o'clock, buddy."

Sam yanked at his baseball cap and headed toward the door. He didn't look back.

The minute he stepped outside, he realized that what everyone said was true: he desperately wanted to take a shower. He would have danced a jig, but he knew Fred was watching from the doorway. He knew in his gut that Mr. FBI was on his cell phone.

Next stop, the satellite offices of the Securities and Exchange Commission here in D.C., and his friend Sinclair Bonaventure. That was going to be a walk in the park. He only hoped he didn't smell like the Blue Goose.

Sam debated with himself as to whether he should call Adam or wait until he left the SEC offices. He knew his old friend was tormented, but a little wait certainly wouldn't hurt him. He felt pleased with himself as he looked around for a trash can to dump the baseball cap and sunglasses. He wanted no more reminders of the Blue Goose and the number he had pulled on Fred about the money. Just because Adam was willing to walk away with nothing more than the shirt on his back did not mean that Sam had to stand by and let him do so.

Chapter Twenty

Dennis West tried his best to make himself invisible, but it wasn't working.

"You might as well tell us what's going on, Dennis," Maggie said, her eyes narrowed into slits.

"Or I can beat it out of you. Then Espinosa and I will bury your body in all that snow out there in Maggie's backyard. You won't be found till the spring thaw. Spit it out, youngster!"

"Okay, okay. I don't think it's a secret anyhow. I didn't say anything because I wasn't sure. I'm driving Manny Macklin out to Pinewood. Myra and Annie are cooking dinner for him. It's to . . . soften him up, I guess. Originally, Macklin was going to invite them to Olympic Ridge, but Myra and Annie vetoed that. At my suggestion, I might add. It always helps to operate on your own turf. Right or wrong?"

"And here I thought you just scooted off

to get out of shoveling snow," Maggie groused. "What else haven't you told us? Don't even think about holding out on us, either."

Dennis spilled his guts. The others nodded their approval.

"So, that leaves us . . . where?" Espinosa asked fretfully.

"Look, I told you everything I know. I have to leave to get ready because I'm supposed to pick Macklin up at his office. He said he'd be waiting out front. I want to give myself plenty of time so I'm not late getting to Pinewood."

"Hold on, kid. What else went down today?"

"Oh, you mean Myra and Annie's going to see the first Mrs. Macklin?"

Ted grabbed the young reporter by his shirt collar and swung him around. "Are you telling us you didn't think that was important?"

"I did tell you at the restaurant. You were sitting right there with the guys. Don't pretend you didn't hear me either."

Ted almost choked when Maggie did an about-face and zeroed in on him. "And what was *that* meeting all about? The one you didn't see fit to tell me about." Maggie erupted then like a seething volcano. *"SIT!"*

she bellowed.

"I can't do that. Sit, I mean. I have to follow orders, and Annie *is* my boss. I have to leave now, or I'll be late. Ted can fill you in," Dennis said as he ran for the door as if the Furies of Hades were chasing him. The arctic air blasting him felt like a balm after Maggie's seething eruption. He raced to the curb and climbed behind the wheel of his car, which was double parked. No ticket. Great. He pulled onto the narrow road and drove as fast as traffic would allow. The dashboard clock said it was 3:50. If nothing else interfered with his plans, he should arrive at Pinewood right on schedule.

Across town, Sam Andover's secretary opened his door and said, "Sam, there's an FBI agent out in the waiting room to see you. He said his name is Fred Barry Isaacson."

Sam grinned from ear to ear. "I do so love it when the Federal Bureau of Investigation sends one of its finest for a chat. Show him in, Irene, and if it isn't too much trouble, could you make us some of that hazelnut coffee you like so much?"

"For you, Sam, anything. How about a raise while you're in such a complimentary mood?"

"I'll think about it. Does he look pissed or

jubilant?"

"The former." His secretary giggled as she closed the door.

"Well, hey there, Mr. FBI. Been a few hours since we spoke. You're looking a little worse for the wear. Did a round or two with the higher-ups, eh? Not to worry. When this is all over you'll be the new director. You can count on it," Sam said expansively.

"Have a seat, my friend. Coffee is on the way. Small talk first? The weather? I see it's flurrying out there again. What a crappy start to the winter season. Don't you agree? And Christmas is still weeks away."

"Stuff it, Sam. Okay, you have a deal. I can't say at this time what your guy's punishment will be, but you said you were okay with anything but prison time. I got that right, didn't I?"

"Well, you did, but within reason. You're going to have to do better than that. We're not signing off on something that is so up in the air. Sending him to live in an igloo in Alaska is not in the cards. I'll go with a ball park, but we need something in writing."

"Not till you give us a name. It's Macklin, isn't it?"

"Yep. My client is his son, Adam. Is his personal bank account in the clear?"

"If you have the paperwork to back it up,

then yeah, it's in the clear."

"The whistle-blower fee?"

"It comes to $7 million, half of which is $3.5 million, so he ends up with $5.5 million if everything checks out. That has to be on the QT. We good on that, Sam?"

"We are absolutely clear on that, Fred."

"The director wants you to swear under oath that you will not — I repeat, will not, in any way, shape, or form — bring Lizzie Fox into this mess. I think he wants it in blood. Yours."

Sam doubled over laughing. In spite of himself, Special Agent Isaacson grinned. "The minute I mentioned her name, you had the director in the palm of your hand. He would have agreed to anything. You got yourself a sterling deal here. That's between us, Pudge."

"When can we expect his share of the whistleblower's fee?" Sam asked.

"After the first sit-down interrogation, which is scheduled for noon tomorrow at the Hoover Building. The director himself will be doing the interrogation. It goes without saying that you are invited. So, hand it all over. He wants to go through everything before tomorrow's meeting."

"I'll have my secretary make copies of everything for you. It's all in the backpack on the sofa. I keep the originals."

"Fair enough. You said something about coffee."

The words were no sooner out of his mouth than Sam's secretary entered the room, carrying a handsome silver tray with fine bone china cups and saucers.

"Irene, take everything in the backpack and divvy it up among the paralegals and make copies for Mr. Isaacson. Try to speed it up. He needs to take it back to the Hoover Building to his boss."

"Just one copy?"

"No, make three copies. The originals go in the safe, along with the backpack.

"What's your game plan, Fred?"

They were just two old friends then, even though they were on opposite sides of the law. In the end, they both knew right would win out and both could walk away with their heads high.

"Not sure. We'll know better after tomorrow's meeting. I think the director wants to strike hard and fast. Before the bastard can take off for parts unknown."

"You should put a tail on him starting right now."

"They're working on it. The director said he should have his best team good to go by six tonight. By the way, how'd it go with

Sinclair at the SEC?"

"No sweat. They're on it, too. He said you were on his list to call. They're swamped over there. He wants the three of us to go to lunch next week. I told him you'd call him, and he's buying. You need to make nice, Fred. You get his jockeys in a knot, and he'll go down another road."

"Damn, I hate prima donnas, and he's one of the biggest ones I know. The guy is so full of himself, he makes me cringe."

"He's a bloodhound is what he is, and a hell of a first baseman. You're just ticked that you got called out when you slid into first."

"Yeah, yeah, yeah."

"So, how's the wife and kids?"

"Sue dyed her hair, said it was time to see if blondes really do have more fun. The twins just got braces. Tommy broke his arm a month ago. He tripped over a bale of hay when we went pumpkin picking at Halloween. Seth got expelled for three days for calling some girl a name that rhymes with witch at school. But after I met the parents, I couldn't punish the kid anymore because the whole family is nutsy cuckoo. Sue was pretty upset, but I wasn't. How are Patty and the kids?"

"Good. Everyone is good. Patty's parents

are coming for Christmas. I am not looking forward to that."

"Know what you mean. Sue's parents came for Easter and forgot to go home. They finally left after Memorial Day."

"Guess that takes care of the small talk," Sam said, pouring more coffee into both their cups. "Just out of curiosity, Fred, what happens if you can't reel Macklin in? What if he slips through and takes off?"

Fred shrugged. "You know better than to ask me something like that. I do have a question for you, though. Do you really believe in your client, that he was a victim like you said?"

"I do, Fred. You'll agree, too, after his interrogation. I told you from the beginning that he wasn't innocent and deserves to be punished. Who the hell knows if you or I wouldn't have done the same thing he did? The good thing is, he finally wised up. It's pretty damn hard to turn on your father, especially if it involves turning him in to the law. That's my opinion. When he came to me, he was expecting to go to prison that day. That has to say something for him.

"You didn't say anything about the sister. You putting a tail on her, too? She is the chief compliance officer. Adam says she knows everything and is totally loyal to her father. But I already told you that, didn't I?"

"Yep, you did, and yes, we're going with the whole ball of wax. The director is out for blood."

Further small talk ground to a halt when Irene walked into Sam's office with a dark brown accordion-pleated file. She handed it to Fred and left the office.

"Treat that file like the Holy Grail, Fred. It's all you've got for now."

"Yeah, I will. Hey, Pudge, thanks."

"Anytime, Mr. FBI. Anytime. Always remember, we're the good guys."

Sam looked at the clock on the wall. Time to wind down and head for home. He wondered what Patty was making for dinner. He felt warm all over when he thought about Patty, who was the love of his life, and the kids he couldn't wait to see. But first he had to call Adam and tell him they had a deal. He closed his eyes for a moment to try to picture his friend's face when he gave him the news. Today was a good day. A really good day. Even better than a really good day.

Life was good.

Chapter Twenty-One

Emanuel Macklin dressed nattily in an outdated polyester suit, with a collarless gray shirt that was actually white, along with a spot-stained Target tie, and exited a run-down building where he leased a one-bedroom, one-bath apartment that he rarely stayed in. Rarely because he hated the ugliness of it. He liked fine things, expensive things, but the apartment and its location was all part of the persona he had cultivated, as well as the game he had spent years playing, and he was the only one who knew the rules. It worked for him. He carried a briefcase that looked to be as old as the barren shade trees that lined the streets. One side of the case was held together with gray electrical tape that was curling loose at the edges. Something to indicate that the case got a lot of use. Again, the briefcase was part of his persona and the game.

Back at Olympic Ridge, he had a ten-thousand-dollar ostrich briefcase he used when he was dealing with billionaires. Or when he went abroad and wanted to make an impression. He'd packed the inside of the worn and battered case with everything he would need to seal the deal with Dennis West's quirky aunts.

Macklin looked down at his feet, at the old-fashioned galoshes that he'd found in a secondhand store years ago. They were ugly and patched with noticeable rubber squares, but he had to admit they did keep his feet dry. All part of his persona. And also part of the game.

He trudged to the curb, the heavy rubber boots weighing him down, and hailed a cab to take him to Adam's office, where he was to meet his daughter, Ava. He looked up at the gunmetal gray clouds scudding across the sky, at the flurrying snow that never seemed to end, as he settled himself in the cab and fastened his seat belt against his wide girth. He sighed.

Something wasn't right — he could feel it in his bones — and it wasn't just Adam thumbing his nose at him. He was thinking more than he should about his ex-wife, Adam and Ava's mother, which then turned his thoughts to Marie and Sally. As always, he wondered where they were and what they were doing since he had left their lives so many years ago. He always felt sad, guilty, and unhappy when he thought of his two best friends from childhood. He warned himself not to go down that road again. Instead, he stared out the window at the snowflakes swirling about. He knew that if he stared at them long enough, he would zone out and fall asleep. He gave himself a hearty shake to bring himself back to the here and now. He needed to be wide eyed and bushy tailed.

Fifteen minutes later, the cab pulled as close as it could to the piled-up snow at the curb. Macklin handed the driver a twenty-dollar bill for the $18.50 cab ride and told him to keep the change. A big tipper he was not.

Macklin looked down at the Timex watch with the black plastic band he'd bought in a Rite Aid drugstore years ago. Back at Olympic Ridge, he had a custom-crafted hundred-thousand-dollar Rolex encrusted with diamonds that he only wore when he carried the ostrich briefcase. He decided that he had time for coffee before heading up to the office to go head to head again with his greedy, mouthy, disrespectful daughter and still have a few minutes left over before it was time to meet Dennis West outside the building. He looked around and saw a diner that he considered a greasy spoon and headed that way.

While Macklin was ordering his coffee, Ava Macklin was spewing hatred at her brother over her cell phone. "You bastard! Tell me you didn't do that! Tell me you're just yanking my chain! Did our mother put you up to that to get even with Daddy? Damn you, Adam, do you realize what you've done? Well, are you going to say something or not? Daddy's on his way here right now."

Ava cringed when she heard her brother's laughter on the other end of the phone. "If you shut that mouth of yours long enough for me to answer, I will be happy to address your questions. By your standards, I suppose I am a bastard. I did do *that.* At 9:00 this morning to be precise. No, I am not yanking your chain. No, *our* mother did not put me up to anything. As far as Pop is concerned, he's just someone Mom used to know. Of course I realize what I've done. Now I can sleep at night. Now I can take a deep breath and not worry about the FBI or the SEC dragging me off and slamming me in prison. In case you aren't getting what I'm saying, Ava, I blew the whistle on all of us and cut my own deal. You know how it goes: I told them where all the bodies are buried. At least the ones I know about. I told them you and Pop could fill in the rest of the blanks. I asked you if you wanted to go with me yesterday, and you took off like a scalded cat. I really could not care less anymore what happens to you and Pop. I really, truly, absolutely do not. So, if we're done here, I'm hanging up. Oh, one more thing for you to think about. All those reports Pop showed us about hiring a private eye to track down Mom. Well, that never happened. Do you hear me, Ava? He lied to us: That never happened. He filled out all those bogus reports himself. Pop never tried to find Mom because he could not have cared less about her walking out. As long as she did not want any of his precious money, he was obviously glad to get rid of her. The only downside to her leaving, according to him, was that he had to hire a housekeeper. He admitted all this to me — to my face. Chew on that, little sister."

"You son of a bitch! How dare you —" The rest of whatever Ava was going to say in her tirade was cut off when she realized she was spewing her venom to dead air.

Ava bounced out of Adam's rickety chair and started pacing the dusty office. What the hell was she doing here anyway? She needed to leave, to breathe some fresh air so she could *think.* She really needed to think. She knew her brother well enough to know he'd done exactly what he said he'd done. He was looking out for himself. Selfish bastard. She couldn't even begin to imagine what her father was going to say when she told him what Adam had done. For sure, he'd go nuclear. More to the point, what was *she* going to do? Get her own house in order, of course. Hire the best attorney money could buy. Money. She knew how it worked. The first thing they'd do would be to freeze all her bank accounts. Then where would she get the money to pay a top-dollar lawyer? Her friends, if they were actually friends and not merely hangers-on, would shun her. They wouldn't let her in the tony health club anymore. Her hairdresser and masseuse would refuse to deal with her because they wouldn't want the exposure. Facials would be something to dream about in the future. She'd be shunned everywhere. They'd take her cars, her furs, her jewelry. She'd be left with dark roots showing, straggly eyebrows, and zits on her face.

Ava started to cry. This couldn't be happening. It was all a bad dream, and she was going to wake up any second now. She pinched her arm. It hurt, and she yelped. This was no dream, and she was wide awake. The word *nightmare* came to mind.

Suddenly, Ava couldn't breathe. She struggled, knowing she was in the midst of a full-blown panic attack. The same kind of attacks she'd had when her mother had left so many years ago. She bolted from the office, ran down the steps, and literally crashed through the grimy lobby door. She took a deep breath and sucked in snowflakes. They felt good on her parched throat. That's when she realized it was snowing again. She'd had plans to go to St. Barts this weekend on the company's private jet. She'd invited six friends, and now she was going to have to cancel the trip and concoct some lie to her friends. Friends who would no longer be her friends once her world came tumbling down around her. She had to get back to New York so she could clean out her bank accounts and take all her jewelry out of the safe-deposit box. And put it where?

"I hate you, Adam, for doing this to me. I hope you rot in hell. Forever and ever, you selfish bastard." She was sobbing. People on the street were looking at her, but she didn't care. She saw her father then, walking toward her. He looked like such a mess, but he always looked like a mess. She wondered what her mother looked like these days. Probably a lot better than her father, but her father was filthy rich, so it didn't matter what he looked like. Her thoughts were like a runaway train she couldn't control, and she was standing right on the tracks. *Splat!*

"What's wrong, Ava? Why are you standing out here in the cold crying? Isn't the heat working?"

"You want to know what's wrong? Well, Daddy dearest, let me tell you what your son just did. Then you'll know why I'm crying. I'm not even crying, I'm bawling. There's a difference. Not that you care."

"Not here, Ava. Let's go up to the office. You know better than to act like this in public. Not another word until we're behind closed doors. I won't tell you again. Turn around and go through the door." The ring of steel in her father's voice told Ava she would be wise to follow his instructions.

Once they were in Adam's office, with the door closed and bolted, she let loose. She enjoyed the look of horror on her father's face. "Okay, now you know as much as I know. I'm outta here. I'm going back to New York to try to salvage something, so I'm not living on a park bench."

"Ever the drama queen. You'll do no such thing. In fact, I'm taking you to dinner to clinch a megadeal. I'm sure our hostesses won't mind another table setting. Meat loaf is a meal that can be stretched." Macklin looked at the Timex on his wrist. "We have ten minutes until my soon-to-be client picks us up. Go into the bathroom and wash your face. That's an order, Ava, not a suggestion."

Ava turned around and walked into an ugly bathroom with a hundred pipes hanging from the peeling walls. She splashed cold water on her face and looked around for a towel or paper towels, but there were none. She used toilet paper and gagged as she did it. She thought about her own beautiful tile bathroom with the monogrammed, thick, thirsty, pristine white towels back in New York.

Once again in Adam's office, she stared at her father. "Did you understand what I just told you, Daddy?" Her voice was calmer now, almost resigned.

"Yes. My son, your brother, is a traitor. I refuse to give Adam another thought. We'll deal with any fallout when it happens. It's not like we haven't been investigated before. We have, and our attorneys have always handled the matters satisfactorily. This time is no different. If your brother is so desperate to go to prison, let him. Now, let's get downstairs, so young Dennis West can take us out to McLean to finalize the megadeal I was telling you about earlier.

"I want you to act sweet and demure. Do not mouth off the way you usually do. I want you to be complimentary on the food, polite and effusive about the ladies' culinary endeavors. You can speak when I ask you a direct question. The ladies might like seeing a knowledgeable female dealing with large sums of money. More than anything, be respectful. Do you understand me, Ava?"

"Fine, but the minute we get back, I want to be dropped off at the airport. I don't care if I have to sit there all night to wait for a flight. Do you understand that, *DAD*?"

Right then, Ava would have agreed to anything just to get out of Adam's office. A dinner was just a dinner. And then she could go back to New York and make her own plans. As smart as she knew her father was, he was also stupid, in her opinion. There was no doubt in her mind that if it benefited him, he'd kick her under the bus. The deal, the con, was a way of life for him and took precedence over anything else. Just the way he wasn't giving Adam another thought because he'd already moved on to the con he was going to execute with two old ladies and some dumb young guy who had inherited close to a billion dollars, with a B. She didn't need to hear the words spoken aloud; what wasn't said was more meaningful, which was that it was every man for himself. Or in her case, every woman.

Outside, in the gray gloomy day, it was colder than it had been a short while ago. The temperature must have dropped at least ten degrees. Ava could hardly believe that her father was discussing the weather given what she'd just told him. She wished she was a child again, so she could run to her room; grab Mitzi, her old rag doll; and burrow under the covers, all the while sucking her thumb. She'd been safe back then. Now she was teetering on a precipice, if what Adam had told her was true, and there was no reason to think Adam would lie to her. *Do-gooder* Adam was what she and her father had both called him. She felt sick and wondered how she would be able to eat a dinner she knew she wouldn't like.

A large white van with the words WASHINGTON POST in bright red letters on the side panel pulled to a stop in front of the building. Dennis hopped out and walked around to the front, shook Macklin's hand, then waited to be introduced to Ava. Then he shook her hand, too. "Is she coming with us?" he asked bluntly. "If so," he said, worry etching his features, "I need to call my aunts to set another plate. They don't . . . ah . . . like to be surprised."

"No problem, young man. Go ahead and call. If it's inconvenient, Ava can take a cab to the airport. She lives in New York. I just thought it would be good to have another female in attendance, one who knows the business. Women relate to other women," Macklin said in his sweet, syrupy voice.

Macklin and his daughter stood shivering on the curb while Dennis pressed numbers on his cell phone. He turned his back when he started speaking. When he turned around he said, "They said it's okay. More than okay, actually. They are really looking forward to meeting your daughter. My aunts do not have any nieces, only nephews. You have no idea how many times they have spoken about how nice it would be to have a niece." As usual, Dennis was babbling again to cover his nervousness.

Macklin beamed his pleasure. Ava scowled as she climbed into the back of the van. Her father sat up front with the young reporter.

Dennis waited for a break in traffic and pulled out slowly. His wipers whipped across the windshield in a frenzy as they battled the swirling snow. He wondered if there would be any kind of serious accumulation. He didn't like driving in snow. And he didn't like driving this big van either. But he had his instructions from Annie, and he was wise enough to know you didn't ever argue with your boss. His thoughts were so scattered that he didn't see the black Lincoln Navigator belonging to Joe Espinosa two cars behind him.

While Ava sulked in the backseat, Manny Macklin realized that his young driver was nervous. It bothered him that a young man like Dennis was so uptight when he'd just inherited a fortune. He should be on top of the world, babbling about what he was going to do with all his money. For all his talk about his aunts, Macklin couldn't help but wonder if they would be the ones who controlled the purse strings when it came to the boy's money. Did they intimidate the youngster?

Whatever it was, it was unnerving to Macklin. "Tell me a little about your aunts, Dennis."

"Ah . . . what do you want to know? They're my aunts. I like them. Actually, I love them. They're . . . ah . . . sweet ladies."

"I'm sure they are. What do they do? Do they work, do they have hobbies? You never said how old they are. Not that age makes a difference. Some people can be old at forty and some people who are forty act like they're seventy. I suppose it's a mind-set. I was never able to figure that out."

What to say, what not to say? Dennis felt his mind go into overdrive. "They travel some. They do some volunteer work sometimes. Did I say they travel? They do. They sit on some boards." *Ooops, oh shit.* He realized right then he wasn't cut out for this cloak-and-dagger stuff even though he sort of, kind of, enjoyed it.

"They sit on boards?" Ava and Macklin said at the same time. "What does that mean?"

"I don't know. I just know they do. They don't work."

"Well, that's a good thing. That means they don't have to worry about finances in their advancing years," Macklin said, trying to keep the excitement from showing in his voice.

Dennis decided right then that since he had already put his foot in his mouth he might as well go for his whole leg. "They don't have a financial worry in the world. As a matter of fact, they're rich."

"How rich?" Ava asked sweetly.

Here we go, Dennis thought to himself.

"Rich enough that they don't ever have to worry about money, that's for sure. Is it important for you to know that?" He hoped he looked as stupid as he sounded.

"Well, yes and no. It's important that they give you sound advice and that you follow that advice. Do they have financial people they trust?"

"I guess so. I never asked."

"Did they inherit their fortunes?" Macklin asked in what he hoped was a disinterested tone of voice.

"I guess Annie did. She's the second richest woman in the world. Well, she was second last year, she might be first this year. My auntie Myra is a candy heiress. She's almost as rich as Annie. They argue over it all the time. Oh yeah, you asked me what they do. They spend hours counting their money. They even have a board game they made up."

Macklin almost choked at the reporter's words. He coughed so hard, his daughter had to pound him on the back. He was so dizzy with what he was hearing, he thought he was going to black out.

"That's really interesting, isn't it, Ava?" Macklin finally said when he got his tongue to work.

"What I think is interesting is that Annie

owns this big casino in Las Vegas," Dennis said. "I love to gamble. Within reason, of course. Auntie Myra got so jealous over that, she went out and bought a whole island and set up her own gambling paradise. She flies high rollers out there twice a day. Don't get the idea the two of them fight, they don't. It's all a big game between the two of them. I need to warn you, they think they can cook, but they really can't, so do me a big favor and pretend you like dinner." Damn, this was like leading the lambs to a slaughter. He wasn't sure how he felt about that thought.

Ava almost fainted in the backseat.

"Of course," Macklin said as he fought off another wave of dizziness.

"We're almost there. See that marker, that's the beginning of Auntie Myra's land. She has over a thousand acres. The land to the east belongs to Auntie Annie. She has a thousand acres herself. All undeveloped except for their houses and outbuildings. They have some pretty impressive neighbors, but I can't remember all of them right now except for Judge Easter. Her husband used to be the Director of the FBI. Judge Easter was a federal judge. She's my godmother," Dennis lied.

"How exciting for you," Ava cooed from

the backseat.

"Yeah, I guess," Dennis mumbled. He looked into his rearview mirror and swallowed hard. Was that Joe Espinosa behind him? He deliberately slowed down and watched the Lincoln Navigator slow behind him. Crap! He speeded up, and so did the Navigator. He'd have all the proof he needed if the Navigator followed him at the turnoff. It would be totally dark in a few minutes, and the big van would be just a dark blob except for the headlights. Surely if it was Espinosa, Ted, and Maggie, they wouldn't follow him onto the private road that led to Pinewood but would wait until he was out of sight. They had the code to the gate. They could drive through without headlights and stake out the place. The question burning in his mind was why? Did Annie and Myra send for them for backup? Should he say something to the ladies? Damn, he hated curveballs.

"We're almost there. A quarter mile down the road is the entrance to Pinewood. It's beautiful out here in the spring and summer." Dennis could hardly believe how squeaky his voice sounded. Kind of like one of those chipmunks in that crazy cartoon he'd watched when he was a kid.

"I imagine it is," Macklin said smoothly.

"I think it's gorgeous even now, with all the snow," Ava purred.

Dennis risked a glance in his rearview mirror. He liked pretty girls and beautiful women, but the person in the backseat was neither. Ava Macklin looked like something that should be in Madame Tussauds wax museum and reminded him of a sleek panther ready to strike, fangs bared. She smiled, and Dennis felt his insides start to shrivel. He wouldn't ever want to be on the receiving end of whatever she doled out.

"We're here." Dennis slowed as he made the right-hand turn. The Navigator roared on past. He relaxed. "The driveway is a mile and a half long, so be patient. We're right on schedule, too."

Macklin stared out into the darkness. His brain whirled and twirled. Two thousand acres of prime real estate right in the middle of horse country between the two aunts was probably the equivalent of his crown jewel, and if he had to guess, he would guess that both parcels were free and clear and not mortgaged to the hilt the way Olympic Ridge was.

For sure the gods of something or other were smiling on him.

Adam Macklin felt the same way his father

did. The moment his attorney stopped speaking, he was convinced that God had smiled on him. Not gods of something or other but the Supreme Being. He felt his mother, who was standing next to him, sag. He reached out to put his arm around her. "I don't know how to thank you, Sam."

"Hey, what are friends for. You did hear everything I said, right? You are *not* off the hook. Be on time tomorrow. I'll meet you there. The half of the whistle-blower fee you are to receive will go into an escrow account that I will control. You'll never get a job around here in this lifetime, but that money and your own honestly accumulated funds will see you through the rest of your life. You should have no problem, financially speaking, living on the earnings of $5.5 million. I'll let you know when you can draw on the escrow account. For now, they're going to keep this on the down low. It will hit the fan soon, though. Day after tomorrow, they're going to arrest your father and sister. No one knows where you are but me, the FBI, and the SEC. My advice is to stay under the radar until the Fibbies are done with you. You okay with this, Adam?"

"I'm okay with it, Sam. You sure you don't want to stay for dinner?"

"No, thanks. Appreciate the invitation, but

I have a rule that I eat dinner with my wife and kids no matter what."

"That's a wonderful rule, Mr. Andover. Thank you for helping my son."

Sam smiled, hugged his old friend, kissed his old friend's mother, then left the pretty little house, knowing Adam was in good hands.

Sometimes the good guys did win. Not that Adam was exactly a good guy, but he had seen the light and did the right thing. He knew in his gut Adam would never touch the whistle-blower money. If anything, he'd donate it to worthy causes. He knew that because that's what the good guys did.

"Jeez, Mom, do you believe this?"

"I do. I am so happy for you, Addy. I prayed all day long. I won't say it's a miracle, but it's close. What do you think will happen to your sister and father?"

Adam shivered. "Nothing good. He'll fight it every step of the way. He's not a believer in the two P's."

"What are the two P's, Addy?"

"Prison and penniless."

Mary had to fight to suppress a smile. "Come along, Son, it's time for dinner, but first I have to make a phone call. You can set the table if you want."

Mary walked into the den and called Pinewood. The time was exactly 5:35. She identified herself and repeated virtually verbatim all that Sam Andover had said. She then listened as Myra updated her. Mary did smile then when she broke the connection.

Before Mary made her way to the kitchen, she stopped long enough to say a prayer for her daughter. She brushed at the tears gathering at the corners of her eyes. She drew a deep breath and walked through the swinging doors that led to her bright yellow kitchen.

Life was good.

Chapter Twenty-Two

"Okay, here we are," Dennis said in a jittery-sounding voice. "Welcome to Pinewood! Hold on, Miss Macklin, and I'll slide the door open for you. Watch your step; there might be a light coating of ice under this fresh snow."

Manny Macklin let himself out and stepped gingerly down onto the snow-covered bricks that made up the courtyard. The last thing he needed now was a broken bone. He wished he could see more of this large estate. He knew it had to be gorgeous and historical as well. It was one of the things he regretted the most, that he had no background, no roots, no blood family. To his mind, the orphanage didn't count. He didn't even know if William Bailey had been his real name. Everything after the orphanage was invented, make-believe in a sense, bogus. He could have all the money in the world and never have what was surrounding him at Pinewood. A past. Something he could discover at one of the genealogy sites he had heard one could search on the Internet. He felt sad at the thought.

He shook away his disquieting thoughts and concentrated on the yellowish lighting on the side of the doorway. It looked eerie in the falling snow. Almost *Halloweenish*. Possibly an omen of some kind. He could hear barking dogs inside. It sounded like a whole pack of animals. He hated dogs and cats, probably because as children they were never allowed pets at the orphanage. What he could never have, he had learned to hate.

"Let's get this over with, Dad. Why are you just standing here like some ice statue?"

At his daughter's chiding remarks, Macklin picked up his feet and followed the young reporter. Not that he ever listened to her, but it was time to move on. Memories never worked for him, no matter where he was.

He could feel a tightness in his shoulders, and he didn't think it was from the arctic cold. The fine hairs on the back of his neck seemed to be moving. He didn't think that was from the cold either. For one wild moment, he almost turned and walked back to the van, but he took one deep breath, then another. The cold air in his lungs propelled him even closer to Dennis. And then they were inside a very large, very warm, modern kitchen. Just as the door was about to close behind him, he thought he heard the sound of a powerful engine. He actually turned to look but could see nothing past the yellowish glow the outside lights cast on the snow. The fine hairs on the back of his neck continued to dance. *Not good,* he thought as he listened to Dennis make the introductions.

Macklin smiled his most affable smile. He blinked and hoped his eyes were twinkling. He'd worked hard on that twinkle over the years. The media always somehow managed to remark on his twinkling eyes. He watched his daughter, Miss Charm herself. He relaxed and allowed the one named Annie to take his down jacket. She more or less tossed it on the clothes tree by the back door. Ava's fur-trimmed coat followed.

"It smells wonderful in here. Like my mother's kitchen used to smell."

Liar liar, pants on fire, Annie thought. She gave no indication that she knew otherwise. Emanuel Macklin, aka Billy Bailey, never knew any mother. He was an orphan.

Myra was trying to hustle Dennis to the door, but he was having none of it. "You need to go now; we can handle this," she hissed.

"I'm not leaving you two alone with those . . . those people," Dennis hissed in return.

"Yes, you are."

Annie, seeing the reporter's resistance, intervened. "This is just so sweet of you, nephew. Make sure you get back on time. Look," she said, pointing to the monitor above the door, "your friends are here to pick you up. Run along, sweetie."

"Call us, honey, if you and your friends get stuck." Myra opened the door and literally pushed Dennis out, then snapped the dead bolt so he couldn't get back in. Before the door slammed shut, Myra caught a glimpse of a black Lincoln Navigator, engine running, with its lights off. She recognized Joseph Espinosa and Ted Robinson. And even though she couldn't see her, she knew that Maggie Spitzer was in the backseat.

"Isn't the young man staying for dinner?" Macklin asked. His hand went to the back of his neck to calm the dancing hairs, which were starting to itch.

"Well, that was the original plan, but then things . . . ah . . . changed. Please sit down. Annie, pour the wine. It's an excellent vintage, a Lafite-Rothschild something or other. I'm not good on names. It's 1854, maybe 1855."

Macklin almost choked. He knew for a fact that a bottle of Lafite-Rothschild of those vintages went for around five thousand dollars a bottle. If you could even find one to buy. No way was he going to pass up this wonderful wine. He could almost savor the dark chocolate, the cherries, a faint taste of mold or wet leaves or something similar. He hoped the one named Annie would be generous when she poured the delightful vintage.

"I thought we would get more done with just the four of us. Dennis . . . well, Dennis really isn't interested in money. All he cares about is his career and getting a second Pulitzer. So, business first or after dinner?" Myra asked brightly. *What were Ted, Espinosa, and probably Maggie doing here?* From the look on Annie's face, she was wondering the same thing. A hitch? A snafu of some kind? She'd seen the startled look on Annie's face when she pushed Dennis through the door. At least they were on the same page now.

Dreading the meat-loaf dinner, Ava said, "Why don't we get the business out of the way first. Then we can enjoy your wonderful dinner. It smells marvelous, by the way."

"Ah, ever the professional" — Macklin twinkled at his daughter — "but I tend to agree. Why not get the business done first so we can enjoy dinner. Personally, I never like doing business over dinner, but that's what's done these days. Worse than that is doing business on the golf course. Dennis said you liked to do it this way, and I always try to accommodate our clients." He held out his wine flute, and Annie poured, a smile on her face. She poured just as generously into Ava's glass.

"Aren't you going to join us?" Macklin asked when he saw Annie return the bottle to the counter.

"Yes, but my sister and I only drink bourbon." Annie handed a squat tumbler to Myra and held hers up. "What should we toast to?"

"I think we should toast your nephew Dennis. May he handle his new inheritance wisely and well, with you ladies and me as backup, guiding him all the way," Macklin said.

"Wonderful, Daddy!" Ava clinked her wine flute against her father's, then against Myra's and Annie's tumblers. The two ladies watched as their guests gulped greedily. Fine wine was to be sipped.

Myra and Annie sat down. "Tell us what you think we need to know. First, though, bottoms up. She reached behind her for the priceless bottle and poured again. "Is it as delicious as the wine connoisseurs say it is?" Myra asked, feigning curiosity.

"Oh, absolutely," Ava gushed as she brought the flute to her lips for another happy pull. Macklin did the same.

Annie and Myra were like two precocious squirrels as they leaned into the table as though each word the two con artists were saying was a pearl of wisdom.

Macklin started to expound ad nauseam, with Ava adding little tidbits when she saw her father slowing down. "That sounds so interesting. And you guarantee 12 to 14 percent?"

"I do guarantee it," Macklin said, his head bobbing up and down.

"If Daddy guarantees it, then you can take it to the bank," Ava gushed.

Macklin continued to expound for another thirty minutes.

"Where do we sign, or is it Dennis who has to sign?" Myra asked. "Annie, shame on you, what kind of hostess are you? Our guests' glasses are empty."

"Young Dennis has to sign," Macklin said, looking around as though Dennis would appear out of nowhere. Annie quickly filled his glass.

"Drink up, dear," Annie said to Ava, who gulped the last of the wine.

"Well, I guess he can sign when he gets back to take us home," Macklin said happily. He couldn't be sure, but he thought he was slurring his words. Good Lord, he wasn't drunk, was he? Of course not, he'd never been drunk in his life. He was just feeling exceptionally good. He looked across the table at his daughter. He blinked when he saw two of her. *TWO AVAS!* Dear God. The world could hardly deal with one Ava. That was when he started to laugh and couldn't stop.

Myra and Annie smiled.

Ava slumped sideways in her captain's chair. If the chair hadn't had arms, she would have slid to the floor. She looked up to see her hosts smiling at her. "You bitches put something in that wine, didn't you? Daddyyyyyy!" she screeched.

"Oh, is it time to eat?" Macklin asked. He started laughing again. "Oh, for heaven's sake, Ava, be quiet. Do not give my daughter any more of that priceless wine."

"Okay," Annie said as she bent over to open the oven door. She yanked out the roasting pan and set it on top of the stove.

Myra peered over her shoulder to stare down into the pan. "I don't think meat loaf is supposed to look like this," she whispered.

"It does look kind of *loose,*" Myra said.

"It's not loose, Myra, it's *soupy.* Or is that the gravy? If it's the gravy, what happened to the meat loaf?"

Myra shrugged. "You have to admit it smells good, though. You can't go wrong with the smell of bacon, onions, garlic, and celery. Who cares, Annie, we aren't going to be eating. This is all a charade, remember?"

"You're right. I'll just dump this in the sink. You clear the table, and we can get to it. The daughter is about out, doncha think?"

"As long as she's not completely out of it. I'll make some coffee. The old geezer looks quite happy. I can't wait to squeeze him. That stuff we put in the wine is just supposed to turn their legs to jelly and render them immobile. We do need them reasonably alert so they know what's going on."

"Ooh Myra, that sounds so . . . exciting." Annie laughed.

While the coffee dripped into the pot, Myra cleared the table. When Annie joined her at the table, she looked across at Macklin, and said, "We saw what you brought to the table, and we understand everything.

Now, I want you and your daughter to see what we are bringing to the table." She looked across at Macklin's daughter and said, "Look alive here, Missy. I don't want you to miss a thing. And we are going to need some input from you."

Manny Macklin looked at all the dogs circling the table and felt uneasy. Then he looked at his daughter and the two women sitting across from him. "What do you mean?"

"What we mean is we want all your money. We want a list of all your investors, and we want your ledgers. You know, the two sets that you keep and have been keeping all these years. And we also want to know the location of whatever it is you have been renting all these years and why. We already know about the foreign accounts you have in the names of your first wife, Marie, and Sally, and all those properties you purchased in their names. We know all that, as I said. We also know your name is not Emanuel Macklin. It's Billy Bailey. We know all about Marie and Sally and how you lost them when you went to New York, how you taught them to panhandle and steal," Myra said.

The fine hairs on the back of Macklin's neck were doing their crazy dance again.

He heard the words Myra was saying, but he couldn't get his mind or his tongue to respond. He had to think. *Think,* he told himself. Was his daughter right, had these two women drugged them? He tried to move but froze in place when the big golden dog in front of him showed her teeth and growled deep in her throat. What the hell was happening to him?

"Mr. Macklin, look at me," Annie ordered. Macklin ripped his gaze from the big dog. "You and your daughter will not be leaving here tonight or anytime soon. You are going to be our guests until you give us what we want. Tell me you understand what I just said."

Ava reared up. "You're kidnapping us! You can't do that!"

"Would you like to bet on that?" Annie barked.

Myra got up and opened one of the drawers in the kitchen. She pulled out a small tape recorder and placed it in the middle of the table. "I'm going to turn this on. When I do that, you need to start talking. If you do not start talking, we will begin to inflict pain on you that will make you wish you were dead."

"Should I start to boil the water, Myra?"

"Yes, Annie, it's time to boil the water."

Ava looked around. She shook her head, trying to clear her thoughts. "Where are we?" she mumbled.

"Well, if you subscribe to Catholicism, which the media says you do, I'd say you are in limbo right this moment. That's on the border of hell, in case you haven't kept up with your religious studies."

"Daddy, did you hear that?" Ava screeched. "Why are you boiling water? I want to go home. Where's that fat kid that brought us here? Dadddyyyyy!"

Manny Macklin tried to put together what he'd heard this crazy woman say. She said she knew about Marie and Sally and that his real name was Billy Bailey. How in the hell could she know all that? They knew about the properties and the bank accounts. He knew he heard them say that. How? Even Ava and Adam didn't know about those things. He seriously doubted his first wife Mary knew either. Or did he tell her? He simply couldn't remember.

Suddenly his daughter screamed. "I know who you are!" Her glazed eyes spewed hatred, and spittle flew from her mouth. "Look at them, Daddy, they're those Vigilantes! They are! I thought I knew them from somewhere. Daddy, do something! These women make people disappear. Daddyyyyy, are you listening to me?"

Myra swatted the screaming woman alongside the head. "That's enough. Do not speak again unless I tell you to speak." She turned to Macklin and said, "Your daughter is correct, we are the Vigilantes. And yes, we do know how to make people disappear. Unless you want to become a member of that particular club, you need to tell us what we want to know. In case you don't already know this, your son Adam already cut a deal and has talked to the FBI. He's turned over everything he had in his possession to try to right all the wrongs you've done. Right now, there is a task force that has been assigned to trail you. But lucky you, or maybe not so much, we got to you first. That goes for you, too, Ava."

"Which means you are dead meat," Annie said. "Think of us now as your new best friends. Your *only* friends. Drink the coffee in front of you. I want you both to wake up a little more."

"Don't drink it, Daddy, they probably doped it up, too. You're crazy. You'll go to jail when we file charges against you."

Myra leaned over and glared at Ava Macklin. "You aren't getting it, dear. You are not leaving here. You will never go back to that wicked life you led in New York, and your father will never ever dupe another investor. You are in our hands. We are going to punish you because if we don't and leave it up to the authorities, you could stay free for a number of years with all those high-powered lawyers you both have. We can't allow that. It's not fair to all the people you've taken advantage of. They deserve to get back their money *NOW,* not years from now, if ever. Putting Bernie Madoff in jail did precious little for the people he swindled over the years. We are going to improve the odds that the same thing does not happen in your cases. The world needs to see your faces on the big screen. And they will with our help. Are you getting it now?"

Macklin got it. All of it. So did Ava. In unison, they both said, "We are not telling you anything."

"We'll see about that," Annie snapped.

"In a way, it really doesn't matter. Your son can fill in the blanks," Myra singsonged.

Macklin sat up straight. "My son only knows what I want him to know. No more, no less. Maybe you should be looking to him for nefarious deeds instead of me and my daughter. You can't keep us here."

Annie threw her hands in the air. "Mr. Macklin, did you just fall out of the stupid tree and hit every stupid branch on the way down? Didn't you hear what we just said? You are not leaving here. Is that polyester you're wearing?"

"What does it matter what I'm wearing? Are you the fashion police?" Macklin's words were still slurred but not as badly as before.

"It matters because we're going to press your suit with you still in it. Polyester will stick to your body, and you'll be burned within an inch of your life. Why do you think I'm boiling all that water? We need a lot because you're a big fat guy. I really do not see what Marie and Sally ever saw in you."

"Oh my God!" Ava yelped.

"Why are you yelping like a dog? We haven't even gotten to what we're going to do to *you.* So I'll tell you what we're going to do right now. Whoever talks first gets to walk out of here and take their chances with the Feds. You might even be able to make a getaway, depending on what kind of exit plan you have in place. Of course, I'm assuming you have an exit plan because you had to know this day was coming at some point.

"Your son was smart enough to realize it. Are you telling us he's smarter than the two of you? Or are you telling us the two of you are so greedy you actually think you're going to get away with what you've done and keep all that money you have squirreled away? Who wants to go first?" Myra asked.

Ava squirmed in her chair. "How do we know you'll keep your end of the bargain?"

"You don't, but I have to say we're a lot more reliable and dependable than the two of you. We do have a certain amount of integrity depending on the circumstances and have been known to keep our promises. Bear in mind this is not our first rodeo. Read my lips. We-are-in-control-not-you," Annie said.

Ava licked her lips as she looked at the stove, where steam from the boiling pots of water was spiraling upward.

"Ava!" Macklin said, steel ringing in his voice. Ava ignored him. She closed her eyes and took a deep breath, but she said nothing.

Manny Macklin continued to watch his daughter. He knew she'd crack — it was just a matter of time. There had to be a way out of this — a solution; he just had to find it. He'd gotten this far dancing on the edge and pulling out miracles at the eleventh hour. But he had to admit he had never been under lock and key before. Asa Bellamy's words echoed in his ears, the warning that this time was not like all those other times, when they'd managed to pull rabbits out of the hat for him.

Macklin looked at the Wolf range with the six big pots of water that were boiling. The kitchen felt wet and steamy. He tried for nonchalance and leaned back in his chair. The big yellow dog never took her eyes off him. He glared back, his gaze following Annie de Silva as she pulled something out of a kitchen drawer and plugged it into a wall outlet. The one named Myra reached in and pulled out a duplicate and plugged it into another outlet. Electric shears! He watched in horror as Annie whipped out a strip of plastic and yanked Ava's hands behind her. Flex cuffs. He heard the plastic snap into place just as his own arms were yanked behind him and secured by Myra.

Panic engulfed him when he saw Annie yank at his daughter's perfectly coiffed hair. The shears made a low, humming sound. Ava's screams were unearthly as the shears in Annie's hand took on a life of their own. When he felt his own head being pulled back, he tried to struggle. He roared his outrage at what was happening. Lady didn't like all the noise and made it known. She pounced and sunk her teeth into his fat thigh.

"Good girl, sweetie. You just hold him right there, and if he moves again, you have my permission to go for the jewels," Myra said happily. Lady's tail wagged furiously.

Frustrated with Ava's screams, Annie reached for a dish towel and gagged her. "You ready to give it up yet?" Tears rolled out of Ava's eyes like a waterfall as her long, dyed-blond thick hair carpeted the tile floor. "Done!" she chortled happily. "You are now officially bald. Shoot, I forgot the eyebrows!" Zip, zip, and Ava was browless. Annie stood back to view her handiwork. "What do you think, Myra?"

"Not even one little bit pretty. Not that she was pretty before. Perhaps you should show Ms. Macklin a mirror so she can see what she looks like, then explain the boiling water."

"That makes sense," Annie drawled as she headed off to the downstairs lavatory to return with a large, handheld mirror.

Ava Macklin fainted.

Macklin looked down at the dog holding on to his leg and decided to remain quiet. His head felt cold. These women were monsters. Evil monsters.

Annie prodded Ava with a spatula from the kitchen counter. "Wake up, Ava. You need to hear what's coming next." She turned to Myra, who was now buzzing Macklin's snow-white Santa beard. She looked down at the floor. The man had as much hair as a sheep. He looked like a bowling ball without all his hair. She also noticed that he had a weak chin and thin lips. He definitely looked better with all his hair.

"We could make a pillow with what you have and what I have," Myra said, pointing to the floor. "But then, who would want to sleep on such a pillow?"

"Not anyone I know. Okay, Goldilocks here is waking up." Annie dropped to her haunches till she was eye level with Ava. "Listen carefully. I have the feeling you're a very vain woman and care a great deal about your appearance. Here's what we have planned for you if you don't tell us what we want to know. We are going to pour the boiling water all over you. That means you will be one *HUGE* blister. Your head will scar. Same for your eyebrows. That means you will never grow hair on your head; nor will you have those well-defined eyebrows ever again. I'm not sure about your eyelashes, but I think it's safe to say they'll go the way of your hair and eyebrows. Same goes for you, Macklin. Now, who wants to tell us what we want to know?"

Macklin could no longer contain himself.

He knew Ava was going to give it up any minute. "Ava, stop and think. You can always wear a wig. You paint your eyebrows on anyway. You told me yourself you have false eyelashes and wear them all the time. You give these people what they want, and it's all over. Once we get out of here, our lawyers can fight this. Are you listening to me, Ava?"

"You bastard! Adam was right about you. I should have listened to him. Oh no, I fell for your bullshit again. No more!"

Macklin forgot he was tethered to the chair he was sitting on. He tried to lunge. Lady released her hold on Macklin's leg and followed Myra's earlier instructions, her tail swishing a mile a minute. Macklin's roar of pain and outrage ricocheted off the kitchen walls.

"Did you say I could wear a wig? Is that what you said? I should wear a damn wig? I'm not wearing a wig. Not now, not ever!" Ava turned to Myra and Annie and tried to focus her gaze. "Tell me exactly what my brother told you. I'll tell you if he's lying or not. He'd do anything to save his own skin, even throwing me and my father under the bus."

"It doesn't work that way," Myra said. "We are not here to give you answers. We're here to ask the questions. You either answer and answer truthfully, or you suffer — and I do mean suffer — the consequences." Myra pointed to the boiling, steaming pots of water on the stove. "Remember now, the FBI did not arrest your brother. He's walking around free as the breeze and enjoying his mother's company, which he was denied for so many years. I think the FBI is giving him immunity for testifying against you and your father. What that means to you is that while you languish in prison, he'll be walking around scot free."

"Not when we tell them what his role was in the company," Ava blustered. She couldn't take her eyes off the boiling pots of water on the stove.

"Ava, you obviously have a hearing problem. Your brother cut his deal with the aid of a lawyer. Everyone signed off on it. It's a done deal. No one is going to renege now. Your brother got a free go-past-Go card. He's already collected the five hundred dollars. You and your father are the ones who are going to go to jail. You missed the deadline. Adam asked you to go with him and you decided not to.

"The only chance you have is to talk to us and tell us what we want to know. Like now, my dear. We offered each of you a deal:

whoever talks first walks out of here. And yet neither one of you is taking us up on our offer," Myra said. "Now, why is that?"

Annie had the feeling the effects of the drug she'd put in the woman's drink were wearing off. She was becoming too smart, too fast with her responses.

Ava snorted. "We don't even know if you're telling us the truth. Let me call my brother. I want to hear him tell me what you just told me and my father."

"And put him on speakerphone. I want to hear what my son has to say, too," Macklin said through clenched teeth, his eyes never leaving the dog, who had her teeth locked on his groin.

Myra and Annie walked into the laundry room to confer. "What can it hurt, Myra? Let them hear it from Adam directly. It's possible they'll switch up in a heartbeat. We certainly don't have anything to lose. But I'm going to have to add some more water to those pots; a lot has evaporated."

While Annie poured more water into the pots, Myra placed her cell phone on the table and nodded.

"Remember what I said: put him on speakerphone," said Macklin.

"I can't very well do that, now can I? They have me tied to this chair," Ava snarled.

"Give me the number, and I'll call for you," Myra said. "You can lean over and speak into the phone on the table."

Ninety miles away, Adam Macklin dried the last pot his mother handed him just as his cell phone vibrated in his pocket. "I bet it's Ava!" he said to his mother. He fished the phone out of his shirt pocket, nodded to his mother, then hit TALK. He listened as his sister started to screech in his ear. "Slow down, cut the venom, and talk to me like a normal person or I'll cut you off right now." Either Ava didn't hear him or didn't believe her brother because she kept right on screeching at the top of her lungs. Adam pressed END and snapped his phone shut. He looked at his mother and said, "She'll call back, trust me."

Just as he had said, the phone rang minutes later. Ava's controlled voice was arctic cold, the venom snaking out of the phone to circle Mary's pretty yellow kitchen. "Daddy and I have been kidnapped by two crazy women and some reporter from the *Post.* We're being held in someplace called Pinewood. The women are those crazy Vigilantes. Are you listening to me, Adam? You need to call the police right now so they can come here and get us. They shaved my head and my eyebrows. They shaved all

Daddy's hair and his Santa beard. How cruel is that? Some damn dog just bit Daddy in the crotch and he's bleeding and they don't care. They said they're going to press Daddy into his polyester suit with boiling water. It's boiling on the stove. I can see it!" she screamed. "My God, they're crazy, they're going to pour the water on my head and Daddy's, too, and it will blister. I'll have to wear a wig for the rest of my life. Say something, you bastard; this is all your fault."

"Not much I can do from here. Have you looked outside? The weather has turned bad again. Only emergency vehicles are permitted on the roads. All the phone lines are tied up. Guess you'll have to wing it, Ava."

"You son of a bitch! This was undoubtedly all your idea in the first place. You're probably in cahoots with these crazy women. They said you cut a deal with the FBI. Is that true? God help you if it is."

"It's true. I did cut a deal, and the FBI agreed to no prison time for me. I am now an official whistle-blower, and you know what, Ava, it feels damn good. I'll get some fines, some kind of punishment, which I deserve. I told them everything I know, and I did not hold anything back. Nor did I try to shield you or Pop. I handed over everything I had in my possession. I even told them about that fancy-dancy two-hundred-thousand-dollar bathroom you had built for yourself with investors' money. I told them all about Pop's secret accounts.

"You know what, Ava, maybe you got lucky after all. You wouldn't do well in prison. All you get in your cell is a stainless-steel toilet without a designer seat. Actually, I understand that the toilets don't have any kind of seat. Oh, and you get a stainless-steel sink. You have to shower with the masses. No one-of-a-kind shower curtains with eighteen-carat-gold thread woven through it. One showerhead, nothing like the twenty-seven you have in yours. Everyone will see you without all that makeup you slather on your face. I always said you need to go through a car wash to get it off. I'm thinking wherever you are has to be better than that, so maybe you need to cooperate with those . . . *ladies.*"

"Are you saying you won't call the police?" Ava shrieked. *Stainless-steel toilet without a seat.*

Lady's four pups didn't like the sounds coming from Ava's mouth. They started to howl as they circled her chair, their fangs bared. Ava tried to shrink into herself as Myra calmed the dogs.

"Gee, you're smart tonight, little sister. That is precisely what I am saying." Ava could hear her brother laughing, and it incensed her even more. *No shower curtain.*

"You . . . you . . . you *pimp*!"

Determined to have the last word, Adam replied, "Well, you would know, wouldn't you. Your father has been pimping you out to investors for years, and you allowed it. Good-bye, Ava, and don't bother to call me again."

Ava's legs lashed out as she kicked at the table legs. She turned a venomous look on her father. "I guess you heard all that."

"The boy is sick. He's delusional. He's trying to turn you against me. Can't you see that?"

Ava slumped in her chair as she sobbed.

"Showtime!" Annie said. "The early bird gets the worm! Who wants to go first?" Her hand shot out to press the PLAY button on the recorder.

CHAPTER TWENTY-THREE

"Last chance!" Myra said.

Emanuel Macklin looked at the two women. He'd always been a shrewd judge of character, but these two women were from some other planet. They had no rules, that was obvious. No concocted story would fly with either of them. It was all or nothing. He wished his head weren't so fuzzy. It was hard to think with the fierce pain in his groin and the dog eyeballing him. He wondered if it was part wolf and lived for the taste of blood. His. He could feel something wet trickling down his leg. How much could he safely say to satisfy these two crazy weirdos and still walk away from this? If only he could think straight. If only a lot of things. He looked over at Ava, who looked like she'd zoned out. These women were also crazy smart. He had to accept that and the fact that they meant business. They knew how to get to Ava just the way her brother knew how — through her vanity. Which just went to show that women were inferior to men. Stupid, actually.

If he managed to walk away from this hell-hole, he'd head straight for Olympic Ridge, grab his golf bag, and beat feet. He felt a twinge when he thought about leaving his daughter behind to face the courts and the court of public opinion. He hoped she had enough money left to buy a really good wig.

"Time is money, Mr. Macklin!" Myra said.

"Get this dog off me first. Let me use the bathroom and give me some medical supplies. Show me the transportation you will provide, and we can have a serious discussion about what you want to know so badly."

"Well, that's not going to happen anytime soon, Mr. Macklin. You talk first, then we'll let you know if the information you provide works for us," Annie said. "Talk fast because I'm getting really tired of having to refill those pots on the stove."

Macklin sighed. He thought that would be the women's response, but it was still worth a try. He looked at his daughter, who appeared to be asleep. Or else she was in shock. He shrugged. Bluff. He'd always been good at that. A sweet charmer. In his gut, however, he knew there was nothing in the world that could charm these two harridans. They'd spot a lie in a nanosecond. Plus, he had no clue how much Adam had really divulged. Adam and the women could both be lying.

For the first time in his life as Emanuel Macklin, he did not know what to do. He wondered if his daughter was faking sleep? He wouldn't put it past her.

Myra risked a glance at Annie, who was starting to look concerned. It looked to her like the slick old geezer wasn't going to talk. The longer they waited, the less credibility they would have in his eyes. He'd start to think they were bluffing. Annie rolled her eyes, which meant it was time to make a decision.

"All right, Mr. Macklin, your time is up. We gave you every opportunity to help us out here."

And then it was like a lightbulb suddenly went off in Myra's head. "You know, we were actually going to give you . . . a bonus for fessing up. We were going to tell you about Marie and Sally. By the way, they're the ladies that hired us to . . . make you come to your senses. Now, I guess you'll never get to meet them. At least, not in this lifetime."

At the mention of Marie and Sally, Ava reared up. "Who?"

"Ah, Sleeping Beauty has awakened. Marie and Sally were childhood friends of your father."

Macklin was so stunned, he thought he was going to black out. "You know where Marie and Sally are?"

"We do. I told you, they hired us to go after you. They did not like the person you turned into. They told us how you all left the orphanage and how you taught them how to panhandle and steal. They said you took care of them." Myra rattled on and on, saying everything she could remember of what Sara and Tressie had told them. She finished by explaining about the fire at the rooming house and the telephone booth on the corner being demolished. "Now what do you have to say, Mr. Macklin?"

"Who are Marie and Sally? What orphanage? What are they talking about, Daddy?" Macklin ignored his daughter as he stared at the two women towering over him. They had to be telling him the truth; there was no other way in this whole wide world that they could know about the orphanage, Marie, and Sally.

Macklin cleared his throat. "Bring them here, and I'll tell you everything you want to know. But you have to agree to let the three of us walk away from here. Agree to that, and you have a deal."

"What about me?" Ava shrieked.

"What a guy!" Annie said.

"Well, that's not going to work either. Marie and Sally don't want to see you. Why else do you think they hired us? They want you brought to justice. Get the water, Annie. Start with this sterling fellow."

Ava was still shrieking, saying that if her father walked out of here, she was going, too. Myra gave her a light swat and told her to quiet down.

Annie opened the cabinet and withdrew a four-quart Pyrex measuring cup. She dipped it into the pot of boiling water, filled it, and walked over to the table. "Last chance!" Macklin squeezed his eyes shut. Myra snapped her fingers and Lady backed away to stand at her side.

Annie poured. Steam wafted upward as Macklin roared in pain.

"Don't stop now, Annie. Hit the daughter!"

Two things happened at that moment. Annie poured the boiling water over Ava's head and the kitchen door blew open to reveal Ted, Espinosa, Maggie, and Dennis, who took in the scene, their faces full of shock.

Maggie recovered first. "Looks like you've been busy. Need any help?"

"Actually, no, dear. I think we have it all under control. They were quite . . . reticent, so we had to act. We did bend over backward for them, but they couldn't see their way to cooperating. Now we'll have to get an extraction team in here to tidy up. What's the weather?"

"Bad," Maggie said, peering at Ava's bald red head. "Ooh, this is going to bubble up. Bet she's going to be scarred. Hope she has a good wig. What's up with that skank?" she said, jerking her head in Macklin's direction.

"He didn't want to cooperate. We had no other choice. He doesn't look very pretty right now," Myra said.

Espinosa clicked and clicked his camera.

Dennis grabbed hold of a chair and held on for dear life. He was as white as the snow outside. "Something wrong, Son?" Annie asked.

"Absolutely not." Oh God, everything they said about the Vigilantes was true. He needed to hold it together and think Pulitzer. He wondered if Maggie and Ted would include him on the byline. He could handle this. He wasn't a wuss.

"We need to get these two down in the dungeon. At least until we can get Avery out here," Myra said. "I just don't know how we're going to do that."

Dennis walked across the kitchen to the laundry room and looked around. He found what he was looking for behind the pantry door. He carried out a professional-looking ironing board. "Just slide them one at a time on it and we can slide it down the steps."

"Son, that is a positively brilliant solution. And one that will work. Well, boys and girls, let's get to it so we can get Myra's kitchen back to normal," Annie said. "Once we get them in the cells, we can put the antibiotic ointment on their heads. The rest will be up to Avery and his people. Not to worry, they aren't going to die." This last was said for Dennis's benefit. "The Vigilantes do not allow their targets to die," Annie added. The young reporter almost swooned at her words.

The transition from the main house to the underground dungeon did not go smoothly. Twice, Espinosa lost control of his end of the ironing board, and it resulted in Ted's slamming the board against the stone wall. They finally got the big man to his cell and dumped him on a cot loaded with blankets. He moaned and groaned. Maggie told him to pipe down or she'd gag him.

The second trip down the steep stairs went no better than the first. Ava looked like a rag doll. An ugly rag doll. When Espinosa felt the board slide out of his grip, Ted jumped to the side and the board bounced every step of the way down to the bottom. Ted shrugged as he picked up his end and, between the two of them, got Ava situated in her own cell. He eyed the toilet and sink between the two cells that Charles had installed several years ago when they had a few long-term guests. It wasn't the Ritz, but it would do.

It was left up to Maggie to smear the antibacterial ointment, using sterile gauze pads, all over father's and daughter's heads. She washed her hands, took a last look around, and headed back through the dungeon, following the sounds of the tinkling bells that Myra had installed for her young daughter years and years ago when she used to play down here with her friends.

The kitchen was back to normal, everyone sitting around the table. Coffee was dripping into the pot. Dennis was making peanut butter and jelly sandwiches for everyone.

"Did you call Avery?"

"We did. He'll be here as soon as he can. Early morning was his best guess. I gave him the addresses of every apartment Macklin has leased, Ava's apartment in New York, and the house at Olympic Ridge. With this weather, we might luck out, allowing them to clean everything out before the Feds take over."

"I can't believe those two wouldn't give it up," Ted said. "I would have sung like a canary. They've got to be in a world of pain. No amount of money is worth going through what those two just went through. No amount," Ted repeated.

Myra's cell phone took that moment to ring. The others watched her as she listened to the caller on the other end of the phone. When she finally hung up, they looked at her expectantly.

"Good news. That was Avery. He's got people already inside Ava Macklin's penthouse apartment. His people are using an ambulance, and he said he lucked out here also. He said he was closer to Olympic Ridge than here at Pinewood, so he's using ambulances out there at Olympic Ridge. He said the weather right now works for them. He said he would be inside the Ridge house in about an hour. If there's anything in there, he will find it. He couldn't give me a definite time when he would make it out here to pick up . . . ah . . . his patients."

"Who is Avery?" Dennis asked.

"Someone you don't want to know,"

Espinosa snapped.

Maggie's cell phone buzzed. She looked at the caller ID and grinned. "It's Abner." As with Myra, they all watched her as she listened to Abner. When she broke the connection, she smiled. "He's faxing a boatload of stuff. Said it's just what we need. It should come through shortly."

Myra clapped her hands. "Wonderful!"

Dennis paced the kitchen. "Will the patients be okay?"

"Yes, Son, the patients will be okay," Myra said. "Didn't you see me give them a shot of painkiller? They'll sleep through the night. I'm sure Avery will be here by morning, and he will make sure the . . . patients will receive expert medical aid. Trust me, they are not going to die. That's not to say they might not long for death. All you have to concern yourself with is that we have saved many, many people's retirement funds, erased many sleepless nights for others, and, hopefully, his secret funds will be returned to the innocent people who trusted Emanuel Macklin by believing in his lies."

"Myra, I think you should call Mary and her son and bring them up to date," Annie said. "I . . . ah . . . wouldn't go into too much detail. Just hit the high spots." Myra nodded and headed off to the laundry room to make her call.

When Myra returned to the kitchen, she said, "They both thanked us profusely. There was no joy or jubilation. Just a calm acceptance that justice is served where Emanuel and Ava Macklin are concerned."

"Where is that person Avery going to take the patients?" Dennis asked.

"We never know, Dennis," Myra answered. "And we never ask. When a mission is over, it's over. Period. We move on and put it behind us. I think that Marie and Sally, aka Sara and Tressie, can now rest in peace. That's what this was all about, Dennis. We did what they wanted, and we were successful, we did not fail. If you have any problems with any of this, now is the time to voice them."

Dennis felt his head bob up and down with no conscious thought that he himself was nodding. "I'm good."

"Then let's check the weather and go to bed. We're going to need to get up early in case Avery finds a way to get out here sooner rather than later."

And that was what they did.

At the top of the steps, Myra looked at Annie and raised her eyebrows. "Case closed, right, Annie?"

"Case closed, Myra. Now we can make

plans to go to Vegas."

"Not so quick. We need to get it all together so we can present it to the FBI in one neat package. And we want to do that at the same moment the kids get their Pulitzer."

Annie wrapped her arm around Myra's shoulders. "The end justifies the means, right?"

"Yes, Annie, the end in this case justifies the means."

Three days before Christmas a huge box wrapped in silver paper and tied with a bright red velvet ribbon was delivered to the Federal Bureau of Investigation at the Hoover Building. The package was simply addressed to the Director of the FBI. It was delivered at 5:50.

The following morning the early edition of the *Post* carried a warlike black headline on its front page. The byline carried the names of Maggie Spitzer, Ted Robinson, Joe Espinosa, and Dennis West.

The twenty-four-hour news channels went crazy.

Wall Street shut down.

The Hoover Building doubled its lobby security.

In Las Vegas, where it was three hours

earlier, Myra and Annie were seated at side-by-side slot machines.

"Here goes nothing! It's my last dollar!" Myra watched as three golden bars danced across the screen. "Oh look, Annie, I won thirty-three dollars. Enough to take you to breakfast!"

Just then it sounded like every bell and whistle in the casino went off. Even at that hour, the crowd of people started to scream and holler that someone had won a million dollars. Myra stood up to see where the machine was and looked across the room, straight at her husband, Charles, and Fergus. People rushed by. Myra blinked, and when she opened her eyes, all she could see were people rushing to the winning slot machine.

"Myra! What's wrong? You're whiter than the snow back in Virginia. You're scaring me, Myra. Talk to me."

Myra sat down on the stool and took a deep breath. "Annie, I just saw Charles, and Fergus was with him."

"Are you sure, Myra?"

"I should know my own husband, don't you think? And there was no mistaking Fergus. We just stared at each other."

Annie looked around but could see neither man. "What does it mean?"

"I don't know, Annie, and I am not going to worry about it. Come along, I promised to take you to breakfast. I just have to cash this out."

"Nah, leave it for someone else. Come on, I'll sign for breakfast. Remember, I own the damn joint."

Myra laughed. "So you do, my friend, so you do."

Epilogue

Christmas Eve
Las Vegas, Nevada

It was four o'clock in the afternoon, and the din inside Babylon was at an all-time high. The excited squeals of winners, the bells and whistles, the loud buzz of thousands of people trying to hear one another over the noise were mind bending. On top of that, the voice blaring over a loudspeaker at ten-minute intervals, a voice that sounded suspiciously like the voice of the owner of Babylon, only compounded the frenzy of the patrons wanting to cash in and win *big* before the casino closed its doors at six o'clock, something totally unheard of in Las Vegas.

Not to be outdone, the other casino owners conferred and decided to do the same thing. After all, it was all for charity, and what better place or time to enact good deeds than Christmas Eve in Las Vegas.

They all decided, with Annie de Silva leading the pack, that it would not be the end of the world to close their doors for twelve hours. It would be win win for every charity in Las Vegas. Thousands of kids would get to meet Santa, receive gifts, enjoy a kid's menu of kid-favorite food. There would be Christmas carols, Santa himself, picture taking, fun, and games.

The owners balked a little but gave in when they heard that Babylon employees were going to be outside dressed in elf costumes and pleading for donations for underprivileged children, with the promise that whatever amount was collected would be doubled by Babylon. Annie de Silva meant business.

The numerous chapels in the area got into the act because, as everyone knew, Christmas Eve was their biggest marrying day, with couples standing in line for their turn at the altar. The ministers promised to donate all marriage fees to the cause but only if the couples wanting to get married were sober. As one pastor put it, he did not give refunds.

Inside Babylon, at the Tiki Hut, Jack Emery commandeered a large table and ushered his friends in to sit down. A waitress dressed in a red outfit trimmed in white fur and wearing a rakish Santa hat complete with white tassel took their order. "Double cheeseburgers, fries, and strawberry milk shakes all around."

"I don't think I ever worked so hard in all my life," Ted Robinson said as he rubbed at his neck. "Those women are slave drivers. I personally decorated five Christmas trees, strung three miles of colored lights, up and down ladders all day. I don't know if I'll be able to walk tomorrow."

"Look at my hands!" Espinosa said, holding out his resin-covered hands. "It won't come off."

"Lava soap," Harry Wong said.

"I'm so glad they kicked us out," Jack said wearily. "I think I must have wrapped three hundred presents. But you know what? I'd do it again, too. This is a really great thing Annie is doing. And she got the other owners to do the same thing."

"I had the poop detail," Dennis volunteered. "Annie put me in charge of the animal parade. We had over two hundred dogs, ninety-seven cats, nine parrots, a bunch of other birds, and a baby alligator. And more were expected. I was never so happy as when Maggie came in and took over. It stinks in that place, too, but Maggie said she had some magic stuff to spray around. It was bedlam until she walked in, blew a whistle, and it all came together." He looked down at his phone to see an incoming text:

No one has pooped since you left.

He shared the news with the guys at the table just as their food arrived. No one cared as they dived into the juicy Kobe burgers the Tiki Hut was known for.

Harry Wong looked around the table. Everyone stopped eating. Because . . . everyone knew that Harry rarely spoke unless he had something to say. "This is going to sound weird, but when I came out of the men's room, I thought . . . I'm sure I must be wrong, but I could swear that I saw Charles. Then people got in my way, and whoever it was that I saw was gone. I actually walked around to see if I could see whoever it was I had seen, but the guy was gone."

"Well, I can top that," Abner Tookus said. "I thought I saw that guy Fergus, who hooked up with Annie for a while. The one who used to work for Scotland Yard. I only ever saw him twice, but I have a good eye and a really good memory. I'd swear it was him."

Espinosa said, "Just goes to prove everyone in life has a double." Everyone agreed and went back to eating.

Jack changed the subject. "I handed in my resignation to the firm before we left to come out here. As of January 1, I am a free agent." Congratulations were offered all around.

"What are you going to do?" Espinosa asked.

"Well, I tried talking to all of you over Thanksgiving out at Pinewood. None of you got back to me. I'm going to look for a moneyman who will back my enterprise. Because to do what the girls did all those years, I'm going to need serious funding."

Dennis sat up straight and squared his shoulders. "Then I'm your man!"

The others stared at Dennis, their jaws dropping.

"I have been wondering what I was going to do with all that money. I think my benefactors would approve. No strings. We put it in a pot and take it out as needed. Deal?"

"Kid, I like your style," Jack said as he grinned from ear to ear.

A lot of backslapping started as Dennis beamed.

It was great to be one of the guys. His fist

shot high in the air.

"This calls for another round of milk shakes. Chocolate this time," Ted said as he flagged down the waitress.

Harry was so excited, he stood up and bellowed at the top of his lungs, "Merry Christmas!" Everyone in the Tiki Hut clapped as Annie's voice blared over the loudspeaker, telling everyone they had ten minutes to clear the building.

"Merry Christmas, everyone!" she bellowed.

ABOUT THE AUTHOR

Fern Michaels is the *USA Today* and *New York Times* bestselling author of *A Family Affair, Blindsided, Classified, Gotcha! Breaking News, Tuesday' Child, Late Edition, Betrayal,* and dozens of other novels and novellas. There are over seventy-five million copies of her books in print.

Fern Michaels has built and funded several large daycare centers in her hometown, and is a passionate animal lover who has outfitted police dogs across the country with special bulletproof vests. She shares her home in South Carolina with her five dogs and a resident ghost named Mary Margaret. Visit her website at www.fernmichaels.com.

The employees of Thorndike Press hope you have enjoyed this Large Print book. All our Thorndike, Wheeler, and Kennebec Large Print titles are designed for easy reading, and all our books are made to last. Other Thorndike Press Large Print books are available at your library, through selected bookstores, or directly from us.

For information about titles, please call:
(800) 223-1244

or visit our Web site at:
http://gale.cengage.com/thorndike

To share your comments, please write:
Publisher
Thorndike Press
10 Water St., Suite 310
Waterville, ME 04901